"YOU'RE NOT *THE* SMOKE JENSEN, ARE YOU?"

"One and the same, pardner. Now," Smoke said as he pulled his Bowie knife from its scabbard and held it up so the light sparkled off the blade, "I'll ask you a question, and you'll answer. For every question you don't answer, I'm gonna remove one of your fingrs. After ten times, if you're still reluctant to answer, I'll start on your toes. *Comprende?*

The man shook his head. "You can't do that," he cried.

Smoke grabbed his right hand, bent all the fingers over except the index finger, and held the knife against it. "First question. What's your name?"

"Blackie. Blackie Johnson."

"Who sent you to brace Sheriff Carson?"

"I . . . I can't tell you that. He'd kill me!"

Smoke stroked the finger lightly with his knife. "Last chance, Blackie," he said, "or they're gonna start calling you Stubby."

"Big Jim Slaughter sent us," Blackie said.

"And where is Slaughter going to take Carson's wife?"

Blackie licked his lips, his eyes staring at the blood oozing from his finger. "He's gonna take her up to the hole in the wall."

Smoke gestured to Pearlie. "Get this man a bandage for his hand," he said. "He's gonna draw us a map."

HEART OF THE MOUNTAIN MAN

William W. Johnstone

PINNACLE BOOKS
Kensington Publishing Corp.

http://www.kensingtonbooks.com

PINNACLE BOOKS are published by

Kensington Publishing Corp.
119 West 40th Street
New York, NY 10018

PUBLISHER'S NOTE
Following the death of William W. Johnstone, the Johnstone family
is working with a carefully selected writer to organize and complete
Mr. Johnstone's outlines and many unfinished manuscripts to create
additional novels in all of his series like The Last Gunfighter, Mountain Man, and Eagles, among others. The new novel excerpted in the
back was inspired by Mr. Johnstone's superb storytelling.

All Kensington titles, imprints, and distributed lines are available
at special quantity discounts for bulk purchases for sales promotions,
premiums, fund-raising, educational, or institutional use. Special
book excerpts or customized printings can also be created to fit spe-
cific needs. For details, write or phone the office of the Kensington
special sales manager: Kensington Publishing Corp., 119 West 40th
Street, New York, NY 10018, attn: Special Sales Department; phone
1-800-221-2647.

PINNACLE BOOKS and the Pinnacle logo are Reg. U.S. Pat. &
TM Off.
The WWJ steer head logo is a trademark of Kensington Publishing
Corp.

ISBN-13: 978-0-7860-2845-0
ISBN-10: 0-7860-2845-9

First printing: December 2001
Tenth printing: July 2012

18 17 16 15 14 13 12

Printed in the United States of America

One

Smoke Jensen came fully awake, his heart hammering as he sat up straight in the bed, his hand automatically reaching for the Colt .44 that was never very far from his grasp.

Sally opened her eyes, blinked twice, and asked in a sleepy voice, "What is it, darling?"

Smoke shook his head, forgetting for the moment she couldn't see him in the darkness. "I don't know," he answered, the hairs on the back of his neck stirring at some as yet unexplained noise or movement.

He turned his head toward the window, where a light breeze was billowing the curtains, bringing into the room the sweet scent of mountain laurel and pine needles along with a hint of ozone that foretold of fall showers on the way.

Sally glanced at the glint of moonlight on the barrel of Smoke's gun and sat up herself, reaching for the Colt Navy .36-caliber pistol on the table next to her side of the bed.

"Something wrong, dear?" she asked.

Smoke slipped out of bed and pulled on his buckskin trousers, which he'd flung over the back of a chair the night before. "I'll let you know in a minute, sweetheart. Go back to sleep."

"Not on your life, Smoke. I've learned never to ignore

your instincts." She threw the covers back and grabbed a robe from the foot of the bed. "If something woke you up, then I'm going to go with you to find out what it is."

She could see his teeth gleaming in the semidarkness as he grinned at her. "Well, there's no need for both of us to lose sleep. Why don't you check it out and I'll go back to bed?"

She put her hands on his shoulders, turned him around, and pushed him toward the door. "I'll be right behind you."

"So that's the way it is, huh?" he whispered over his shoulder. "I take all the risks and you stay safe behind me."

"That's why God gave you such big shoulders, dear, so I could hide behind them," she answered with a chuckle.

Smoke snorted. "That'll be the day."

They walked through the darkness of the cabin and stepped to the back door. Smoke eased it open, eared back the hammer on his Colt, and stepped outside. Sally followed him out the door and stepped to his side, her Colt Navy held in front of her.

The night was typical for early fall in the high lonesome of the Rocky Mountains where they had their ranch, Sugarloaf. The sky was crystal clear with millions of stars shining down like diamonds on a field of black velvet. The moon, though not full, shown with brilliance through the thin air, illuminating the area around the cabin with a ghostly yellow light. Lightning danced in dark, roiling clouds over distant mountaintops and the faint sounds of thunder could be heard.

Smoke's eyes stopped their movement and he pointed to the hitching post off to the side. "There's a horse," he said.

Sally followed his gesture and could see a solitary horse standing next to the hitching post, its head down as it calmly munched on nearby grass. Its reins were hanging loose, as if it'd wandered to the post by itself.

"It's wearing a saddle so there must be a rider somewhere close by," Sally whispered back.

Smoke reached inside the cabin and grabbed his Greener ten-gauge short-barreled express gun off a rack next to the door. He stuck his Colt in his waistband and held the Greener in both hands as he stepped off the porch and approached the riderless horse.

"Be careful, Smoke, there may be more than one of them out there," Sally called softly, her eyes flicking back and forth as she tried to cover his back. Since Smoke had once been a notorious gunfighter, she knew there was always the possibility of men tracking him down, looking to get revenge for some perceived wrong Smoke had done them.

"There's something familiar about this horse," Smoke said, a puzzled expression on his face as he turned back to look at Sally. "I've seen that blaze on his forehead before."

Sally took a closer look at the horse and realized she knew who its owner was. "Wait a minute, Smoke," she said, putting her hand on the barrel of the shotgun and pushing it toward the ground. "I think that's Monte Carson's horse."

Smoke walked over to the horse and examined the saddle. "You're right, Sally. It is Monte's mount."

Monte Carson was the sheriff at Big Rock, Colorado, the closest town to the Jensen ranch, and a dear friend of Smoke and Sally.

When Sally got to Smoke's side, she noticed the look on his face. "What's wrong, Smoke? You look like you've seen a ghost."

He pointed at the side of the saddle. The leather was covered with a large stain, looking almost black in the moonlight, that ran down the sides of the saddle onto the fender skirts of the stirrups. Smoke put his finger on the stain and held it under his nose. The coppery scent brought back unpleasant memories of times he'd been shot. "It's blood. Something bad's happened to Monte."

He eased the hammers down on the shotgun and laid

the barrel on his shoulder as he looked around, searching for his friend in the semidarkness. "I guess I'd better get some of the hands up and we'll do a search. If this blood's his, he's injured pretty bad. It won't do to leave him out here too long."

Sally pulled her robe close around her against the chill of the mountain air. "I'll get some water on the stove to boil and have my medical kit handy."

Smoke nodded his approval. "Put some coffee on too, please. We're gonna need it if we spend too much time out here in the cold."

Sally walked back toward their cabin and Smoke proceeded to the bunkhouse across the wide yard. He opened the door and moved to the wood stove in the corner, which was still warm from the evening before. He lit a lantern on a shelf and picked up a coffeepot and banged it on the stove a couple of times.

His foreman, Pearlie, sat up in his bed, yawning and rubbing sleepy eyes, a puzzled expression on his wrinkled, sunburned face. "Pearlie, get everybody up!" Smoke said. "Sheriff Monte Carson's horse showed up here covered with blood. I think Monte may be out there in the night bleeding to death. We need to find him."

Pearlie scrambled out of bed, clapping his hands and shouting, "Off yore butts an' on yore feet! We got work to do and we got to do it fast!"

The cowboys, most of whom knew Monte and liked him, didn't argue. They swung out of their beds and began to pull their clothes on.

"Sally'll have coffee ready over at the cabin. Report there when you're finished dressing," Smoke said as he left the bunkhouse.

By the time Pearlie had the hands gathered outside the cabin, Sally had biscuits and sausage patties cooked along with a large pot of fresh coffee.

Pearlie, a renowned chowhound, made sure he was at

the front of the line for food. "Havin' some of your fresh-cooked biscuits and sausage almost makes gettin' up at this ungodly hour worth it, Miss Sally," he said, as he grabbed a handful of the sausage and biscuit sandwiches.

Cal Woods, Pearlie's best friend and unofficial son to Smoke and Sally, spoke up from behind the foreman. "Hey, go easy there, Pearlie. Anybody'd think you ain't eaten for days the way you grabbin' those sinkers."

Pearlie puffed out his chest. "The man who has to do most of the work gets the most food, Cal, my boy. That's the way it's always been and that's the way it always will be."

"Huh," Cal snorted through his nose. "The only time you move faster'n molasses in January is when you're rushing toward a mess tent."

Pearlie shook his head. "Boys! You just don't understand the difficulty being in charge of a bunch of lazy galoots like you causes a man. Why, I get plumb wore out just thinkin' on ways to get you to earn your salary."

He paused to stuff another sandwich into his mouth as Smoke stepped up on the porch to address the group of men.

"Boys, we need to get moving. Monte is out there, so let's go find him." He glanced at Pearlie. "Pearlie, you organize the men to cover all the territory between here and the gate to the road to Big Rock. If we don't find him there, we'll move on down toward the town."

"Yes, sir, Smoke," Pearlie said, and he turned and began giving orders to the men on where to search.

Sally put a hand on Smoke's arm. "Perhaps we ought to send someone to Big Rock to fetch Doc Spalding."

Smoke nodded. "Cal, hold on a minute. I want you to saddle up and ride as fast as you can to Big Rock and get Doc out here. And tell him to bring what he needs for a bullet wound."

Cal nodded once and sprinted toward the barn to get his mount.

It took the men less than thirty minutes to find the wounded Monte Carson and carry him to Smoke's cabin.

"Put him on the bed," Sally said.

She tore open his shirt and looked at his wounds. She glanced up at Smoke. "Looks like he's been hit twice, once just below the left shoulder and once in the chest."

"Is it in his lung?" Smoke asked.

She shook her head. "I don't think so. He doesn't have any bloody froth on his lips and he seems to be breathing all right."

As Sally took cloths and dipped them in hot water and began to wash his wounds, Smoke bent over the bed, his lips close to Monte's ear.

"Monte, can you hear me?"

Monte's eyes flickered and opened, his lips curling in a half smile. "Of course I can hear you, Smoke. I've been shot, but I ain't deaf."

Smoke grinned. It was a good sign his friend could still joke in spite of having two bullets in him. "Who did this to you, pal, and why?"

Monte's eyes moved to look at Sally, then back to Smoke. "Big Jim Slaughter and his men."

"I thought Slaughter was up around Wyoming, near the hole-in-the-wall area."

Monte nodded, then groaned with the pain the movement caused. "He was. He decided to pay me a visit and talk over some old times."

Smoke pursed his lips. He hadn't been aware that Monte used to ride with Slaughter, who was one of the most vicious and bloodthirsty killers still roaming the countryside. Before he could ask any more questions, the door opened and Doc Cotton Spalding walked in, followed by Cal.

Sally stepped back from Monte's side and she and the doc began to discuss his wounds and what to do next.

Smoke grabbed Cal by the arm and led him out to the kitchen. "Let's let the doc do his work in peace, Cal."

Smoke went out on the porch and told the men waiting there he thought Monte was going to be all right and they could go back to bed if they wanted.

Pearlie laid his hand on the butt of his Colt pistol. "Who did this to him, Smoke? Me and the boys'd like to have a talk with them galoots."

Smoke held up his hands. "There'll be plenty of time for that later, Pearlie. Soon as we find out what's going on, we'll do whatever is necessary to help Monte."

Pearlie scratched his chin, a glint in his eye. "Any of Miss Sally's sausage and biscuits left?"

Smoke laughed, "Cal, go in and get that platter and hand 'em out before Pearlie faints from hunger."

"Man ain't allowed hisself to get hungry in ten year at least," Cal muttered as he went back inside the cabin.

Two

Monte had just finished the lunch of beef broth Sally had prepared for him when Smoke sat down next to his bed. "Hey, partner," Smoke said, "you ready to tell me what happened last night?"

Monte's face changed and he got a far-away look in his eyes as he glanced out the window. Smoke followed his look, observing the distant mountaintops already covered with snow down to the tree line, the bright yellow leaves on the grove of aspen just down from the cabin, and the deep green of the evergreens mixed with the reds and yellows of maple trees on the mountainsides. Fall was as beautiful as ever in the high lonesome of the Rocky Mountains, but Smoke knew Monte wasn't seeing the scenery so much as he was looking into his past.

He and Monte Carson had become very good friends over the past few years. Monte had once been a well-known gunfighter, though he had never ridden the owl-hoot trail. Or so Smoke believed.

A local rancher, with plans to take over the county, had hired Monte to be the sheriff in Fontana, a town just down the road from Smoke's Sugarloaf spread. Monte went along with the man's plans for a while, till he couldn't stomach the rapings and killings any longer. He put his foot down and let it be known that Fontana was going to be run in a law-abiding manner from then on.

The rancher, Tilden Franklin, sent a bunch of riders in to teach the upstart sheriff a lesson. The men killed Monte's two deputies and seriously wounded him, taking over the town. In retaliation, Smoke founded the town of Big Rock, and he and his band of aging gunfighters cleaned house in Fontana.

When the fracas was over, Smoke offered the job of sheriff in Big Rock to Monte. He married a grass widow and settled into the job like he was born to it. Neither Smoke nor the citizens of Big Rock ever had cause to regret his taking the job.

When Monte didn't speak, Smoke leaned back and crossed his arms, signaling he was there until he got some answers. "Why don't you start by telling me how you know Big Jim Slaughter?"

After he picked up a glass of fresh milk from the tray and took a deep draft, Monte began talking, still without meeting Smoke's eyes.

"It was a lot of years ago, Smoke, when I was still in my teens and thought I was a big man with a gun. It was just after the big war, when the country was still wild and gangs were on the prowl everywhere. Slaughter's bunch, Slaughter's Marauders, invited me in when I didn't have a whole lot of other choices. All the men were back from the war and there just wasn't much honest work to be found. Anyway, I began to ride with 'em, doin' little jobs at first, stealing a few horses or cattle or boosting a wagonload of freight here and there. Then, Slaughter decided to hit it big in one job. He found out from a drunken sergeant in a bar that an Army payroll was coming in on a train in a few days. After he got all the details, he planned out how to rob the train."

"How many men did he have riding with him at the time?" Smoke asked.

" 'Bout ten or so, countin' me. Well, we pried up some tracks and hid nearby. When the engine ran off the rails, we spurred our hosses and charged that old train like Pickett did in the war. We managed to get the payroll out of the boxcar pretty quick, and then Slaughter had me put the money in my saddlebags. He'd divide it up later, he said. We rode off free and clear. Only, somehow an Army patrol managed to catch up with us."

"What did you do?"

Monte grinned, his eyes looking inward as he remembered the day. "Slaughter told me to git the hell outta there. He said we'd all meet up in two weeks down at Del Rio, and split up the money and head on down into Mexico. Then we all rode off in different directions with the blue-bellies coming on like dogs on a coon's trail."

"Did you meet up later?"

Monte shook his head. "No. I waited around Del Rio for almost three weeks, spending most of my time in bars and cantinas, drinking myself to sleep every night. You see, Smoke, I'd never done anything that serious before. Now I knew that I'd never be able to stay in the country, not with the whole government after me. I didn't much like the idea of spendin' the rest of my life tryin' to learn to speak Mexican."

"What did you do when Slaughter didn't show up?"

"I heard from some men in a bar that he'd been shot and killed and his band of Marauders was broken up and scattered across the whole territory, so I packed the money in my saddlebags and headed north. I drifted for a while, but never spent any of the money. Finally, I came to work for Tilden Franklin and ended up with you offerin' me the job as sheriff in Big Rock."

"So you still have the money?"

Monte wagged his head. "You remember, after you offered me the job, I told you I'd need a week or so to think it over?"

"Yeah."

"Well, during that week, I rode over to the U.S. marshal's office in Denver and traded that money in for a pardon for the robbery. The government was right proud to get the money back, and they knew Slaughter had been behind the whole thing, so they let the little fish, me, go. That way I was free to take the job you'd offered with a clear conscience and not have to live my life lookin' back over my shoulder at my back trail."

Smoke nodded. "And then you met Mary."

Monte smiled for the first time since Smoke came into the room. "Yeah, Mary saved me, Smoke. She showed me what life is all about. Fallin' in love with her and marryin' her was the rightest thing I've ever done in my life."

"So, that brings us up to last night. What happened and what does Jim Slaughter have to do with it?"

Monte cut tortured eyes toward Smoke, eyes that were wet with unshed tears. "I got home late from the office, 'bout eight o'clock. As I rode up to our house, I saw three men sitting on their horses out front . . ."

Monte pulled back on the reins, letting his right hand fall to his side and unhook the hammer-thong on his Colt pistol. "Howdy, gents," he called. "What can I do for you?"

As he spoke, he let his eyes flick to his house, trying to see if Mary was in sight, or if the door was shut. There were no lights on in the house, which worried him, for she always left a lantern burning on the porch when he was late getting home.

"Carson, we came to give you a message from Big Jim Slaughter," one of the men said. He was tall and skinny, with a beard hanging down to his chest and scraggly hair sticking out from under his hat. He wore two pistols, butts forward, on each hip. They were tied down low, so Monte knew he wasn't a cowboy but made his living with his guns.

Monte's heart beat faster when he heard Slaughter's name. "I heard he was dead."

One of the other men laughed, and then began to choke on his chaw of tobacco. "Pardner, you gonna wish he was dead 'fore all this is over, that's fer sure," he finally managed to say.

"Before what's over?" Monte asked, his hand drifting down to rest on his thigh next to his pistol.

The third man heeled his horse closer to Monte and stared at him from under the brim of his hat. "Slaughter wants his money, Carson, the whole fifty thousand."

Monte recognized the man. He'd ridden with Slaughter back when Monte had. His name was Boots Malone, and he was as nasty a specimen of humanity as Monte had ever met. He liked to slice up bar girls with his Bowie knife, just for fun, and Monte had seen him gun down women and children for no reason other than they were in his way.

"What if I tell you, Boots, that I don't have it?"

Boots shifted the toothpick in his mouth from one side to the other, his dead eyes never leaving Monte's. "Then I'd say it's too bad for that pretty little wife of your'n."

"What do you mean?"

Boots leaned back against the cantle of his saddle. "Slaughter took her on over to Robber's Roost, near Jackson Hole, Wyoming. He said to tell you he'd keep her there for four weeks, free from harm, to give you a chance to bring him his money. Then, he's gonna start handin' her out to the men there in the hole-in-the-wall area. You know the type, men on the run who ain't seen a woman in months."

"You bastard!"

Boots started to rein his horse around, "You got thirty

days, Carson. Then if you want to see your wife, you're gonna have to stand in line."

Monte's pistol appeared in his hand as if on its own volition. His first slug took Boots in the chest, knocking him backward off his horse to land spread-eagled on the ground, his eyes wide and surprised until the life slowly winked out in them.

The second man had his pistol half out of his holster when Monte shot him in the face, the bullet entering his mouth and blowing out the back of his head, showering the third man with hair and brains and blood as he pulled the trigger on Monte.

Monte felt the bullets tear into him, twisting him sideways in his saddle. As his horse danced and whirled, trying to escape the explosions of gunfire, Monte snapped off a shot at the man as he rode away. The man flinched and leaned over his saddle horn, but Monte couldn't tell if he'd hit him or he was just ducking.

Monte tucked his useless left arm into his belt and ran to search the house. Mary was gone . . .

Monte looked up at Smoke, his voice hoarse from the tale. "All I could think of was to get to you, Smoke, and see what you thought I should do."

Smoke thought for a moment. "A lot will depend on whether you hit the galoot that was running away, and how hard you hit him. If you planted him forked end down, we've got some time to plan what to do. On the other hand, if he made it back to Slaughter and told him you don't have the money, Mary's time is a lot shorter than I like to think about."

"Yeah. As long as he thinks there is a chance he'll get the money, he'll keep her safe. At least until I see her and hand over the payroll."

Smoke hesitated. "Monte, you know Slaughter and his

reputation better than I do, but I don't think there's any way in hell you and Mary are going to be allowed to walk away from this."

Monte nodded. "You're right, Smoke. Even if I had the money, which I don't, I got to plan some way to get Mary out of there and put an end to Slaughter once and for all."

Smoke stood up. "First things first, Monte. Cal and Pearlie and I'll head out to your place and see if we find two bodies or three. If there's three men down, I'll go up into the mountains and talk to some friends of mine about the hole-in-the-wall area, see if there's some way we can get in without being seen."

"What if the man got away?"

"Then we don't have time to do it the easy way. I'll have to get moving right away and work something out on the way to Wyoming."

Monte started to get up, struggling to use his bandaged left arm.

"Hold on, pardner. Doc Spalding says you got at least a week in bed, and then another few days before you're gonna be able to use that arm."

"But I can't let you and the boys do this alone. It's my mess and I need to get myself out of it."

Sally, who had been standing in the doorway for most of their talk, stepped into the room. "Monte Carson, you sit yourself back down in that bed right now. You'll be of no use to Mary if you get those wounds to bleeding and end up killing yourself. You let Smoke and Cal and Pearlie do what they need to while you heal. After that, we'll see what the doc says about how soon you can go to Wyoming. All right?"

Though she said it as a question, Sally left no room for discussion. Monte knew she was right and he'd have to let his friends do the initial investigation into the happenings out at his ranch.

He flopped back down on the pillow. "All right, Sally. You win. Smoke, would you let me know what you find out at the ranch?"

Smoke nodded. "One way or another, Monte, we'll keep you informed. Now, you rest up and eat whatever Sally brings you, 'cause you got a lot of blood to make up for what you spilled all over the country between here and your place."

He turned to Sally. "Keep him down until we get back. We should know something by supper time."

Sally stood on tiptoes and kissed Smoke's lips. "You ride with your guns loose, Smoke Jensen. I don't want to have to call Doc Spalding back out here to patch you up, too."

"Yes, dear," Smoke said as he strapped on his Colt .44.

Three

As Smoke and Cal and Pearlie approached the Carson house, Smoke pulled his Colt and eared back the hammer.

"You expectin' trouble, Smoke?" Pearlie asked, resting his palm on his own pistol butt.

Smoke shrugged, "You never know. Monte said he may've put some lead into the man trying to ride away. He may be wounded and lying around here somewhere just waiting to put a bullet into whoever might come looking."

Cal and Pearlie looked at each other and pulled their guns.

When they got to the house, they found the two dead men right in front of the porch. Both had been killed with clean shots.

"Jimminy," Cal said, "I remember you sayin' Monte was a gunslick 'fore he joined up with you and became sheriff, but he must've been pretty doggone good to draw down on three men and get 'em all."

Smoke nodded. "There isn't any back-up in Monte, that's for sure. And it looks like he hasn't lost much of his skill with a six-killer either."

He pointed at the bullet hole over one man's heart and the other in the center of his face. "Dead center with both shots," Smoke said with some admiration.

Pearlie shook his head. "And then, after gettin' hit twice, he managed to possibly put some lead in the third man as he was ridin' off. That takes some *cojones,* Smoke."

Smoke looked at his friend. "I've never had any doubts about Monte's courage, boys. Now let's spread out and see if we can find the last man."

As Cal and Pearlie reined their horses off to opposite sides of the yard surrounding Monte's house, Smoke got off Joker, his blanket-hipped Palouse stud, and walked bent over, staring at the ground.

An experienced tracker, he could almost see what had happened from the way the horses' hooves tore up the sod around the bodies. Once he found the trail of the third man, he began to follow the hoofprints, glancing up frequently so he wouldn't be caught off guard if the man were still around.

About thirty yards from the original confrontation, he found spots of dried blood on the ground. "You did hit him, Monte," Smoke mumbled. He looked back over his shoulder at the distance. "And at thirty yards on the back of a moving horse. That was a hell of a shot, partner," he said, as he followed the trail of blood toward a copse of trees nearby.

As he approached the trees, he whistled shrilly through his lips to get Cal and Pearlie's attention. When they rode into view from opposite directions, he pointed at the grove of trees and held up his gun.

The men dismounted and approached the trees from different directions, guns drawn and ready.

All of their precautions were unnecessary. Smoke found the man lying on his stomach, a bullet hole surrounded by dark crimson stains on the back of his shirt. He was still alive, but unconscious.

"Pearlie, go get a wagon out of Monte's barn and hitch a couple of his horses to it. We need to get this man to town and see if Doc Spalding can save him."

Cal leaned over and spat in the dirt. "Why go to all that trouble to save pond-scum like that, Smoke?"

Smoke glanced up. "Because if he lives, he can give us important information about Slaughter and how many men he has and where they're holding Mary."

Cal's face colored. "Oh, I didn't think of that."

"What if he won't talk, Smoke?" Pearlie asked.

Smoke looked at him with an expression on his face that made Pearlie glad he was the big man's friend and not his enemy.

"Oh, he'll talk, Pearlie. He'll talk or he'll wish he'd never seen either Big Jim Slaughter or Monte Carson."

Smoke took a slab of fatback pork out of his saddlebag, placed it over the bullet hole in the man's back, and tied it in place with a strip of cloth torn from the gunny's own shirt. When Pearlie brought Monte's buckboard up next to him, he bent and lifted the man off the ground as if he weighed no more than five pounds, placing him in the back of the wagon.

"We're gonna ride for town, Cal. You go on ahead and have Doc Spalding ready to do some cutting on this man. Tell him Mary Carson's life depends on keeping this snake alive!"

Four

Big Jim Slaughter pulled his Winchester from its saddle boot and waved it over his head at the sentry standing on a nearby ridge. It was the third such sentry he and his gang had passed in the last few miles as they approached their hideout known only as the "hole-in-the-wall." It was a natural valley high in the mountains surrounding the small Wyoming town of Jackson Hole. Accessible only by a narrow pass that meandered between several higher peaks, it had been a hiding place for men on the run for longer than anyone could remember. Easily defended, it had simply never been worth the trouble or the many dead men it would take to roust the criminals out of the place.

Slaughter led a column of twenty men, all hard cases who were wanted by the law across the country for everything from rape to armed robbery and murder. Riding next to him was an attractive woman in her late thirties. She had long brown hair, tied loosely behind her neck with a small, silk ribbon, and was wearing a man's shirt and trousers. She rode her horse with practiced ease, as if she spent a lot of time on horseback. Her face was serene and composed and she showed no trace of fear or trepidation, a fact that bothered Jim Slaughter.

As they rode down a dry gulch, cut out of the surrounding mountainside by hundreds of years of seasonal snowmelt runoffs, he glanced at her, his face showing his puzzlement.

"Mrs. Carson," he said, his voice neutral, "excuse me, but all the way here from Colorado, you've acted like you were out for a ride in the park. Doesn't the fact that you've been kidnapped by a gang of men and taken from your home to a strange place bother you?"

Mary Carson turned her calm eyes to Slaughter and gave a half smile. "Does it bother me? Yes. Do I fear you? No."

Slaughter shook his head. He was beginning to admire this woman more and more. Monte Carson was a lucky man.

"Why not?" he asked. He'd raped and killed and beaten hundreds of times before, and he'd never failed to see the haunted look that appeared in someone's eyes the moment they knew for certain they were going to die or be seriously injured, the acknowledgment of defeat and terrible sadness. It was a look he knew well, and he had come in some perverted way to look forward to it and enjoy instilling it in others.

"Because I know my husband will come for me eventually."

Slaughter snorted. "Even assuming he tries, and assuming he is able to make it past the sentries and guards we have set up to discourage visitors, what makes you think you'll be alive when he gets here? How do you know I won't just turn you over to this"—he hesitated as he glanced at the scum riding with them, then back at her—"pack of animals ridin' along with us?"

She raised an eyebrow. "Are you trying to frighten me, Mr. Slaughter?"

"No, just wondering why you seem so unconcerned about your fate."

Mary looked away from him, her eyes taking in the mountains that surrounded them, the blue sky, and the grass-covered slopes still layered with wildflowers and blooming shrubs. Finally, she took a deep breath and spoke. "I've lived a good life, Mr. Slaughter. I was married to a fine man for five years, and when he was killed I was lucky enough to find another wonderful man. Out here on the frontier, we learn to accept death as just another part of life, and not necessarily the worst part either. So, if I die . . . if you kill me, then so be it. I've had more than my share of goodness, and I'll die knowing I've had more than you'll ever have if you live to be a hundred years old."

Slaughter nodded. There was more than a little truth in what she said. He stared ahead down the trail without answering, thinking back on his life. It'd been a hardscrabble existence ever since he was a kid. After his mother died when he was no more than five or six, his father dove into a whiskey bottle and lived there until he died, at Jim's hands, ten years later.

Daily beatings became a way of life for the young Slaughter, until finally, one day when he was sixteen, he took the razor strap out of his father's hands, knocked the surprised man down, and beat him to death with an ax handle. Instead of burying him to hide his crime, young Jim threw his dad in the hog pen, figuring they had to eat too, just like worms or buzzards. When he saddled the plow horse and rode off to make his way in the world, he never looked back.

"All right, Mrs. Carson, you're right," he finally said. "I haven't got anything against you, so you have nothing to fear from me or my men, if your husband does what he's been told to do."

Mary stared at him for a moment, before asking in a low voice, as if she feared the answer more than anything Slaughter could do to her, "What about my husband, Mr. Slaughter? What business do you have with him?"

Slaughter laughed, a sound many of his men who'd

ridden with him for years had never heard. "Old business, Mrs. Carson. A matter of some money he's owed me for a long time."

Mary's face showed her surprise. "Money? Why would Monte owe you money?"

"I suspect there's lots of things about your husband you don't know, Mrs. Carson." He pursed his lips, thinking. "Perhaps I'll let him explain them to you . . . if he's got the *cojones* to come after you like you think he does."

Mary faced forward and put her heels to her horse's flanks, causing it to move forward so she wouldn't be riding next to Slaughter any longer.

He shook his head, thinking how lucky Carson was to have such a woman, and wondering if he knew it.

Smoke glanced across the operating table at Doc Spalding. "Doc, why don't you mosey on over to Louis's place and have a steak, on me?"

Doc Spalding looked up from where he was washing blood off his hands. He glanced at Smoke, then at the injured man on the table. He'd just taken two bullets out of him. "I take it you want to have a private word with this miscreant, Smoke."

"If you don't mind, sir."

Doc sighed and threw the dirty towel in a basket next to the table. "Try not to make any more work for me today, all right? The man's lost a lot of blood and his heart won't stand much more . . . grief."

"You got my word on it."

Doc stared at Smoke, his eyes narrowing at the expression on his friend's face. He shook his head. It went against everything he'd ever believed in to leave the gunman with Smoke looking like that, but Mary Carson was a good and kind woman and a dear friend of everyone in town. If a little judicious absence was what it took to get her back, then so be it.

After Doc left the room, Pearlie and Cal lined up on the other side of the table, hands on hips, waiting to see what Smoke had in mind.

Smoke reached down and slapped the man lightly across the face, causing his eyelids to flicker open.

"What's your name, mister?" he asked.

The man's eyes moved from Smoke to Cal and Pearlie, and his lips tightened into a white line. Evidently he wasn't prepared to speak just yet.

Smoke nodded to Pearlie, and they both took leather straps Doc used to tie down unruly patients on whom he was doing surgery, quickly fastening the man's hands to rails alongside the table.

"Hey," he said, a look of fear entering his eyes, "what the hell do you think you're doin'?"

"I'm fixing to do a little surgery on you, pardner, and I don't want your hands to get in the way. And I don't intend to use any of that chloroform the doc used either."

Smoke inclined his head toward Cal. "Cal, shut that window over there, would you? I don't want any citizens to be scared by any hollering that might occur."

"Sure, Smoke."

"Smoke?" the man asked. "You're not THE Smoke Jensen, are you?"

"One and the same, pardner. Now," Smoke said as he pulled his Bowie knife from its scabbard on the back of his belt and held it up so the light from the lantern in the room sparkled off the blade. "I'll ask you a question, and you'll answer. For every question you don't answer, I'm gonna remove one of your fingers. After ten times, if you're still reluctant to answer, I'll start on your toes. *Comprende?*"

The man shook his head. "You can't do that," he cried, his voice trembling with terror.

Smoke grabbed his right hand, bent all the fingers over except the index finger, and held the knife against it where the man could see.

"First question. What's your name?"

"Blackie . . . Blackie Johnson."

"Who sent you to brace Sheriff Carson?"

"I . . . I can't tell you that. He'd kill me!"

Smoke stroked the finger lightly with his knife, the razor-sharp blade slicing through skin as easily as if it were butter on a July afternoon.

"Wait! Hold on!" Blackie screamed.

"Last chance, Blackie, or they're gonna start calling you Stubby," Smoke growled, his eyes glittering hate.

"Slaughter, Big Jim Slaughter sent us," Blackie said, his voice hushed as if he was afraid to say the name out loud.

"What were your instructions?"

"We was supposed to tell 'im to bring the money to Jackson Hole an' Slaughter'd find him there and give him his wife back."

"And where is Slaughter going to take Carson's wife?"

Blackie shook his head, flinging fear-sweat off his forehead. "Please, Mr. Jensen, don't ask me that. Slaughter'd skin me alive if he found out I tole you any of this."

Smoke smiled, but there was no friendliness in his face. "How's he gonna find out, unless you tell him?"

Blackie licked his lips, his eyes staring at the blood oozing from his finger. "He's gonna take her up to the hole-in-the-wall."

"How many men does he have up there with him?"

Completely defeated now, Blackie made no more pretense of hesitation. He spoke in a low voice. "Anywhere from twenty to thirty, depending on the time of year and how many men are off spending the loot they've earned."

"Is there a back way in?"

"No. Only one way in and one way out, an' it's always

guarded real well. Jensen, if you're thinkin' of tryin' to get in there without Slaughter knowin' it, you're crazier than he is."

Smoke looked at Pearlie. "Get this man a bandage for his hand. He's gonna draw us a map of the area around the hole-in-the-wall and Jackson Hole, then we're going to keep him locked up here until we get back."

"What . . . what if you don't make it back?" Blackie asked, sweat pouring off his face in a steady stream.

"Why, then the good citizens of Big Rock will hang you by the neck until you're as dead as we are, Blackie, so you'd better put everything you can remember in that map."

Five

Smoke sat at the kitchen table in his cabin with Sally, Cal, and Pearlie, finishing a plate of scrambled hen's eggs, bacon, flapjacks, and sliced tomatoes.

Cal was watching Pearlie, who had his head down and was shoveling eggs into his mouth as if he hadn't eaten for days.

"I swear, Pearlie, you got to have a hollow leg," Cal said with some astonishment. "There ain't no other explanation for you bein' able to put away that much grub at one sittin'."

"Don't say ain't, Cal," Sally said without thinking about it. She'd been a schoolteacher when she met Smoke, and had tried her best, without much luck, to teach Cal proper English usage in the few years he'd been staying with them.

She glanced up at Smoke and he looked back, smiling, both of them remembering the first time they'd met Cal . . .

Calvin Woods, going on eighteen years old now, had been just fourteen four years ago when Smoke and Sally had taken him in as a hired hand. It was during the spring branding, and Sally was on her way back from Big Rock to the Sugarloaf. The buckboard was piled high with supplies because branding hundreds of calves made for hungry punchers.

As Sally slowed the team to make a bend in the trail, a rail-thin young man stepped from the bushes at the side of the road with a pistol in his hand.

"Hold it right there, miss."

Applying the brake with her right foot, Sally slipped her hand under a pile of gingham cloth on the seat. She grasped the handle of her short-barreled Colt .44 and eared back the hammer, letting the sound of the horses' hooves and the squealing of the brake pad on the wheel mask the sound. "What can I do for you, young man?" she asked, her voice firm and without fear. She knew she could draw and drill the young highwayman before he could raise his pistol to fire.

"Well, uh, you can throw some of those beans and a cut of that fatback over here, and maybe a portion of that Arbuckle's coffee, too."

Sally's eyebrows raised. "Don't you want my money?"

The boy frowned and shook his head. "Why, no, ma'am. I ain't no thief. I'm just hungry."

"And if I don't give you my food, are you going to shoot me with that big Navy Colt?"

He hesitated a moment, then grinned ruefully. "No, ma'am, I guess not." He twirled the pistol around his finger and slipped it into his belt, turned, and began to walk down the road toward Big Rock.

Sally watched the youngster amble off, noting his tattered shirt, dirty pants with holes in the knees and torn pockets, and boots that looked as if they had been salvaged from a garbage dump. "Young man," she called, "come back here, please."

He turned, a smirk on his face, spreading his hands. "Look lady, you don't have to worry. I don't even have any bullets." With a lightning-fast move he drew the gun from his pants, aimed away from Sally, and pulled the trigger. There was a click but no explosion as the hammer fell on an empty cylinder.

Sally smiled. "Oh, I'm not worried." In a movement every bit as fast as his, she whipped her .44 out and fired, clipping a pine cone from a branch, causing it to fall and bounce off his head.

The boy's knees buckled and he ducked, saying, "Jimminy Christmas!"

Mimicking him, Sally twirled her Colt and stuck it in the waistband of her britches. "What's your name, boy?"

The boy blushed and looked down at his feet. "Calvin, ma'am, Calvin Woods."

She leaned forward, elbows on knees, and stared into the boy's eyes. "Calvin, no one has to go hungry in this country, not if they're willing to work."

He looked up at her through narrowed eyes, as if he found life a little different than she described it.

"If you're willing to put in an honest day's work, I'll see that you get an honest day's pay, and all the food you can eat."

Calvin stood a little straighter, shoulders back and head held high. "Ma'am, I've got to be straight with you. I ain't no experienced cowhand. I come from a hardscrabble farm and we only had us one milk cow and a couple of goats and chickens, and lots of dirt that weren't worth nothing for growin' things. My ma and pa and me never had nothin', but we never begged and we never stooped to takin' handouts."

Sally thought, *I like this boy. Proud, and not willing to take charity if he can help it.* "Calvin, if you're willing to work, and don't mind getting your hands dirty and your muscles sore, I've got some hands that'll have you punching beeves like you were born to it in no time at all."

A smile lit up his face, making him seem even younger than his years. "Even if I don't have no saddle, nor a horse to put it on?"

She laughed out loud. "Yes. We've got plenty of ponies and saddles." She glanced down at his raggedy boots. "We can probably even round up some boots and spurs that'll fit you."

He walked over and jumped in the back of the buckboard. "Ma'am, I don't know who you are, but you just hired you the hardest-workin' hand you've ever seen."

Back at the Sugarloaf, she sent him in to Cookie and told him to eat his fill. When Smoke and the other punchers rode into the cabin yard at the end of the day, she introduced Calvin around. As Cal was shaking hands with the men, Smoke looked over at her and winked. He knew she could never resist a stray dog or cat, and her heart was as large as the Big Lonesome itself.

Smoke walked up to Cal and cleared his throat. "Son, I hear you drew down on my wife."

Cal gulped, "Yessir, Mr. Jensen. I did." He squared his shoulders and looked Smoke in the eye, not flinching though he was obviously frightened of the tall man with the incredibly wide shoulders standing before him.

Smoke smiled and clapped the boy on the back. "Just wanted you to know you stared death in the eye, boy. Not many galoots are still walking upright who ever pulled a gun on Sally. She's a better shot than any man I've ever seen except me, and sometimes I wonder about me."

The boy laughed with relief as Smoke turned and called out, "Pearlie, get your lazy butt over here."

A tall, lanky cowboy ambled over to Smoke and Cal, munching on a biscuit stuffed with roast beef. His face was lined with wrinkles and tanned a dark brown from hours under the sun, but his eyes were sky-blue and twinkled with good-natured humor.

"Yessir, Boss," he mumbled around a mouthful of food.

Smoke put his hand on Pearlie's shoulder. "Cal, this here chowhound is Pearlie. He eats more'n any two hands, and he's never been known to do a lick of work he could get out of, but he knows beeves and horses as well as any puncher I have. I want you to follow him around and let him teach you what you need to know."

Cal nodded, "Yes, sir, Mr. Smoke."

"Now let me see that iron you have in your pants."

Cal pulled the ancient Navy Colt and handed it to Smoke. When Smoke opened the loading gate, the rusted cylinder fell to the ground, causing Pearlie and Smoke to laugh and Cal's face to flame red. "This is the piece you pulled on Sally?" Smoke asked.

The boy nodded, looking at the ground.

Pearlie shook his head. "Cal, you're one lucky pup. Hell, if'n you'd tried to fire that thing it'd of blown your hand clean off."

Smoke inclined his head toward the bunkhouse. "Pearlie, take Cal over to the tack house and get him fixed up with what he needs, including a gun belt and a Colt that won't fall apart the first time he pulls it. You might also help pick him out a shavetail to ride. I'll expect him to start earning his keep tomorrow."

"Yes, sir, Smoke." Pearlie put his arm around Cal's shoulders and led him off toward the bunkhouse. "Now the first thing you gotta learn, Cal, is how to get on Cookie's good side. A puncher rides on his belly, and it 'pears to me that you need some fattin' up 'fore you can begin to punch cows."

Smoke and Sally grinned at each other, and Smoke glanced across the table at Pearlie, who was still stuffing food in his mouth as if he were in an eating contest at a state fair.

Pearlie had come to work for Smoke in as roundabout a way as Cal had. He was hiring his gun out to Tilden Franklin in Fontana when Franklin went crazy and tried to take over Sugarloaf, Smoke and Sally's spread. After Franklin's men raped and killed a young girl in the fracas, Pearlie sided with Smoke and the aging gunfighters he had called in to help put an end to Franklin's reign of terror.*

Pearlie was now honorary foreman of Smoke's ranch, though he was only a shade over twenty-two years old. Boys grew to be men early in the mountains of Colorado.

Sally wiped her lips daintily with the edge of a linen napkin, her eyes on Smoke's. "What are your plans now, Smoke? Did the map that man Blackie made give you enough information to try and rescue Mary?"

Smoke shook his head. He held his coffee cup in both hands, his elbows on the table, and looked at Sally over the brim. "It shows how to get into the hole-in-the-wall, and the approximate location of the sentries, but we're going to need to know more than that to get in and back out alive, especially if we're bringing Mary out with us."

Pearlie looked up from his plate. "You know, we could get fifty men from Big Rock to ride with us if they knew we was goin' after Mary Carson. There ain't a man within fifty miles don't owe the Carsons more'n they can repay for favors the two of them have done."

Smoke shook his head. "It's not a question of numbers, Pearlie. If we go blasting our way into the hole-in-the-wall, Slaughter'll kill Mary before we can get within a mile of him."

"Well, what's the answer, then?" Cal asked.

"I'm going to have to find out more about the mountains around Jackson Hole, and the hole-in-the-wall," Smoke said.

"How're you gonna do that?" Pearlie asked.

*Trail of the Mountain Man

Smoke grinned. "Why, from the men who know more about mountains than anyone else, of course."

Sally nodded. "You're going to go up into the high country and ask some of your mountain man friends about the area."

"Yes. Fall's coming on so they'll be down from the higher peaks, getting ready for the winter. It shouldn't be too hard to find a couple of old cougars up there who've been to Wyoming before." He took a final drink of his coffee and put the cup down. "And if they've been there, they'll know every path and pass and crevice in the area like the back of their hands."

Cal cleared his throat. "Uh, do you mind if Pearlie and I go with you up into the mountains, Smoke?"

Smoke grinned. "No, as a matter of fact, I'm looking forward to it, boys. Mountain lore is a part of your education that's been sorely missing until now. You might even learn a little about how to survive in the mountains from those old beavers."

Sally laughed. "And if you're not careful, the Last Mountain Man might also teach you a few things he's learned over the years," she said.

"Go get your gear packed, and put in some heavy clothes, 'cause it's going to be twenty degrees colder up in the high lonesome than it is down here," Smoke said, his eyes glittering at the prospect of once again traveling the peaks where he grew to manhood.

Six

Sally stood on the porch and waved as the three men rode off toward the high lonesome. Smoke turned in his saddle and stared at her for a moment just before they got out of sight, and she knew it meant he'd be thinking of her on his journey.

Smoke, Pearlie, and Cal were all riding horses that were crosses from Smoke's Palouse mares and Joey Wells's big strawberry roan stud, Red. Joey and his wife had bought the old Rocking C ranch in Pueblo, Colorado, after killing Murdock, the man who owned it. Sally, as a gift to Joey's wife, had given them some Palouse mares to breed with Red and start their remuda.*

The offspring Joey had sent to the Sugarloaf were all beautiful animals that had inherited their father's big size and strength and the Palouses' speed and endurance.

Smoke's stud was a blanket-hipped Palouse, red or roan-colored in front with hips of snow white, without the usual spots of a Palouse. He'd named him Joker because of his funny coloring.

Pearlie's descendant of Red was a gray-and-white Palouse he'd named Cold. When Smoke asked him why he'd named him that, Pearlie said it was because the sucker

*Honor of the Mountain Man

was cold-backed in the morning and bucked for the first ten minutes every day when Pearlie saddled him up.

Cal's mount was a quicksilver gray and was actually almost pure white, differing from a true albino by having blue eyes instead of pink. The bronc was a pale gray in front with snow-white hips without the usual Palouse spots. Cal had named him Silver and had formed a deep and immediate bond with the animal the first time he rode him.

As they approached the mountains, with the peaks hanging in the air and looking as if they were right overhead, Cal pulled out his makin's and began to build himself a cigarette.

"Miss Sally'd whup you if she saw you doin' that," Pearlie said.

Smoke glanced at Cal and smiled. "She would that, all right."

"But Smoke," Cal protested, "if I'm old enough to ride the herd and go after *bandidos,* I ought'a be old enough to smoke if'n I want to."

"You get no argument from me, Cal. I agree with you. A man old enough to strap on a gun and saddle a horse is old enough to make his own decisions about how he lives his life. Like I always say, a man's got to saddle his own horse and kill his own snakes."

"But Miss Sally . . ."

Smoke nodded. "You're right, Sally don't agree with you starting to smoke, or drink, so young. It's that mothering instinct all women have, son, to try and tell a man what's best for him, even if he doesn't want to hear it. Don't pay it no mind, Cal. Just try not to light up in front of her and everything'll be all right."

As they rode up the slope, the sun hung over the distant peaks, gleaming a dull orange-red, like a frying pan left on the fire too long, surrounded by clouds a dull gray in color.

Smoke nodded toward the clouds. "Tell me what kind of weather we're going to be facing up there, boys."

Pearlie pursed his lips. "Well, clouds like that usually mean rain down in the valley, so I 'spect there'll be some snow off and on at the higher places and maybe some freezing rain down lower."

"Heavy or light?" Smoke asked.

"Heavy," Cal replied. "When the clouds are kind'a flatlike and fluffy, it means a light fall. When they're high and thick like that, it means it's gonna be a frog-drownin' son-of-a-buck of a storm."

Smoke grinned. "Looks like I don't have much to teach you boys about how to read the weather. We'll have to see what little bits of knowledge you can pick up from the mountain men we're going to meet."

"Who do you think'll be up here, Smoke?" Pearlie asked.

"Old Bear Tooth for one. He always makes his camp up in this area in the winter. And maybe Long John Dupree or Bull Durham will be somewheres nearby."

"Bull Durham, like the tobacco?" Cal asked.

Smoke laughed. "Yeah. His real name is Christopher Durham, but he's called Bull 'cause he's always got a chaw in his cheek, even when he drinks coffee or eats." He shook his head. "I don't know how he does it, but it doesn't seem to bother his appetite any. He eats about as much as Pearlie."

"Man knows what's good for him then," Pearlie said.

"Better shag those mounts, boys. We've got a long way to go and we're going to need to have time to make a good camp before nightfall or we're going to freeze our *cojones* off when the snow starts to fall."

It was mid-afternoon before they arrived at a place Smoke said would be suitable for a campsite.

"This place looks good enough for our first night," he said. "We've got that ledge over there to block the north wind, the ground is fairly level, there's a stream of water for drinking and washing, and there's plenty of wood-fall for our fires and good grass for the broncs nearby."

"Where do you want us to set up?" Cal asked.

Smoke stepped down off Joker and sat with his back against a tall fir tree. He built himself a cigarette and looked at them over the flame of a lucifer as he lit it. "I'll let you boys decide that. I'll just sit here and relax while you get the fire and coffee going."

Pearlie nodded. "You do that, Smoke. Makin' camp is young men's work, an' old codgers like you need your rest after bein' in the saddle all day."

Smoke leaned back against the tree, tipped his hat down over his eyes, and smoked. "Damn right, Pearlie, couldn't've said it better myself."

"Do you think we'll find any mountain men today, Smoke?" Cal asked.

"Ought to," Smoke replied from under his hat. "They've been watching us for the past three hours."

Pearlie glanced around over his shoulder. "I haven't seen anybody."

Smoke chuckled. "You weren't supposed to, Pearlie."

The smell of bacon and beans cooking on an open fire woke Smoke up.

"Coffee's ready," Cal called from where he and Pearlie sat next to a campfire.

Smoke got to his feet and stood and stretched for a moment, letting his eyes wander around the trees and bushes and boulders surrounding them.

As he walked to the fire, he called, "Might as well come on in and get warm, Bear Tooth. No need squatting out there in the cold."

A tall hulking man well over six feet tall and wearing a bearskin coat and moccasins stepped from behind a nearby fir tree. He was carrying a Sharps Big Fifty rifle that was almost as long as he was tall, and had a coonskin hat on. His face was covered with a dark, scraggly beard, and as he got closer he gave off an odor like he hadn't bothered to clean the bearskin particularly well before making it into a coat.

"How do, Smoke," he growled, his voice husky and deep, as if he didn't get much practice speaking.

"Right well, Bear Tooth. Light and set and draw up a cup of *cafecito* with us."

"Don't mind if I do, young'un."

As he got closer, he could be seen to be older than he'd first looked. In spite of still-dark hair and beard, he had to be in his seventies, but he moved and acted like a man much younger.

He wrapped his hands around the coffee cup Pearlie handed him and took a deep swig. "Just right," he said, "strong enough to float a horseshoe."

Smoke nodded. "Remember old Puma Buck?"

"Shore," Bear Tooth replied with a grin.

"He used to say, the thing about makin' good coffee is it don't take near as much water as you think it do."

Bear Tooth laughed. "Old Puma had a way with words, all right." He hesitated a moment, then asked, "By the way, Smoke, whatever happened to ol' Puma? I heared some rumors he was kilt down Colorado way, but never met nobody who knew fer shore."

Smoke nodded. "You heard right, Bear Tooth. Puma was killed while trying to help some folks out that sorely needed helping." Smoke's eyes were unfocused as he thought back to that night, and in a low voice he told Bear Tooth the tale . . .

* * *

Puma Buck walked his horse slowly through under-brush and light forest timber in foothills surrounding Murdock's spread. His mount was one they'd hired in Pueblo on arriving, and it wasn't as surefooted on the steep slopes as his paint pony back home was, so he was taking it easy and getting the feel of his new ride.

He kept a sharp lookout toward Murdock's ranch house almost a quarter of a mile below. He was going to make damned sure none of those *buscaderos* managed to get the drop on Smoke and his other new friends. He rode with his Sharps .52-caliber laid across his saddle horn, loaded and ready for immediate action.

Several times Puma had seen men ride up to the ranch house and enter, only to leave after a while, riding off toward herds of cattle that could be seen on the horizon. Puma figured they were most likely the legitimate punchers Murdock had working his cattle, and not gun hawks he'd hired to take down Smoke and Joey. A shootist would rather take lead poisoning than lower himself to herd beeves.

Off to the side, Puma could barely make out the riverbed, dry now, that ran through Murdock's place. He could see on the other side of Murdock's ranch house a row of freshly dug graves. He grinned to himself, appreciating the graves, some of them the result of his shooting, and appreciating the way Smoke had deprived the man of water for his cattle and horses.

Puma knew that alone would prompt Murdock to make his move soon; he couldn't afford to wait and let his stock die of thirst.

As Puma pulled his canteen out and uncorked the top, ready to take a swig, he saw a band of about fifteen or more riders burning dust toward the ranch house from the direction of Pueblo. Evidently they were additional men Murdock had hired to replace those he and Smoke and Joey had slain in their midnight raid.

"Uh-huh," he muttered. "I'll bet those *bandidos* are

fixin' to put on the war paint and make a run over to Smoke's place."

He swung out of his saddle and crouched down behind a fallen tree, propping the big, heavy Sharps across the rough bark. He licked his finger and wiped the front sight with it, to make it stand out more when he needed it. He got himself into a comfortable position and laid out a box full of extra shells next to the gun on the tree within easy reach. He figured he might need to do some quick reloading when the time came.

After about ten minutes, the gang of men Puma was observing arrived at the front of the ranch house, and two figures Puma took to be Murdock and Vasquez came out of the door to address them. He couldn't make out their faces at this distance, but they had an unmistakable air of authority about them.

As the rancher began to talk, waving his hands toward Smoke's ranch, Puma took careful aim, remembering he was shooting downhill and needed to lower his sights a bit, the natural tendency being to overshoot a target lower than you are.

He took a deep breath and held it, slowly increasing pressure on the trigger so when the explosion came it would be a surprise and he wouldn't have time to flinch and throw his aim off.

The big gun boomed and shot a sheet of fire two feet out of the barrel, slamming back into Puma's shoulder and almost knocking his skinny frame over. Damn, he had almost forgotten how the big Sharps kicked when it delivered its deadly cargo.

The targets were a little over fifteen hundred yards from Puma, a long range even for the remarkable Sharps. It seemed a long time, but was only a little over five seconds, before one of the men on horseback was thrown from his mount to lie sprawled in the dirt. The sound was several seconds slower reaching the men, and by then

Puma had jacked another round in the chamber and fired again. By the time the group knew they were being fired upon, two of their number were dead on the ground. Just as they ducked and whirled, looking for the location of their attacker, another was knocked off his bronc, his arm almost blown off by the big .52-caliber slug traveling at over two thousand feet per second.

The outlaws began to scatter, some jumping from their horses and running into the house while others just bent over their saddle horns and burned trail dust away from the area. A couple of brave souls aimed rifles up the hill and fired, but the range was so far for ordinary rifles that Puma never even saw where the bullets landed.

Another couple of rounds were fired into the house, and then Puma figured he had done enough for the time being. Now he had to get back to Smoke and tell him Murdock was ready to make his play, or would be as soon as he rounded up the men Puma had scattered all over the countryside.

Several of the riders had ridden toward Smoke's ranch and were now between Puma and home. "Well, shit, old beaver. Ya knew it was about time for ya ta taste some lead," he mumbled to himself. He packed his Sharps in his saddle boot and opened his saddlebags. He withdrew two Army Colt .44s to match the one in his holster and made sure they were all loaded up six and six, then stuffed the two extras in his belt. He tugged his hat down tight and eased up into the saddle, grunting with the pain it caused in his arthritic joints. He kept to heavy timber until he came to a group of six men standing next to a drying riverbed, watering their horses in one of the small pools remaining.

There was no way to avoid them so he put his reins in his teeth and filled both hands with iron. It was time to dance with the devil, and Puma was going to strike up the band. He kicked his mount's flanks and bent low over his saddle horn as he galloped out of the forest toward the gunnies below.

One of the men, wearing an eye patch, looked up in astonishment at the apparition wearing buckskins and war paint charging them, yelling and whooping and hollering as he rode like the wind.

"Goddamn, boys, it's that old mountain man!" One-Eye Jackson yelled as he drew his pistol.

All six men crouched and began firing wildly, frightened by the sheer gall of a lone horseman charging right at them.

Puma's pistols exploded, spitting fire, smoke, and death ahead of him. Two of the gunslicks went down immediately, .44 slugs in their chests.

Another jumped into the saddle and turned tail and rode like hell to get away from this madman who was bent on killing all of them.

One-Eye took careful aim and fired, his bullet tearing through Puma's left shoulder muscle, twisting his body and almost unseating him.

Puma straightened, gritting his teeth on the leather reins while he continued firing with his right-hand gun, his left arm hanging useless at his side. His next two shots hit their targets, taking one gunny in the face and the other in the stomach, doubling him over to leak guts and shit and blood in the dirt as he fell.

One-Eye's sixth and final bullet in his pistol entered Puma's horse's forehead and exited out the back of its skull to plow into Puma's chest. The horse swallowed its head and somersaulted as it died, throwing Puma spinning to the ground. He rolled three times, tried to push himself to his knees, then fell facedown in the dirt, his blood pooling around him.

One-Eye Jackson looked around at the three dead men lying next to him and muttered a curse under his breath. "Jesus, that old fool had a lot'a hair to charge us like that." He shook his head as he walked over to Puma's body and aimed his pistol at the back of the mountain man's head. He eared back the hammer and let it drop. His gun clicked . . . all chambers empty.

One-Eye leaned down and rolled Puma over to make sure he was dead. Puma's left shoulder was canted at an angle where the bullet had broken it, and on his right chest was a spreading scarlet stain.

Puma moaned and rolled to the side. One-Eye Jackson chuckled. "You're a tough old bird, but soon's I reload I'll put one in your eye."

Puma's eyes flicked open and he grinned, exposing bloodstained teeth. "Not in this lifetime, sonny," and he swung his right arm out from beneath his body. In it was his buffalo skinning knife.

One-Eye grunted in shock and surprise as he looked down at the hilt of Puma's long knife sticking out of his chest. "Son of a . . ." he rasped, then he died.

Puma lay there for a moment. Then with great effort he pushed himself over so he faced his beloved mountains. "Boys," he whispered to all the mountain men who had gone before him, "Git the *cafecito* hot, I'm comin' to meet 'cha."*

Bear Tooth, instead of looking sad, smiled as he nodded his head. "That's the way a mountain man ought'a go out, with his guns blazin' and spittin' death and destruction all round him."

Smoke smiled, too. "You're right, Bear Tooth. Old Puma wouldn't't've wanted to die in bed, that's for sure."

Bear Tooth inclined his head at Cal and Pearlie. "You gonna introduce me to yore *compadres,* Smoke?"

Smoke introduced the boys, who both stood to shake hands with Bear Tooth.

*Honor of the Mountain Man

"What you boys doin' up here on the slopes, Smoke? Teachin' the young beavers some'a the lessons 'bout mountain life ole Preacher taught you?"

Smoke hesitated a moment, then looked directly at the mountain man. "No, actually, we came up here to see you, Bear Tooth."

Bear Tooth pursed his lips, making his beard move as if it were home to tiny animals. "Ya came all the way up here to see me? Pardon me fer sayin' so, Smoke, but the idee of that kind'a makes the skin on my back crawl."

Smoke smiled. "Oh, there's nothing to worry about, Bear Tooth. I just need some information about a place you used to trap a few years back."

Bear Tooth pulled a long rope of tobacco from his shirt pocket, bit off a sizable portion, and began to chew. "You talkin' 'bout Wyomin'?"

Smoke nodded. "A friend of mine's wife was taken by some hard cases and word is they're camping at the hole-in-the-wall near Jackson Hole."

Bear Tooth narrowed his eyes. "An' I reckon you want to know if'n there's some back way into the hole so's you can go in and get the woman out?"

Smoke nodded.

Bear Tooth scratched his beard, his eyes far off as he thought about it. "There's only one way in where they won't see ya comin'. On the back side of the second-highest peak there's a cave. It'll be kind'a hard to find this time of year 'cause of the snow, but the cave goes all the way through the mountain and comes out on the other side in a group of boulders. I'm bettin' those flat-landers won't know 'bout it."

"That's just what we're looking for. Can you tell me how to find it?"

Bear Tooth shook his head. "Nope, but an ole friend of mine, Muskrat Calhoon, can. I hear tell he's still trap-pin' up in those peaks round Jackson Hole."

"How can I find him?"

"He comes into town 'bout ever two, three weeks to get his tobaccy and a little hair of the dog. Usually buys it at Schultz's general store as I recall. You ask round town an' they'll let him know yore lookin' fer him. Feel free to tell him yore a friend of mine."

Cal cleared his throat. "Mr. Bear Tooth, how come they call him Muskrat? Is it because he traps 'em?"

Bear Tooth leaned his head back and laughed, showing a row of yellow-stained teeth ground down almost to the gums. "No, son, he don't trap 'em, he smells like 'em."

Smoke laughed along with Cal and Pearlie as he got up and walked to Joker. He pulled a paper bag out of his saddlebags and brought it over to the fire. "Bear Tooth, thanks for your help," he said, setting the bag in front of the mountain man. "My wife, Sally, made these bear sign before we left our ranch, and I'd be honored if you'd share them with us."

"Bear sign?" Bear Tooth asked, his eyes lighting up. He reached into the sack, pulled out a large, homemade doughnut, and stared at it for a moment before dunking it in his coffee, then popping the whole thing in his mouth.

Pearlie licked his lips and turned imploring eyes on Smoke. "Uh, Smoke, do you think there's enough bear sign there for all of us to share?"

Smoke nodded. "I guess so, Pearlie, long as you let Cal and me take one or two before you attack that bag."

"That's for danged sure," Cal said. "Otherwise won't none of us get a chance at any if'n Pearlie digs in first."

Seven

On the way back to Sugarloaf, Smoke decided to stop by Big Rock and see if the wounded man Monte had shot had any more information for them before heading up to Wyoming.

Pearlie slowed Cold as they pulled next to Longmont's Saloon. "You think we might have time to get a bite or two to eat at Longmont's 'fore we head back to the Sugarloaf?" he asked, a hopeful expression on his face.

"That hollow leg of your's beginning to feel empty, Pearlie?" Smoke asked, winking at Cal.

"Yes, sir. I'm so hungry my stomach thinks my throat's been cut."

Smoke glanced at the sun, nearing the middle of the sky but not giving off much heat as cold autumn air flowed down from the mountain passes and chilled the day.

"Well, it has been a few hours since you cleaned us out of fatback and sinkers, so I guess it won't hurt any if we stop and have a meal before bracing that gunny over at Doc's."

They tied their horses to the rail in front of Longmont's and got down out of the saddle. Smoke stood and looked at a trio of horses already tied there, noting the trail dust covering the animals and the strange brands on their flanks.

"Looks like we've got some strangers in town," he said, as they walked through the batwings.

By force of long habit, Smoke stepped to the side as he entered the saloon and diner and let his eyes adjust to the darkened room while he studied the men inside. When he'd lived by his guns, it'd been a trait that had saved his life on more than one occasion. Saloons were the most dangerous places in the West, accounting for more than three quarters of the deaths in most towns.

Cal and Pearlie, trained by Smoke, stepped to the other side of the door and also waited, checking out the customers to see if any appeared dangerous. They both knew there were many men in the country who would like nothing better than to get a reputation for being the one who planted Smoke Jensen forked end up.

Smoke noticed his gambler friend of many years, Louis Longmont, sitting at his usual table in the saloon he owned, where he plied his trade, which he called teaching amateurs the laws of chance.

Louis was a lean, hawk-faced man, with strong, slender hands and long fingers, nails carefully manicured, hands clean. He had jet-black hair and a black pencil-thin mustache. He was, as usual, dressed in a black suit, with white shirt and dark ascot—something he'd picked up on a trip to England some years back. He wore low-heeled boots, and a pistol hung in tied-down leather on his right side. It was not for show, for Louis was snake-quick with a short gun and was a feared, deadly gunhand when pushed.

Louis was not an evil man. He had never hired his gun out for money. And while he could make a deck of cards do almost anything, he did not cheat at poker. He did not have to cheat. He was possessed of a phenomenal memory and could tell you the odds of filling any type of poker hand, and was one of the first to use the new method of card counting.

He was just past forty years of age. He had come to the West as a very small boy, with his parents, arriving from Louisiana. His parents had died in a shanty-town fire, leaving the boy to cope as best he could.

He had coped quite well, plying his innate intelligence and willingness to take a chance into a fortune. He owned a large ranch up in Wyoming Territory, several businesses in San Francisco, and a hefty chunk of a railroad.

Though it was a mystery to many why Longmont stayed with the hard life he had chosen, Smoke thought he understood. Once, Louis had said to him, "Smoke, I would miss my life every bit as much as you would miss the dry-mouthed moment before the draw, the challenge of facing and besting those miscreants who would kill you or others, and the so-called loneliness of the owlhoot trail."

Sometimes Louis joked that he would like to draw against Smoke someday, just to see who was faster. Smoke always allowed as how it would be close, but that he would win. "You see, Louis, you're just too civilized," he had told him on many occasions. "Your mind is distracted by visions of operas, fine foods and wines, and the odds of your winning the match. Also, your fatal flaw is that you can almost always see the good in the lowest creatures God ever made, and you refuse to believe that anyone is pure evil and without hope of redemption."

When Louis laughed at this description of himself, Smoke would continue. "Me, on the other hand, when some snake-scum draws down on me and wants to dance, the only thing I have on my mind is teaching him that when you dance, someone has to pay the band. My mind is clear and focused on only one problem, how to put that stump-sucker across his horse toes-down."

Today, Louis was, as usual, sitting at his personal table, playing solitaire and drinking coffee, a long, black cheroot in the corner of his mouth. Louis looked up and saw Smoke, but he didn't smile as he usually did when Smoke paid him a visit. Instead, he cut his eyes toward the bar and gave his head a slight toss.

Smoke followed his gaze, letting his right hand unhook the hammer-thong on his Colt .44. There were three men standing at the bar, leaning on elbows and drinking whiskey with beer chasers. They looked like hard men, and all had their guns tied down low on their legs, showing they weren't typical cowboys.

Smoke spoke low, out of the side of his mouth. "Watch those three, boys, and keep your guns loose. Something tells me they ride for Slaughter."

Smoke and Cal and Pearlie joined Louis at his table, all three adjusting their chairs so they could watch the men at the bar.

"Howdy, Louis," Smoke said.

"Good afternoon, Smoke," Louis replied, his eyes too on the strangers.

"I notice you got some new customers. Anyone I might know?"

Louis tilted smoke out of his nostrils toward the ceiling and shook his head. "I don't believe so. But these men are very curious about the whereabouts of our sheriff, Monte Carson. They've asked just about everyone who's come in where he might be."

Smoke had filled Louis in on the happenings at Monte's, and had asked him to spread the word that Monte was away on a trip, letting his deputy Jimmy cover things for him in his absence. "Did they believe the story about Monte gone fishing?"

"Not for a moment."

Smoke leaned back in his chair and pushed his hat back on his head. "Do you think you could get Andre to fix us up some lunch? Pearlie's about to starve to death."

Louis grinned for the first time since they entered. "And when is he not?"

He motioned for the young black man who was the waiter to come to his table. "Bobby, would you ask Andre to fix three steaks, not too well done, and to fry some potatoes for Mr. Jensen and his friends?"

"Shore, Boss, and I'll bring some fresh coffee right over too."

While waiting for their food, Smoke got to his feet. "I think I'll mosey on over to the bar and say hello to our friends there," he said.

Longmont sighed. "I'll tell Bobby to keep the mop handy. I have a feeling he'll be having a mess to clean up before long."

Smoke smiled, but there was no mirth in his eyes as he walked to the bar. He leaned on it next to the three men.

Smoke, who stood a few inches over six feet in height and had shoulders as wide as an ax handle, dwarfed the men next to him. The closest turned his head and looked up at Smoke's face.

"Howdy, boys," Smoke said, leaning his left elbow on the bar, keeping his right hand free hanging next to his pistol.

"You want somethin', mister?" a short, dark-haired man with a scraggly mustache growled out of the side of his mouth.

Smoke stared into the man's eyes, his gaze as hard as flint. "I hear you've been asking a lot of questions about our sheriff, Monte Carson."

"What's it to you, feller?" the man asked, a sneer turning up the corners of his lips.

Smoke hesitated for a moment, then backhanded the man across the mouth, slamming his face to the side and almost taking his head off. The man spun on his heels and fell facedown on the floor, his eyes crossed and vacant as blood spurted from his flattened nose and torn lips.

The gunny next to him reached for his gun, but before he could clear leather Smoke drew and slammed his .44 down on the man's head, driving him to his knees with blood spurting from his forehead.

Smoke turned the barrel of the Colt toward the third man, who was standing there with his eyes wide and his mouth hanging open. "I live in this town," Smoke said in a low voice ringed with steel, "and I don't like pond scum like you three smelling up the town."

Sweat appeared on the man's forehead as he slowly moved his hand away from the butt of his pistol. "Uh . . . yes, sir," he mumbled.

"Now, I'm going to ask you once more, why are you fellows so interested in the whereabouts of Monte Carson?"

The man on his knees glanced up, wiping blood off his face, but didn't answer. The third man, who hadn't moved a muscle, looked at Smoke, his eyes switching from the hole in the Colt's barrel to Smoke's face. "We had a message from an old friend of his, that's all. We were just supposed to tell him hello." His face slowly drained of color as he spoke.

"And what was this friend's name?" Smoke asked, earing down the hammer on his .44 and putting it back in his holster.

The two men who were still conscious glanced at each other, sudden fear in their eyes. "I don't rightly remember," the man on his knees said as he grabbed the bar and pulled himself to his feet, swaying slightly. He had a slight quaver in his voice and his eyes fixed on Smoke's pistol.

The man on the floor moaned and rolled on his back, sleeving blood off his mouth with his arm. Smoke reached down, grabbed a handful of his hair, and hauled him to his feet; the man squealing in pain.

Smoke smiled and dusted the man's clothes off. "Well, like I said, this is a nice town, but as you can see, it's not too healthy to go around asking a lot of questions about things that don't concern you."

"Yes, sir, we can see that," the third man said, relieved that Smoke's gun was back in his holster.

"Now, why don't you fellows head on back to Wyoming and learn to mind your own business?"

"How'd you know we was from Wyomin'?" the second man said, before the third slapped him on the shoulder and said, "Shut up, Max."

Smoke leaned forward and whispered, "I know a whole lot more than you think I do, and I want you to take a message to your boss, Jim Slaughter."

"We don't . . ." the third man started to say until a look from Smoke silenced him in mid-sentence.

"Tell Slaughter that Smoke Jensen is coming to have a talk with him, and that if Mary Carson has even one hair out of place when I get there, they'll be finding pieces of his carcass all over the territory before I'm done with him."

"Smoke Jensen . . . THE Smoke Jensen?"

"There's only one I'm aware of," Smoke said.

"Gawd Almighty, Joe, you done drawed down on Smoke Jensen," the second man said to the one with blood all over his face.

Smoke looked at each man one at a time. "I'd suggest that after you give Slaughter my message, you boys look for a healthier climate, 'cause if I see you when I get there, I'll kill you deader'n a snake."

"All right, Mr. Jensen," Max said as he picked his hat up off the bar, ignoring the blood running down his face.

"Oh, and you can tell him Blackie Johnson and his friends send their regards from Hell."

The three men's eyes widened and their faces paled as they threw some coins down on the bar and walked rapidly out of the room without looking back.

"Smoke, your steak is getting cold," Louis called from his table.

Smoke glanced over and saw the gambler hooking his hammer-thong back on the pistol he wore on his right hip, and knew his friend had been backing his play.

Pearlie already had his head down and was stuffing his food into his mouth as if he hadn't eaten in days. Cal was smiling and watching the men leave the saloon.

"You shore know how to liven up a place, Smoke," he said.

As Smoke cut into his steak, Louis leaned forward. "Do you mind telling me why you did that?"

Smoke swallowed, took a drink of coffee, and looked up. "I wanted Slaughter to know that Monte got his message. I also wanted him to know what would happen if he hurt Mary."

"Do you think that's wise?"

Smoke shrugged. "Slaughter's not the kind of man to keep his word, so if he's planning to kill Monte when he gets his money, there wouldn't be any reason for him to keep Mary safe."

Smoke cut another piece of steak. "Now there is, and he'll be wondering why I'm dealing myself into this hand. I hope it'll make him nervous, not knowing just what's going on, and a nervous man sometimes makes mistakes."

Eight

Big Jim Slaughter sat at a table in the main room of a cabin and watched Mary Carson work in the kitchen. She was rolling dough into a long tube, fixing to bake a loaf of bread in the oven.

The cabin was one of five situated in a box canyon in the mountains just north of Jackson Hole, Wyoming. They were rough, had been made of weathered pine logs many years before, and had been used by hundreds of outlaws who'd holed up there while waiting for the law to tire of hunting for them.

There was only one road into the canyon, though there were several steep trails that could be used as exits in the event of a raid by lawmen or the Army. The trails were rough and winding and, though passable by men riding in single file, were too steep and narrow to be suitable for a force of men to use as an attack. Because of the remoteness of the area, and the many narrow passes that were heavily guarded, no one had ever attempted to roust the men hiding there, which made it an ideal place for what Slaughter had in mind.

Slaughter tipped his hat back on his head and leaned back in his chair, crossing his legs. He took a deep drink of the coffee Mary'd made and smacked his lips.

"I sure do appreciate you cooking for us, Mrs. Carson.

It's the first time we've had any food worth eating in over six months."

Mary spoke without turning around. "I don't mind. Keeping busy keeps my mind off . . . other things. I'd rather be doing this than sitting and worrying about Monte and what's going to happen when he finds you."

Slaughter smirked as he took a cloth bag out of his pocket and began to build himself a cigarette. "You worried that maybe he'll get himself killed?"

She turned and leaned back against the counter, dusting flour off her hands on the apron around her waist. She shook her head. "No, not really. Monte's been a sheriff for sometime now, and I know that every day there is the chance some drunken cowboy or thief will shoot him." Her lips curled in a small smile. "It goes with being married to an officer of the law."

Slaughter's face puckered in puzzlement as he struck a lucifer on his pants leg. "Then what are you fretting about?"

Mary's eyes bored into his, making the back of his neck tingle, as if he were being watched by a rattlesnake. "I'm worried about how he's going to feel after he kills you and your men. Monte's never liked having to kill . . . it upsets him for weeks afterwards."

Slaughter choked on a lungful of smoke as he reared his head back and laughed and coughed. When he could get his breath, he asked, "You mean you're afraid he might lose some sleep if he manages to put some lead in me?"

"That's right," she answered. "He's not like you, Mr. Slaughter. Killing goes against his nature, though I'm told he's right good at it when he needs be."

Slaughter nodded his head. "Well, let me assure you, Mrs. Carson. If Monte does manage to plant me six feet under, he sure as hell won't lose any sleep over it. Matter of fact, he's liable to dance a jig on my grave."

He stabbed out his butt on the sole of his boot and

dropped it in an empty can on the table that had once held tinned peaches. "But personally," he said, looking back up at her, "I don't think Monte is that good with a gun."

Mary stared at him with sad eyes, making him wonder just what was going through her mind. "Perhaps you've underestimated my husband, Mr. Slaughter. Have you heard back from the three men you sent to tell him what you wanted?"

The itch returned to the back of Slaughter's neck when she reminded him of the strange absence of Boots Malone, Blackie Johnson, and Slim Watkins. They'd had plenty of time to deliver his message to Monte Carson and make their way back to the hole-in-the-wall. If they didn't show up in the next couple of days, or if he didn't hear from Max or the other two he'd sent to find out what had happened to Blackie and the others, he'd have to ride into Jackson Hole and see if there was a telegraph message for him. Slaughter had been planning this operation for several years now, and he didn't much like being in the dark and not knowing how his plan was progressing.

"I'm sure they'll show up eventually, Mrs. Carson," he answered her, though his voice was less sure now.

She gave him a slight smile, her eyes still sad. "If those men told Monte that you'd taken me, then they're probably dead, or in jail." She turned and began kneading the bread dough. "And I wouldn't go making plans on how you're going to spend that money you want from Monte, because there's not a chance in Hell you're going to live to see a single dollar of it."

Slaughter gritted his teeth until his jaw ached and stood up from the table. He wasn't going to let this woman and her faith in her husband's ability get to him. He turned and walked out the door without another word.

Mary glanced at his back as he left, smiling to herself. She knew Monte was coming for her and that they would be together again soon.

* * *

Smoke refilled his coffee cup and sat back after telling Monte and Sally about what had happened at Longmont's.

Monte was healing fast and was already up and walking around the cabin, anxious to get moving toward Wyoming.

Sally glanced at him with worried eyes. "I really don't think you're ready to make that long a journey on horseback, Monte."

He took the bowl of beef soup she'd fixed him in both hands and drank the last of the juice. "There's no other way, Sally. Every day we wait puts Mary in that much more danger. There's no telling what those bast . . . uh, galoots are doing to her."

Smoke put his hand on Monte's shoulder. "Calm down, Monte. I don't think Slaughter will let any harm come to Mary until he's gotten his hands on the money. He's going to know you won't turn it over to him until you're sure Mary is still alive."

Sally nodded. "Smoke's right, Monte. From what you say, Slaughter is no fool, and he knows you're not the kind of man to give in unless he has Mary to hold over your head. I'm sure she is being treated well."

Monte stood up, grimacing at the pain the movement caused him. "Nevertheless, I can't just sit around here while she's in the hands of those outlaws." He looked at Smoke. "It's gonna take us more'n a week to get to Wyoming, longer if we have any early winter storms. By then, I'll be fit as a fiddle and ready to call the dance with Slaughter."

Smoke shrugged. "If that's the way you want it, Monte." He stood up. "I'll have Pearlie and Cal start packing our gear and getting some horses from the remuda for the trip. I figure we'll make better time if we each take a spare to ride when our mounts get tired."

Sally shook her head. "If you men insist on this foolishness, I'll pack enough food for the trip so you won't have to live on beans and fatback." She pointed her finger at Monte. "You're going to need steak if you want those wounds to heal without getting infected."

He grinned. "Yes, ma'am. I ain't never turned down none of your cooking, Sally, an' I ain't about to start now."

The sound of horses' hooves outside the cabin interrupted their talk. Smoke stepped to the window and pulled the curtains aside.

He looked back over his shoulder with a grin on his face. "Louis Longmont's riding up, and he's wearing his winter coat and pulling a packhorse. Looks like he wants to ante up in this game."

Monte smiled. "Good. Louis is the best man with a gun I know, next to you, Smoke, and if those bastards are holed up in the mountains, we're gonna need all the firepower we can muster to blast 'em out."

Tired of waiting for his men to return, Slaughter decided to ride into Jackson Hole to see if any telegrams had arrived for him. He left Mary in the care of Juanita Sanchez, common-law wife of one of the *bandidos* who lived full time in the hole-in-the-wall. He told her that if anything happened to Mary in his absence, he would personally slit her throat.

"You no need worry, Señor Slaughter," she told him, patting the Army Colt in a holster on her hip. "Any *bastardo* try to touch the *gringa* going to have a beeg hole in his gullet."

Slaughter took two of his top guns with him, Whitey Jones and Swede Johanson. Whitey, an albino with silver hair and snow-white skin and pink eyes, was a stone killer who favored a short-barreled ten-gauge Greener shotgun he wore in a cut-down holster on his right hip. Swede Johanson was a six-foot six-inch giant of a man with blond hair, blue eyes, and a sweet-looking face that belied the fact that he had killed over twenty men, most of whom he'd beaten to death with his ham-sized fists. He wasn't quick on the draw, but he seldom missed once he cleared leather.

The three men tied their horses up outside the Cattleman's bar, a misnomer since the only patrons were outlaws and footpads and other miscreants who rode the owlhoot trail. There wasn't an honest rancher within twenty miles of Jackson Hole.

As they stepped to the bar, Slaughter stood next to an old man in buckskins and a beaver-skin cap who was leaning on his elbows watching the bartender fill a jug with whiskey.

Slaughter wrinkled his nose and glanced at the old mountain man. "Whew, what's that stink? Don't you ever bathe, old-timer?"

The man cut his eyes toward Slaughter and his companions and grinned. "Shore, sonny. I takes me a bathing ever spring and ever summer. I figger twice't a year is plenty. Any more'n that an' ya tend to git the fever."

"You want me to run this stink-pot outta here, Boss?" Whitey asked, his hand on the butt of his pistol.

Before Slaughter could answer, the mountain man jerked a twelve-inch Bowie knife from a scabbard on his belt and had the point of the blade under Whitey's chin, forcing his head up.

As a trickle of blood ran down the albino's neck, the mountain man said, "Now, fellers, I didn't come in here lookin' fer no trouble, but if'n trouble is what yore hankerin' fer, then I'll be glad to oblige ya."

Slaughter laughed, liking the old man's guts. "No . . . no old-timer," he said, holding his hands out. "We don't want any trouble. Go right ahead and finish getting your . . . supplies."

"Thank yee kindly, mister," the mountain man said with some irony, as if he didn't need Slaughter's permission to do anything he wanted to do.

He holstered his knife and winked at Whitey. "Sorry 'bout that nick, feller, but if'n you reach fer that six-killer again, I'll skin you like a beaver 'fore you can blink."

He took his jug from the bartender and picked up off the bar a Sharps .50-caliber rifle that was almost as long as he was tall.

He nodded at Slaughter and backed out the door, his finger on the trigger of the rifle. "See you gents later," he said, showing yellow stubs of teeth in a wide grin.

Whitey grimaced. "Why didn't you let me drill that sucker, Boss?"

Slaughter smiled, turning back to the bar. "You don't appreciate history, Whitey. That man there is one of the last of a dying breed. Another couple of years and there won't be any mountain men left."

Swede slapped his hand on the bar. "How about some whiskey, barkeep? My friend here needs something to calm his nerves."

Whitey took a step toward Swede, his eyes glittering hate, but Slaughter stopped him with a look. "Whitey, why don't you go on over to the telegraph office and see if there's any messages for me? I'll order us some food while you're gone."

"Yes, sir," Whitey said, glaring at Swede as if he could kill him.

By the time Whitey returned, Slaughter and Swede were digging into steaks that looked as if they'd been burned to a crisp. "Damn," Slaughter said as he tried to chew the tough meat, "this is making me appreciate Mrs. Carson's cooking more and more."

Swede nodded. "Yeah, maybe we shouldn't kill her after we get Carson's money. We can keep her around for the winter to keep us warm on cold nights."

Slaughter gave him a flat look. "Swede, Mrs. Carson is a lady and I don't want to hear any more talk like that. It's not her fault she married the wrong man."

"You're not gettin' soft on us, are you, Boss?" he asked, a funny look in his eyes.

Slaughter glared at him. "Anytime you think that, Swede, just give me a try and you'll find out how soft I'm gettin'."

Whitey sat at the table, glancing at the two men as if wondering what he'd interrupted. "Here's a telegram for you, Boss. It's from Max."

Slaughter took the paper and opened it up. As he read, his brow furrowed. "Well, I'll be damned."

"What's it say, Jim?" Swede asked, evidently willing to forget their words of a few moments before.

"Max says a man name of Smoke Jensen braced him in Big Rock. Said to tell me if anything happened to Mary Carson he was going to cut me to pieces."

"Smoke Jensen?" Whitey asked, "The old gunfighter? I thought he was dead."

Slaughter looked at him. "So did I. Haven't heard anything 'bout him in years. Evidently he's joined forces with Monte Carson and wants to deal himself into this little fracas."

"What's he say about Blackie and Boots?" Swede asked.

"According to this, they won't be coming back. Jensen says they send their regards from Hell."

Swede leaned back in his chair, pushing his half-eaten steak away. "This is gettin' complicated, Boss. I thought you said Monte would bring us the money once he knew we had his wife."

Slaughter nodded, a thoughtful look on his face. "I must've figured him wrong. Now it looks like we may have a little more trouble getting our hands on our money than I thought."

"Is Max on his way back here?" Whitey asked.

Slaughter glanced at the telegram. "I don't think so. His last line says he wishes us luck, but he didn't figure on having to face Smoke Jensen for his share and he doesn't think it's worth it."

"That yellow-bellied bastard!" Swede said. "I told you he was the wrong man to send to Big Rock."

Slaughter looked over at him. "Like I said, Swede, anytime you think you're good enough to take over leadership of this gang, you're welcome to give it a try."

Swede's eyes dropped. "It's not that. You're still the boss, Jim, but I don't like the idea of some gunslick friend of Carson's joinin' up with him. It complicates matters."

"Don't worry. There ain't no way they can get into the hole-in-the-wall without us knowing about it first, and we've still got Mary Carson as our ace in the hole. Monte's got to come through with the money. He doesn't have any other choice in the matter, whether he's got some old geezer ex-gunman to ride with him or not."

Whitey caressed the butt of the Greener ten-gauge in his cut-down holster on his hip. "I wouldn't mind mixin' it up with this old Jensen feller. Might be fun to see what he's made of . . . see if all those stories 'bout him are true or not."

Swede cleared his throat. "Uh, he ain't all that old, Whitey."

The albino turned to look at his friend. "You know this galoot?"

Swede shook his head. "No, but when I was just a kid, my daddy and I were livin' in this old mining town just west of the Needle Mountains, place called Rico. It wasn't much more than a camp, and was filled with more gunfighters than miners."

"What's that got to do with Smoke Jensen?" Whitey asked impatiently.

"I'm gettin' to it," Swede answered. "Anyway, I was

in the tradin' post there one morning, gettin' supplies for my dad and me, and I saw these two men ride up from the window. One wasn't more'n a boy in his teens, an' the other was this old mountain man went by the name Preacher. Seems somebody had told Smoke Jensen the men who'd killed his father were in town . . ."

Smoke and Preacher dismounted in front of the combination trading post and saloon. As was his custom, Smoke slipped the thongs from the hammers of his Colts as soon as his boots hit dirt.

They bought their supplies, and had turned to leave when the hum of conversation suddenly died. Two rough-dressed and unshaven men, both wearing guns, blocked the door.

"Who owns that horse out there?" one demanded, a snarl in his voice, trouble in his manner. "The one with the SJ brand?"

Smoke laid his purchases on the counter. "I do," he said quietly.

"Which way'd you ride in from?"

Preacher had slipped to his right, his left hand covering the hammer of his Henry, concealing the click as he thumbed it back.

Smoke faced the men, his right hand hanging loose by his side. His left hand was just inches from his left-hand gun. "Who wants to know—and why?"

No one in the dusty building moved or spoke.

"Pike's my name," the bigger and uglier of the pair said. "And I say you came through my diggin's yesterday and stole my dust."

"And I say you're a liar," Smoke told him.

Pike grinned nastily, his right hand hovering near the butt of his pistol. "Why . . . you little pup. I think I'll shoot your ears off."

"Why don't you try? I'm tired of hearing you shoot your mouth off."

Pike looked puzzled for a few seconds; bewilderment crossed his features. No one had ever talked to him in this manner. Pike was big, strong, and a bully. "I think I'll just kill you for that."

Pike and his partner reached for their guns.

Four shots boomed in the low-ceilinged room, four shots so closely spaced they seemed as one thunderous roar. Dust and birds' droppings fell from the ceiling. Pike and his friend were slammed out the open doorway. One fell off the rough porch, dying in the dirt street. Pike, with two holes in his chest, died with his back against a support pole, his eyes still open, unbelieving. Neither had managed to pull a pistol more than halfway out of leather.

All eyes in the powder-filled and dusty, smoky room moved to the young man standing by the bar, a Colt in each hand. "Good God!" a man whispered in awe. "I never even seen him draw."

Preacher moved the muzzle of his Henry to cover the men at the tables. The bartender put his hands slowly on the bar, indicating he wanted no trouble.

"We'll be leaving now," Smoke said, holstering his Colts and picking up his purchases from the counter. He walked out the door slowly.

Smoke stepped over the sprawled, dead legs of Pike and walked past his dead partner in the shooting.

"What are we 'posed to do with the bodies?" a man asked Preacher.

"Bury 'em."

"What's the kid's name?"

"Smoke."*

* * *

*The Last Mountain Man

Whitey raised his eyebrows. "He was that fast, huh?"

Swede smiled. "Faster'n a rattlesnake strikin'. If you do go up against him, Whitey, you'd better get him with your first shot, 'cause you sure as hell won't get more'n one."

Tired of all this talk about Smoke Jensen, Big Jim Slaughter threw a handful of coins on the table and stood up. "Let's get back to the hole-in-the-wall, boys. If Carson's got some help, we need to make sure we're gonna be ready for 'em when they ride in."

"I'm ready for 'em right now," Whitey said, a sneer on his face.

Swede just smiled. "I'll remember you said that, Whitey."

Nine

When Slaughter got back to his hideout in the hole-in-the-wall, he called all of his men together.

"Boys, we may be facing a little trouble. Seems Monte Carson has gotten some other men to ride with him and he's on his way out here."

Johnny Tupelow, who called himself the Durango Kid, leaned over and spat on the ground. He was a young man, barely out of his teens, and dressed in what he thought a soon-to-be-famous gun hawk should wear—black pants and shirt with a vest festooned with silver conchos and a hat slung low over his forehead. He wore a brace of pearl-handled Colt .45 Peacemakers on his hips and highly polished black boots that rose to his knees. "That mean he ain't gonna give us the money, Boss?"

Slaughter's lips curled in a nasty smile. "Oh, he'll give us the money, all right, or he'll be gettin' pieces of his wife in the mail for months to come." He hesitated. "I don't rightly know if he plans on puttin' up a fight or if he's just bringing some extra guns to make sure we keep our end of the bargain. In any case, until we find out just what his intentions are, I want two men at each sentry post around the clock. One to keep anybody who tries to get in here pinned down and the other to ride here to let us know we got company."

The Durango Kid looked around at the others, then asked, "Any idea who he's got ridin' with him?"

Slaughter hesitated. "Max said it was Smoke Jensen."

"Jensen?" the kid asked, "I thought he was dead."

"Evidently not, according to Max," Slaughter said.

"Any others?" the kid asked.

Slaughter shrugged. "Don't have any idea, but if the thought of goin' up against Jensen worries you, Kid, you're welcome to ride outta here anytime."

The kid leaned over and spat again, a smirk on his face. "Not likely, Mr. Slaughter. I reckon my share of fifty thousand is worth killing a couple of old men past their prime."

Slaughter didn't bother telling the Kid that if he went up against Monte Carson alone, Carson would in all probability plant him six feet under without getting his hair mussed. "Good. Whitey will make out a new schedule for standing watch. I figure it'll be a couple of weeks 'fore we see anybody, but it won't hurt to keep a sharp lookout just the same."

Smoke and his men were making good time toward Jackson Hole, Wyoming. The weather had been unusually mild for this time of year and they'd only had to contend with a few short-lived snowstorms. They made their final camp when Smoke figured they were less than a day's ride from Jackson Hole.

As they sat around the campfire, eating the last of the rations Sally had packed for the trip, Louis put down his empty plate. "I'll tell you something, Smoke. If Sally ever feels the need to leave you for someone who will really appreciate her, she's welcome to come to my place and cook for me anytime."

Smoke grinned. "I'll bet you won't say that in front of Andre," he said, referring to the French chef who'd been preparing meals for Louis for as long as Smoke could remember.

Louis shook his head. "Don't even think such a thing, my friend. Andre would gut me like a fish if he even thought I was contemplating letting anyone else cook for me."

Pearlie grunted. "Hell, if Miss Sally ever left the Sugarloaf, Smoke wouldn't have any hands left to tend the stock. They'd all be off following her to wherever she was going. Most of 'em would travel ten mile just for one of her bear sign."

Cal laughed. "They'd have to leave awful early to beat you to 'em, or there wouldn't be any left for 'em to eat."

Smoke held up his hands to quiet the banter. "All right, men. We need to form a plan of action for when we get to Jackson Hole. Slaughter will have gotten my message by now, and if he's as smart as Monte says he is, then he's going to have men in town watching for us to arrive."

"You can bet on that, Smoke," Monte said. "Slaughter hasn't survived this long by not watching his back."

"I would suggest that we split up on the outskirts of town," Louis said as he pulled a long, black cheroot from his coat pocket and lit it off a burning twig from the fire. He tilted smoke from his nostrils and continued. "Slaughter will be waiting for Monte and an unknown number of men to arrive together. If we go in by ones and twos, his men won't know we're associated with Monte."

Smoke nodded. "Good idea, Louis. I propose that Monte camp just outside town, while Cal and Pearlie circle around and go in from the west, Louis from the north, and I'll enter from the south. With any luck, there won't be anyone there who will know who I am. That should give us time to locate this Muskrat Calhoon Bear Tooth told us about and see if he's going to be willing to help us find a back way into the hole-in-the-wall."

"Wait a minute, Smoke. I ain't gonna sit out here cooling my heels while you fellers do all the work," Monte said.

Louis pointed his cigar at Monte as if it were a gun. "You don't have any choice, Monte. Slaughter's sure to have given your description to his men. If they see you in town, they'll know Smoke and whoever else has offered to ride with you is there, too."

Smoke leaned toward Monte. "It's the only chance we have of getting close enough to free Mary without Slaughter getting wind of our presence, Monte."

"Hell, I know you're right, Smoke. It just sticks in my craw having you fellers take risks for Mary and me."

"That's what friends are for," Pearlie said from across the fire. "We all knew what we were gettin' into when we offered to help out, Monte. Hell, you'd've done the same for any one of us."

Monte nodded, accepting the wisdom of the plan Smoke laid out. "All right. I'll set up a camp and when you locate this Muskrat Calhoon you can bring him there."

Pearlie stood up and dusted off the seat of his pants.

"Where you goin', Pearlie?" Cal asked.

"To see if there's any of that apple pie left Miss Sally made," he said.

Louis stared at him in wonder. "Smoke, if you ever run short of money, you can hire Pearlie out to the circus. He could be billed as the man with the bottomless stomach."

Cal and Pearlie slowed their mounts to a walk as they entered the town of Jackson Hole. The light covering of snow on the ground from the last snowfall did little to make the town look any more inviting. The buildings were mostly made of the ponderosa pine logs that were so plentiful on the surrounding mountain slopes, and the streets were dirt and mud, with only a few boardwalks on the main street. Every other building seemed to be a saloon or gambling parlor, though there were several rather seedy boarding-houses and hotels for the mostly transient population.

"Jimminy," Cal said, his eyes wide as he glanced from side to side, noticing the hard-looking men who lounged along the streets, most with bottles of whiskey in their hands even though it was barely past breakfast time. "I can sure see why they call this area Robber's Roost."

Pearlie nodded as he let his hand drift to his hip to loosen the hammer-thong on his Colt. "Yep. 'Bout the only citizens around here that don't make their livin' with a gun are the barkeeps and fallen doves in the whorehouses."

As he spoke, a girl who looked to be no more than fifteen stumbled out of a doorway and grabbed a cowboy leaning against the wall by the shoulder. She wore a tawdry dress made of red silk with green overlay that was cut almost down to her navel. After a few moments talking to the gent, he grinned and followed her back through the doorway.

Cal shook his head. "Not much like Big Rock, is it, Pearlie?"

"Not enough so's you can tell it, Cal." He swiveled his head, glancing to both sides of the street. "You figger there's any place we can rustle up some breakfast around here?"

Cal pursed his lips. After a moment, he pointed to the right side of the street. "There's a sign over that boarding-house sayin' 'Good Eats.' I reckon that's as good a place as any to look. We gotta find us a place to bed down anyway."

They reined in before the building with the sign that read, "Aunt Bea's Boarding House, Clean Sheets and Good Eats."

When they entered they saw an entrance to the dining area off to the left. Pearlie removed his hat and made a beeline for the room, holding his nose in the air. "I smell bacon fryin' an' eggs cookin', Cal, boy. Looks like we struck pay dirt."

Cal just shook his head and followed his partner's nose. Pearlie was like a bloodhound when it came to food, and could smell out vittles as well as a hound could track a rabbit.

They sat at a table near the window, where they could watch the comings and goings along the main street, and put their hats on a chair.

After a moment, a rotund woman wearing a flour-stained apron approached the table.

"Howdy, boys. What can I git ya?" she asked.

She had gray hair done up in a bun and a face full of wrinkles, showing she'd spent considerable time in the sun. Her eyes were sky-blue and seemed to twinkle with good nature.

Pearlie considered her question for a minute, then said, "I'd like four hen's eggs, scrambled, a pound of bacon, not too crisp, and some flapjacks with syrup. And about a gallon of coffee," he added.

"Are you Aunt Bea?" Cal asked.

"That's what most folks call me, sonny, boy, leastways round here."

"I'll have a couple of eggs and some bacon and flap-jacks too," Cal said.

Aunt Bea's eyes narrowed as she studied Cal and Pearlie. "You boys don't exactly look like the usual sort we get around here. You just passin' through?"

Cal and Pearlie glanced at each other. They hadn't had a chance yet to get their story straight about why they were in Jackson Hole.

Finally, Pearlie answered her. "Yes, ma'am. We're just up from Texas way. Had a little trouble crost the border with the Mexican Federales and we figgered it'd be better for our health if'n we moseyed on up north for a spell."

The light seemed to go out of her eyes. "Oh, outlaws, huh?"

Cal, noticing her disappointment, quickly said, "Oh, no, ma'am. Leastways, not here in the States. It's just that the Rangers tend to take a dislike to anybody that causes trouble with the Mexican authorities, so we thought we'd leave Texas until they forgot about our . . . little problems."

Aunt Bea nodded. "Well, I hope you don't plan on stayin' here too long, boys. Jackson Hole ain't exactly a healthy place to hang around 'less you're tougher 'n boot leather. Some of the men round here like to eat young fellers like you for breakfast, if you know what I mean."

"Yes, ma'am," Cal said, putting on his most innocent expression.

Aunt Bea dusted her hands on her apron, causing a cloud of flour dust to rise in the air. "Well, I'll be seein' to your food an' I'll have the boy bring you your coffee right out."

After she left, Cal leaned across the table. "Why'd you tell her we was runnin' from the law?"

Pearlie shrugged. "We got to fit in, Cal, boy. You can't just come to a place full of footpads, thieves, and rustlers and pretend to be choirboys. It wouldn't look right."

Cal leaned back. "I guess you're right, though I hate makin' her think we ride the owlhoot trail."

Pearlie glanced at the kitchen door through which Bea had disappeared. "Unless I miss my guess, that lady likes to gossip, Cal, an' it won't hurt nothin' to have her spread the word we're on the run."

While Pearlie was talking, Cal looked out the window and saw Louis Longmont dismounting in front of the boardinghouse. Cal nudged Pearlie's shoulder and motioned at the window with his head.

Pearlie grinned and nodded, evidently glad to see a friendly face among the hard cases on the street.

Louis sauntered into the dining room, gave Cal and Pearlie a quick glance, but didn't acknowledge them in any other way. He sat at a table across the room and leaned back in his chair, pulling out his trademark long black cheroot and lighting it.

Aunt Bea brought them a large coffeepot and two

mugs, said their food would be ready shortly, then walked over to Louis's table.

"Howdy, mister," they heard her say. "I'm Aunt Bea. You want breakfast or lunch?"

"I believe I'll have lunch, Aunt Bea. How about a steak, cooked just long enough to keep it on the plate, some fried potatoes, and some tinned peaches if you have any."

Bea nodded. "Coffee?"

"Yes, please."

"Ah, a man with manners. Quite a rarity around here," she said, as she walked back toward the kitchen.

A few minutes later a boy that looked to be no more than twelve or fourteen came out of the back room with two large platters in his arms. He placed the plates in front of Cal and Pearlie and walked back to the kitchen.

Pearlie wasted no time. He put his head down and began to eat as if he were starving. Cal glanced over at Louis, smiled, and also began to eat.

Just as Louis was being served, several groups of men entered and the tables in the dining room began to fill up, it being close to the noon hour. Minutes later, Smoke walked in and took a table by himself, sitting as was his custom with his back to a wall where he could keep watch on the entrance to the room.

Soon all the tables in the room were filled. Pearlie, finally finished with his food, poured himself another cup of coffee and leaned back in his chair, building himself a cigarette. "Aunt Bea must do all right, from the looks of the crowd," he said, handing Cal his fixin's so he could make himself a cigarette also.

Just as Cal was lighting his cigarette, four men walked up to their table. The first one, a tall, skinny man with several days' growth of whiskers on his face, a tied-down Colt on one hip, and a large Bowie knife in a scabbard on the other, leaned over and put both his hands on their table.

"If you gents are through eatin', why don't you get

your asses away from my table and let me an' my friends sit down?"

Pearlie glanced up at him through the smoke from the butt in the corner of his mouth, a mannerism he'd copied from his idol, Joey Wells. "Take it easy, pardner," he drawled, making no move to get up. "We'll leave when we're good and ready, an' not a minute sooner."

"You gonna let a pup like that sass you, Billy?" the man behind him said with a chuckle.

Billy backed away from the table and squared off, letting his hand dangle near the butt of his pistol. "Hell, no, I'm not," he growled. "Now, you young'uns can either get up of your own accord, or I'm gonna have to make you."

The three men with Billy spread out next to him, grim expressions on their faces.

"Hold on there, Billy Baxter!" Aunt Bea called from the kitchen door. She was holding a long-barreled Greener shotgun cradled in her arms. "I don't want no trouble in my place, you hear me, you hooligan?"

Before Billy could answer, Pearlie got to his feet. "Don't you worry none, Aunt Bea," he said, his eyes never leaving Baxter. "This *cabron* sounds like all talk to me, an' even if he does have the guts to go for that smoke wagon on his hip, he won't even clear leather 'fore I put his lights out."

Cal got to his feet and unhooked the leather hammerthong on his Colt. "Four to two, Pearlie. Looks even enough for me," he whispered in a gravelly voice, his eyes on the men behind Baxter.

Louis, concerned about the turn of events, cut his eyes over to Smoke, who was sitting smiling and watching. Smoke winked at Louis, indicating he shouldn't worry.

Nevertheless, Louis leaned back and straightened out his right leg, resting his hand next to his pistol just in case.

Baxter's eyes shifted from Pearlie to Cal, seeing no back-up in either man. Sweat popped out on his forehead, though the room was cool. He licked suddenly dry lips, unsure of what his next move should be. The man next to him moved over a little, evidently trying to get out of the line of fire.

Suddenly, Baxter's hand grabbed for his gun butt. Before he could get his pistol halfway out of his holster, Pearlie had drawn and slammed the barrel of his Colt on top of Baxter's head, poleaxing him and dropping him to the floor. Only a shade slower, both Cal's pistols were out with hammers cocked and pointed at the remaining men, who were standing there with mouths open and eyes wide.

"Jesus God Awmighty," one of them croaked, holding his hands out away from his pistols, "that boy's faster'n a snake."

Pearlie slowly turned to the other men. "You gents better drag your friend outta here, 'fore he bleeds all over Aunt Bea's floor."

Aunt Bea rushed over to stare down at Baxter. She looked up. "Damn right! Drag his sorry ass outta here and don't none of you bother to try an' eat here again, you hear me?"

Pearlie picked up his hat and gave a slight bow to Aunt Bea. "Sorry for the trouble, ma'am. I hope I didn't make too much of a mess."

She smiled and clapped him on the shoulder. "A little blood on the floor is better'n hair on the wall, sonny. It's not the first an' it won't be the last blood spilt in this town neither."

"Any chance of us gettin' a room for the night, ma'am?" Cal asked, holstering his pistol as Baxter's friends picked him up and carried him from the room.

"Sure, boys. Be a welcome change to have guests who don't shoot off their guns first chance they git. Come on over to the front and I'll give you a key."

Ten

Later that afternoon, after Smoke and Louis had also gotten rooms at Aunt Bea's boardinghouse, the four men met in Smoke's room.

Louis looked at Pearlie. "Pearlie, you just about gave me a heart seizure when you braced that cowboy and his friends."

Pearlie grinned. "Oh, I wasn't worried, Louis. After all, Cal and me had you and Smoke to back our play."

Smoke chuckled. "Obviously, you didn't need us, Pearlie. You boys handled it just right. By now, everyone in town has heard about your little set-to with Baxter."

Cal frowned. "You don't think they'll be laying for us when we leave, do you, Smoke?"

Smoke shook his head. "I doubt it. Things like that must go on every day here in Jackson Hole. By tomorrow, it'll be old news."

Louis grinned. "Except I'll wager no one attempts to rush you from your table before you're ready again."

"Cal," Smoke said, "I'd like you and Pearlie to head on over to Schultz's general store this afternoon and let it be known that you're looking for Muskrat Calhoon. Bear Tooth said that's where he usually gets his supplies for the winter and I need to know if he's still in town or has already headed up into the high lonesome."

"Yes, sir," Cal said.

"Louis and I will visit a few of the saloons and gambling houses to see what we can find out about Big Jim Slaughter. We'll see if we can get a handle on just how many men he has up at the hole-in-the-wall with him."

"Anything else you want us to do?" Pearlie asked.

"Yeah. Start buying up ammunition and gunpowder and dynamite while you're there. Not too much at one time, and try to spread out your purchases among several different places. We don't want anyone to think we're going to war."

Just after supper, Louis joined a table of men playing poker at a place called The Dog Hole Saloon and Gaming Room. He slipped his coat off and played wearing only his vest, with his sleeves rolled up. He'd found that when he won large sums of money, as he usually did, it eased competitors' minds to see that he had nothing up his sleeves. Of course, he had no need to cheat. Possessed of a remarkable memory and intelligence and a deep knowledge of the odds of drawing certain hands, he rarely lost, especially when playing cowboys who were usually both drunk and stupid.

After a couple of hours, one of the men at the table threw down his hand in disgust. "Boys, that about finishes me for the night. I'm busted."

"Perhaps you can get an advance from your boss and rejoin us later," Louis said as he raked in yet another pot.

The cowboy shook his head. "What boss? I ain't exactly workin' at the present time."

"Oh?" Louis said. He flipped a twenty-dollar gold piece across the table. "Then take this," he said. "I make it a practice never to take a man's food money from him."

The man picked up the gold piece. "Thanks, mister."

"Perhaps you could seek employment with Jim Slaughter."

When the table got quiet, Louis looked around innocently. "Didn't I hear someone saying a gentleman named Slaughter was hiring men?"

The other men at the table seemed to relax slightly, as if the mention of Slaughter's name was risky, even in a town as hard as Jackson Hole.

"Just where'd you hear that, mister?" a man in a fur-lined deerskin coat across the table asked.

Louis shrugged. "Oh, I don't know. I believe a couple of gentlemen were discussing it at a roulette table earlier in the evening."

The man next to Louis leaned over and whispered, "It ain't exactly healthy to go around talkin' 'bout Slaughter's business hereabouts, Mr. Longmont. Word is he don't take kindly to anybody bein' too nosy 'bout his affairs, if you get my drift."

Louis smiled and put his finger to his lips. "Oh, of course. Then mum's the word regarding this Mr. Slaughter, whoever he might be."

"Besides," another man at the table, who was drunk, said, "I heard he's got all the men he needs. Must have over thirty men up there at . . ."

"Shut your mouth, Kyle!" the man in the deerskin coat shouted. "You talk too much an' you're liable to have somebody cut your tongue out for you."

Kyle looked at the man through bleary, bloodshot eyes. "Go to hell, Davis. Just 'cause you work for Big Jim don't give you the right to tell ever'body else in town what they can say."

"Ante up, gentlemen," Louis called, throwing a coin into the middle of the table to change the subject. "I believe it's my deal."

Davis looked pointedly at the stack of money in front of Louis. "And as for you, Mr. Fancy Tinhorn Gambler, make sure you deal off the top of the deck this time. I'm gettin' awfully tired of you winnin' all the pots."

Louis stared at Davis and put the cards down, pushing his chair back from the table. "Then perhaps you should make an effort to learn how to play poker, Mr. Davis, if you're tired of losing. Drawing to an inside straight like you did the last hand is a fool's play."

Davis jumped up from his seat. "A fool, am I?" he shouted, bringing a sudden hush to the room.

Louis looked at him without a trace of fear on his face. "You are either a fool or you are stupid, Mr. Davis. And I wouldn't care to wager which it is."

"Why you . . ." Davis shouted, and went for his gun.

Louis drew without standing up. His Colt exploded, spewing smoke and hot lead across the table before Davis could cock his pistol. The slug took him in the right shoulder, spinning him around and throwing him face-down on the floor.

Louis spun his Colt on his finger and deposited it in his holster without showing the slightest trace of emotion. "As I said, I believe it is my deal," he remarked to the men at the table.

"Uh . . . yes, sir, Mr. Longmont. I believe it is," said the man on his left.

As Louis dealt the cards, Davis groaned and writhed on the floor. "Perhaps someone should send for a doctor, before poor Mr. Davis bleeds to death," Louis said, as if it really didn't matter to him whether they did or didn't.

Smoke was standing at the bar in the Cattleman's Saloon. He was sipping a glass of whiskey and chasing it with beer, drinking slowly so as not to let the liquor cloud his judgment.

He'd spoken with several men, inquiring whether anyone in the area was hiring men who knew how to use a gun. The answer was always the same. The town was full of such men and, since there were no range wars going on at present, no one was actively hiring.

Evidently, word of his inquiries spread, and before long a tall man, broad through the shoulders, with a weathered face and tired eyes, stepped up next to him at the bar. The man wore a Colt low on his hip and a tin star on his vest.

He ordered a beer and after the barman brought it, leaned his elbow on the bar and looked at Smoke.

"Howdy, stranger. I don't believe I caught your name," he drawled in a nonchalant manner.

Smoke lit the cigarette he'd built and let smoke trail from his nostrils as he answered, "I don't believe I threw it."

The man chuckled. "A gunfighter with a sense of humor. That's a new one around here. My name's Pike. Walter Pike, but everyone around here just calls me Sheriff," Pike said, raising his eyebrows in silent interrogation of Smoke.

"Howdy, Sheriff Pike. I'm Johnny West," Smoke said, giving a name he'd once used while on the run years before.

"West, huh? Well, Johnny West, I don't recollect any wanted posters on you at my office, but I'll be sure and check again, first chance I get."

Smoke gave Pike a questioning look. "Sheriff, I understood this town was . . . rather open and understanding of men with a reputation. Are you telling me that's not the case?"

Pike took a deep swig of his beer, sleeving the suds off his mustache with the back of his arm. "No, you heard right, Mr. West. I don't ordinarily hassle men about what they did or didn't do 'fore they entered my town. I figure it's live and let live as long as they don't do anything to cause a ruckus here. However, I do like to let newcomers know that if they bust a cap in my town, they're gonna have me to answer to."

Smoke turned to look at the sheriff. "Are you that good?"

Pike grinned. "Oh, I'll be the first to admit I'm not the fastest gun in town, but I DO maintain an edge." He inclined his head at the door to the saloon.

Smoke turned and looked. Two men were standing just inside the batwings, both cradling short-barreled shotguns in their arms. Their eyes were fixed on Smoke and their fingers were on the triggers with hammers eared back.

Smoke grinned. "I see what you mean, Sheriff. A sensible precaution in a place known as Robber's Roost filled with more gunfighters than Dodge City at its prime."

Doubt showed in Pike's eyes for the first time since he spoke to Smoke. "You sure don't talk like your average gunslick, Mr. West. Just what are you doing here in Jackson Hole?"

Smoke shrugged. "Just a man passing through, Sheriff. Looking to pick up some spare change in the only way I know, by hiring my services out if anybody's interested."

Pike nodded. "Uh-huh. Well, there's nothing illegal about that, so far as it goes, Mr. West." He tipped his hat. "I just thought I'd amble on over and explain the rules of the town to you. You take it easy now, you hear?"

Smoke was about to reply when a man ran into the saloon. "Sheriff, Sheriff Pike. A gambler named Longmont just put some lead in Jack Davis over at the Dog Hole."

Pike loosened his Colt in its holster and smiled at Smoke. "See, Mr. West? Now I've got to go and make sure this Longmont was sufficiently provoked to justify shooting someone in my town."

"And if he wasn't?" Smoke asked.

"Then he'll either leave town of his own accord, or he'll stay forever in boot hill." Pike pulled his hat down tight over his forehead and walked out the batwings, his deputies close behind.

Smoke hesitated. He was tempted to follow and find out what had happened with Louis, but he didn't want to tip his hand by showing too much interest. Besides, he figured, Louis was perfectly capable of taking care of himself. He turned back to his whiskey and took a sip, wondering what Cal and Pearlie were doing.

Cal and Pearlie walked into Schultz's General Store and Emporium and were surprised to find a large, well-stocked establishment.

"Jimminy, Pearlie," Cal said, his eyes wide as he stared around at the wealth of supplies in the store. "This place is bigger'n anything we got in Big Rock."

Pearlie nodded. "Yep, it sure is. I guess it's because this is the only place for hundreds of miles fer folks to buy supplies an' such to git through the winter."

The store was divided into several different parts. On one side was a wall covered with shelves stocked with all manner of foodstuffs—barrels of flour and beans and coffee, row upon row of tinned milk, meat, and fruits, and even cases stuffed with sides of beef and bacon and all manner of fowls.

Another section contained various and sundry mining and trapping equipment from shovels and picks to traps and axes and skinning knives.

The other side of the room was lined with rifles, pistols, cases of ammunition of all calibers alongside small wooden kegs of gunpowder, and cases containing sticks of dynamite and fuses.

A large man wearing an apron over a white shirt, with his sleeves rolled up, approached them with a grin. He was barrel-chested, with a large stomach, dirty blond hair, and ice-blue eyes over a handlebar mustache whose ends hung below ample jowls.

"Howdy, gents. What can I get for you?" he said in a thick German accent. "If I don't got it, they don't make it," he added with a grin.

Pearlie nodded at the section with ammunition and gunpowder. "We came to stock up on some cartridges and blastin' powder, an' maybe a few sticks of that dynamite," he said.

"You came to the right place," Schultz said. "I can fit you out with anything from musket balls to the latest rimfire cartridges from Colt or Smith and Wesson."

As the proprietor helped them load up what they needed, Cal cleared his throat. "By the way, Mr. Schultz, we heard tell an old friend of ours sometimes stopped by here 'fore headin' up into the mountains. His name is Muskrat Calhoon."

Schultz chuckled. "Well, as you can tell from the absence of any stink, ole' Muskrat hasn't been in yet today, but I expect him 'fore too long. He'll likely be here in the next day or two if he wants to get through the mountain passes 'fore they get all snowed in."

Pearlie hefted the crate of ammunition onto his shoulder and handed Schultz a stack of bills. "Would you tell him a couple of old friends of his and Bear Tooth are in town? We're stayin' over at Aunt Bea's boardin' house for the next couple of days."

"Gonna partake of a little night life 'fore you head on out, huh?"

Cal blushed and grinned as he picked up the kegs of gunpowder and crate of dynamite. "Yes, sir, we shore are."

"Well, if ole' Muskrat happens by, an' he ain't too drunk to listen, I'll tell him to look you up."

"Thank you kindly, Mr. Schultz," Pearlie said, and led Cal out the door.

On the way back to the boardinghouse, Pearlie said, "Jeez, Cal, I sure hope we find that old mountain man, or we ain't gonna have a prayer of gettin' to Miss Carson without those *bandidos* knowin' we're comin'."

Cal nodded. "Well, Mr. Schultz said he ain't been by yet, so there's still hope."

Pearlie raised his nose to the air as they neared Aunt Bea's. "Smells like Aunt Bea's cookin' fried chicken fer dinner."

Cal stared at Pearlie. "With a nose that good, maybe you could smell out this Muskrat feller."

Pearlie shook his head. "Only works fer food, Cal, boy, only fer food. If'n it worked fer fellers that needed a bath, it wouldn't get past you!"

Eleven

After eating supper at different tables in Aunt Bea's
dining room, Smoke and the others met in Smoke's room
to compare notes on what they'd learned during the day.

"From what I can gather, Slaughter has all the men he
needs," Smoke said. "At least he's not actively looking
to hire any new gunhands."

Louis nodded. "That squares with what I could glean
from my compatriots at the gaming tables. The best es-
timate I can come up with is he has between twenty and
thirty hard cases up in the hole-in-the-wall with him. No
one knows for sure since they never all come into town
at the same time, but usually in groups of three or four,
and then only when they need supplies or female com-
panionship."

"How about you and Cal, Pearlie? What did you find
out about Muskrat Calhoon?"

"Well," Pearlie drawled as he picked fried chicken
from between his teeth with a toothpick, "Muskrat hasn't
been in the store to buy his provisions yet, so the proprietor thought it'd be any day now since he's got to do
it soon to beat the snows in the passes."

"Proprietor's gonna let him know some old friends of
his and Bear Tooth are hankerin' to meet up with him.
We told him we was stayin' at Aunt Bea's boardin'house,"
Cal added.

"Did you get the supplies we talked about?" Smoke asked.

"Yes, sir. We got four kegs of gunpowder, a case of dynamite sticks, and twenty boxes of ammunition."

"Did you remember to get some shells for my Sharps?" Smoke asked, referring to the Sharps Big Fifty long rifle he'd brought.

"Yes, sir," Pearlie answered, "two boxes of twenty shells each."

Louis raised his eyebrows. "You planning on doing some long-range shooting, Smoke?"

Smoke nodded. "Yeah. Depending on how close Musk-rat can get us to the gang's camp, I figured a long gun might come in handy to spread a little fear and trepidation among the bandits."

"Smoke can hit a squirrel in the eye at fifteen hundred yards with that baby," Pearlie said, pride in his voice.

Just then, they heard a knocking at Pearlie and Cal's door, which was just down the hall from Smoke's.

Smoke stepped to the door, pulled his Colt from his holster, and peeked out into the hall. He could see an older man wearing buckskins waiting outside Pearlie's room.

Smoke holstered his gun and opened his door, stepping into the hallway. "Mr. Muskrat Calhoon?" he called.

The old mountain man whirled, a battered Colt Army revolver appearing in his hand in the wink of an eye.

"Yep, that be me, sonny boy. Who might ye be?"

Smoke held his hands out from his sides showing he wasn't a threat. "My name's Smoke Jensen. Bear Tooth said we should look you up and see if you might be able to do us a favor."

Muskrat narrowed his eyes and studied Smoke for a moment. "Ye be the Smoke Jensen used to ride with Preacher?"

Smoke smiled. "Yes, sir. One and the same."

"Don't be callin' me sir, boy. Onliest ones ever did that was somebody tryin' to sell me somethin'."

"All right, Muskrat. Would you like to join us down here in my room?"

"That depends, young'un. If'n you got a wee mite of whiskey, I could be talked into it."

Smoke laughed out loud. "Well, then, come on in and we'll crack open a bottle of Old Kentucky bourbon, if that suits you."

"If'n it's got a bite, it'll suit me jest fine," the old man answered with a grin, exposing yellow stubs of teeth worn down almost to his gums.

As he passed by Smoke in the doorway, Smoke took a deep breath. Bear Tooth was right, this man was way beyond ripe.

Muskrat walked into the room and leaned his Sharps long rifle against the wall, then turned and looked at the others gathered there.

He pursed his lips. "You boys havin' a prayer meetin' or somethin'?"

Smoke introduced Muskrat to everyone in the room. Louis, having heard his request for whiskey, got up, poured a long draft into a water glass, and handed it to the mountain man. As he took a deep drink, Louis stepped over to the window and opened it, hoping it would let some of the odor out of the room lest they all suffocate.

Muskrat smacked his lips and held up the empty glass for a refill. "How's ol' Bear Tooth doin' these days?" he asked.

"Other than a little rheumatiz, he said he was doing all right," Smoke answered.

Muskrat nodded. "Rheumatiz goes with the territory if'n yore gonna live up in the high lonesome durin' the winter."

He took another drink of his whiskey. " 'Course, Bear

Tooth is gettin' on up in years, an' he ain't as spry as he used to be. Never could keep up with us younger fellers, even in his better days."

Muskrat leaned back in his chair and crossed his legs, looking from one man to another. "Now, I ain't no fool an' I know nobody looks me up jest to give me free whiskey, so jest what is it you young fellers want from ol' Muskrat?"

Smoke pulled up a chair and leaned forward, his elbows on his knees, and told Muskrat the whole story of the kidnapping and transportation of Mary Carson to the hole-in-the-wall.

"We aim to get her back, and put some lead in Big Jim Slaughter for what he did," Smoke said.

Muskrat nodded. "And you need ol' Muskrat to show you a back way into the hole-in-the-wall, eh?"

Smoke decided a little flattery was called for. "That's right. Bear Tooth said no man alive knows the mountains around Jackson Hole better'n you. He said if anyone could get us in there without being seen, it'd be you."

Muskrat grinned. "You don't have to shine me on, Smoke, boy. I never believed much in gettin' involved in other people's business nor feuds, but I surely don't like the idee of takin' a man's woman fer somethin' he did. It jest ain't right to git womenfolk involved in men's doin's. No siree bob, it jest ain't right."

"Then you'll help us?" Pearlie asked.

"Damn straight, young man, damn straight."

Pearlie pulled a rolled-up piece of paper from a sack on the bed. "I got us a map of the surrounding mountains, an' it shows all the passes on it."

Muskrat looked at the paper and sneered. "Ain't never looked at no map in all my born days, young feller. Wouldn't know the first thing 'bout readin' one of those. Nope. I'm jest gonna have to take you up there personal-like and show you the way. Idn't no way I could'splain to you how to git there."

"How soon do you think you can be ready to travel?" Smoke asked.

Muskrat cocked one eye at the whiskey bottle on the dresser. "I reckon that there bottle'll last till dawn. Any time after that'll be jest fine with me."

Louis laughed, took the bottle from the dresser, and poured drinks all around, smiling when Cal noticed he'd only been given half as much in his glass as the other men.

Muskrat pulled a long twist of tobacco from his coat pocket, bit off a sizable chunk, and began to chew on it as he sipped his whiskey.

"Whilst we're waitin' fer this whiskey to run out, Smoke, ol' Preacher once told me you and he'd had a little set-to up near the Plaza of the Lions back when y'all first rode together. He said it had to do with some galoots that'd kilt your brother."

Smoke stared into the amber liquid in his glass, thinking back on his early days riding with Preacher . . .

"A group of men shot and killed my brother and stole some Confederate gold he was trying to return to its rightful owners. My father told me the story just before he died, and I promised him I would avenge his death. Preacher and I went after them after we'd buried my father up in the mountains.

"After I shot and killed Pike, his friend, and Haywood, and wounded Pike's brother, Thompson, Preacher and I took off after the other men who'd been involved in the theft. We rode on over to La Plaza de los Leones, the Plaza of the Lions. It was there we trapped a man named Casey in a line shack with some of his *compadres*. Preacher and I burnt 'em out and captured Casey, then I took him to the outskirts of the town and hung him."

Muskrat's eyebrows shot up. "Just hung 'em? No trial nor nuthin'?"

Smoke began to build himself a cigarette as he talked. "Yeah, Muskrat. I'm sure you remember that's the way it was done in those days. That town would never of hanged one of their own on the word of Smoke Jensen." He put a lucifer to his cigarette and took a deep puff. "Like as not they would've hanged me and Preacher instead. Anyway, after that, the sheriff there put out a flyer on me, accusing me of murder. Had a ten-thousand-dollar reward on it."

"Did you and Preacher go into hidin'?" asked Muskrat as he leaned over and spat brown tobacco juice into the room's trash can.

"No. Preacher advised it, but I told him I had one more call to make. We rode on over to Oreodelphia, looking for a man named Ackerman. We didn't go after him right at first. Preacher and I sat around doing a whole lot of nothing for two or three days."

"How come did you do that?" asked Muskrat.

" 'Cause I wanted Ackerman to get plenty nervous. He did, and finally came gunning for us with a bunch of men who rode for his brand . . ."

At the edge of town, Ackerman, a bull of a man, with small, mean eyes and a cruel slit for a mouth, slowed his horse to a walk. Ackerman and his hands rode down the street six abreast.

Preacher and Smoke were on their feet. Preacher stuffed his mouth full of chewing tobacco. Both men had slipped the thongs from the hammers of their Colts. Preacher wore two Colts, .44s. One in a holster, the other stuck behind his belt. Mountain man and young gunfighter stood six feet apart on the boardwalk.

The sheriff closed his office door and walked into the empty cell area. He sat down and began a game of checkers with his deputy.

Ackerman and his men wheeled their horses to face

the men on the boardwalk. "I hear tell you boys is lookin' for me. If so, here I am."

"News to me," Smoke said. "What's your name?"

"You know who I am, kid. Ackerman."

"Oh, yeah!" Smoke grinned. "You're the man who helped kill my brother by shooting him in the back. Then you stole the gold he was guarding."

Inside the hotel, pressed against the wall, the desk clerk listened intently, his mouth open in anticipation of gunfire.

"You're a liar. I didn't shoot your brother; that was Potter and his bunch."

"You stood and watched it. Then you stole the gold."

"It was war, kid."

"But you were on the same side," Smoke said. "So that not only makes you a killer, it makes you a traitor and a coward."

"I'll kill you for sayin' that!"

"You'll burn in Hell a long time before I'm dead," Smoke told him.

Ackerman grabbed for his pistol. The street exploded in gunfire and black powder fumes. Horses screamed and bucked in fear. One rider was thrown to the dust by his lunging mustang. Smoke took the men on the left, Preacher the men on the right side. The battle lasted no more than ten to twelve seconds. When the noise and the gunsmoke cleared, five men lay in the street, two of them dead. Two more would die from their wounds. One was shot in the side—he would live. Ackerman had been shot three times: once in the belly, once in the chest, and one ball had taken him in the side of the face as the muzzle of the .36 had lifted with each blast. Still, Ackerman sat in his saddle, dead. The big man finally leaned to one side and toppled from his horse, one boot hung in the stirrup. The horse shied, then began walking down the dusty street, dragging Ackerman, leaving a bloody trail.

Preacher spat into the street. "Damn near swallowed my chaw."

"I never seen a draw that fast," a man said from his storefront. "It was a blur."

The editor of the paper walked up to stand by the sheriff. He watched the old man and the young gunfighter walk down the street. He truly had seen it all. The old man had killed one man, wounded another. The young man had killed four men, as calmly as picking his teeth.

"What's that young man's name?" the editor asked the sheriff, taking out a pad of paper and a pencil to record the day's events for his newspaper.

"Smoke Jensen. But he's a devil . . ."*

"What'd you fellers do next?" asked Muskrat.

"Well, we both had some minor wounds, and there was a price on my head, so we took off to the mountains to lay up for a while and lick our wounds and let the heat die down."

Smoke took a last puff on his cigarette and stubbed it out on the sole of his boot. "Except it didn't work out exactly that way. We chanced upon the remains of a wagon train that'd been burned out by Indians, and rescued a young woman. Nicole was her name. She was the lone survivor of the attack. There wasn't nothing else we could do, so we took her up into the mountains with us where we planned to winter."

"And whatever happened to that girl?" Muskrat asked, his eyes sparkling with interest.

"And," Smoke said, glancing at the almost-empty whiskey bottle, "that's a story for another night and another bottle of whiskey."

*The Last Mountain Man

Twelve

Mary Carson was showing Juanita Sanchez how to make biscuits in the small cabin where she was being held prisoner.

"I pretty good with tortillas and tamales," Juanita said as she watched Mary roll dough into a flat sheet and then cut out circular pieces and place them on a sheet greased with lard, "but I never made biscuits."

Mary smiled as she reached up to wipe flour off her nose. "It really isn't all that difficult, Juanita. The main thing you have to remember is not to cook them too long, or they become as hard as rocks." She glanced sideways at the Mexican. "Perhaps that's why some cowboys call them sinkers."

Juanita giggled, just as Jim Slaughter and Whitey and Swede walked into the cabin.

"Well," Slaughter said with a frown, "I see you women are gettin' along all right."

Juanita blushed and stepped back away from Mary, as if she were afraid of seeming too friendly to the *gringa*.

Mary placed the metal sheet with the biscuit dough on it into the stove and closed the metal door. She turned and stared at the three men without a trace of fear on her face. "I was just showing Juanita how to make biscuits. I figured you men might like a change of pace from the Mexican food you seem to eat for every meal."

"I no do nothing wrong, Señor Slaughter," Juanita said, fear making her voice quaver.

Slaughter waved a dismissive hand. "I know you didn't, Juanita. Now, why don't you leave us so we can have a little talk with Mrs. Carson?"

"Si, Señor."

After the woman left, Slaughter stepped to the stove, took a steaming coffeepot off the burner, and poured coffee for himself and his men.

They sat at the table, and he motioned for Mary to take a seat with them.

After she sat down, Slaughter wasted no time in preliminary conversation, but got right to the point of his visit.

"I hear from my men that a man named Smoke Jensen has joined your husband and they're on their way here."

He watched Mary's expression closely to see what effect his announcement would have on her.

She smiled and nodded. "I figured he would," she said.

"You knew this was gonna happen?" Swede asked, leaning forward and staring at her through narrowed eyes.

"Of course," she replied, looking from one to another of the men. "Big Rock is a small community, and we all tend to help one another out when needs be."

"Just what do you know about this Smoke Jensen?" Slaughter asked.

"He's the only man I know who's faster on the draw and more dangerous than my husband, Mr. Slaughter."

Slaughter's face showed his puzzlement. "But why would a man go so far as to travel several hundred miles and risk his life just to help a neighbor out in something that's none of his business?" he asked.

"Perhaps it's because you kidnapped me, Mr. Slaughter. You see, in the West, men value their womenfolk above all else. I've heard of men being hanged just for showing disrespect for a lady, and to go so far as to steal a man's wife to try and collect a debt . . . Well, it just isn't done where I come from."

"That don't exactly answer my question, Mrs. Carson. This Smoke Jensen has quite a reputation as a gun hawk and a killer. He ain't no gentleman who's likely to go around avenging women who are disrespected, as you put it."

Mary leaned back in her chair and got a strange look on her face. "There's a lot you don't know about Smoke Jensen, Mr. Slaughter. It may well be that this situation has a . . . particular significance to Smoke."

"What do you mean?"

"I'm going to tell you men a story about Smoke that my husband once told me. It may explain why Smoke will never let you get away with what you've done."

Slaughter pulled a cigar out of his pocket, struck a lucifer on his boot, and lit it. As thick clouds of pungent, blue smoke trailed from his nostrils, he said, "Go ahead."

"When Smoke was just a young man, in his first years living in the mountains, he took a young woman as his wife. They lived up in the high lonesome for a couple of years. They had a baby, a son that Smoke loved very much." Mary's eyes misted as she recalled the details of the story.

"At the time, there was a price on Smoke's head and a band of bounty hunters tracked him up into the mountains. As luck would have it, when the men arrived at the small log cabin in the woods where Smoke and Nicole lived, Smoke wasn't there. One of their cows had wandered off and Nicole told him they needed milk for their son to drink, so Smoke went looking for the cow. While he was gone, the bounty hunters burst into the cabin, guns drawn. They were furious when they found Smoke wasn't there, and as men will, they began to do horrible things to his wife and son, trying to find out where Smoke had gone to . . ."

* * *

Some primitive sense of warning caused Smoke to pull up short of his home. He made a wide circle, staying in the timber back of the creek, and slipped up to the cabin.

By then Nicole was dead. The acts of the men had grown perverted and in their haste, her throat had been crushed.

Felter sat by the lean-to and watched the valley in front of him. He wondered where Smoke had hidden the gold.

Inside, Canning drew his skinning knife and scalped Nicole, tying her bloody hair to his belt. He then skinned a part of her, thinking he would tan the hide and make himself a nice tobacco pouch.

Kid Austin got sick to his stomach watching Canning's callousness, and went out the back door to puke on the ground. That moment of sickness saved his life—for the time being.

Grissom walked out the front door of the cabin. Smoke's tracks had indicated he had ridden off south, so he would probably return from that direction. But Grissom felt something was wrong. He sensed something, his years on the owlhoot back trails surfacing.

"Felter?" he called.

"Yeah?" Felter stepped from the lean-to.

"Something's wrong."

"I feel it. But what?"

"I don't know." Grissom spun as he sensed movement behind him. His right hand dipped for his pistol. Felter had stepped back into the lean-to. Grissom's palm touched the smooth wooden butt of his gun as his eyes saw the tall young man standing by the corner of the cabin, a Colt .36 in each hand. Lead from the .36s hit him in the center of the chest with numbing force. Just before his heart exploded, the outlaw said, "Smoke!" Then he fell to the ground.

Smoke jerked the gun belt and pistols from the dead man. Remington Army .44s.

A bounty hunter ran from the cabin, firing at the corner of the building. But Smoke was gone.

"Behind the house!" Felter yelled, running from the lean-to, his fists full of Colts. He slid to a halt and raced back to the water trough, diving behind its protection.

A bounty hunter who had been dumping his bowels in the outhouse struggled to pull up his pants, at the same time pushing open the door with his shoulder. Smoke shot him twice in the belly and left him to scream on the outhouse floor.

Kid Austin, caught in the open behind the cabin, ran for the banks of the creek, panic driving his legs. He leaped for the protection of a sandy embankment, twisting in the air, just as Smoke took aim and fired. The ball hit Austin's right buttock and traveled through the left cheek of his butt, tearing out a sizable hunk of flesh. Kid Austin, the would-be gunhand, screamed and fainted from the pain in his ass.

Smoke ran for the protection of the woodpile and crouched there, recharging his Colts and checking the .44s. He listened to the sounds of men in panic, firing in all directions and hitting nothing.

Moments ticked past, the sound of silence finally overpowering the gunfire. Smoke flicked away sweat from his face. He waited.

Something came sailing out the back door to bounce on the grass. Smoke felt hot bile build in his stomach. Someone had thrown his dead son outside. The boy had been dead for some time. Smoke fought back sickness.

"You wanna see what's left of your woman?" a taunting voice called from near the back door. "I got her hair on my belt and a piece of her hide to tan. We all took a time or two with her. I think she liked it."

Smoke felt rage charge through him, but he remained still, crouched behind the thick pile of wood until his anger cooled to controlled venom-filled fury. He unslung the big

Sharps buffalo rifle Preacher had carried for years. The rifle could drop a two-thousand-pound buffalo at six hundred yards. It could also punch through a small log.

The voice from the cabin continued to mock and taunt Smoke. But Preacher's training kept him cautious. To his rear lay a meadow, void of cover. To his left was a shed, but he knew that it was empty for it was still barred from the outside. The man he'd plugged in the butt was to his right, but several fallen logs would protect Smoke from that direction. The man in the outhouse was either dead or passed out; his screaming had ceased.

Through a chink in the logs, Smoke shoved the muzzle of the Sharps and lined up where he thought he had seen a man move, just to the left of the rear window, to where Smoke had framed it out with rough pine planking. He gently squeezed the trigger, taking up slack. The weapon boomed, the planking shattered, and a man began screaming in pain.

Canning ran out the front of the cabin, to the lean-to, sliding down hard beside Felter behind the water trough. "This ain't workin' out," he panted. "Grissom, Austin, Poker, and now Evans is either dead or dying. The slug from that buffalo gun blowed his arm off. Let's get the hell outta here!"

Felter had been thinking the same thing. "What about Clark and Sam?"

"They growed men. They can join us or they can go to hell."

"Let's ride. They's always another day. We'll hide up in them mountains, see which way he rides out, then bushwhack him. Let's go." They raced for their horses, hidden in a bend of the creek, behind the bank. They kept the cabin between themselves and Smoke as much as possible, then bellied down in the meadow the rest of the way.

In the creek, in water red from the wounds in his butt, Kid Austin crawled upstream, crying in pain and humiliation. His Colts were forgotten—useless anyway; the powder was wet—all he wanted was to get away.

The bounty hunters left in the house, Clark and Sam, looked at each other. "I'm gettin' out!" Sam said. "That ain't no pilgrim out there."

"The hell with that," Clark said. "I humped his woman, I'll kill him and take the ten thousand."

"Your option." Sam slipped out the front and caught up with the others.

Kid Austin reached his horse first. Yelping as he hit the saddle, he galloped off toward the timber in the foothills.

"You wife don't look so good now," Clark called out to Smoke. "Not since she got a haircut and one titty skinned."

Deep silence had replaced the gunfire. The air stank of black powder, blood, and relaxed bladders and bowels, death-induced. Smoke had seen the men ride off into the foothills. He wondered how many were left in the cabin.

Smoke remained still, his eyes burning with fury. Smoke's eyes touched the stiffening form of his son. If Clark could have read the man's thoughts, he would have stuck the muzzle of his .44 into his mouth and pulled the trigger, insuring himself a quick death, instead of what waited for him later on.

"Yes, sir," Clark taunted him. He went into profane detail about the rape of Nicole and the perverted acts that followed.

Smoke eased slowly backward, keeping the woodpile in front of him. He slipped down the side of the knoll and ran around to one wall of the cabin. He grinned. The bounty hunter was still talking to the woodpile, to the muzzle of the Sharps stuck through the logs.

Smoke eased around to the front of the cabin and looked in. He saw Nicole, saw the torture marks on her, saw the hideousness of the scalping and the skinning knife. He lifted his eyes to the back door, where Clark was crouching just to the right of the closed door.

Smoke raised his .36 and shot the pistol out of Clark's hand. The outlaw howled and grabbed his numbed and bloodied hand.

Smoke stepped over Grissom's body, then glanced at the body of the armless bounty hunter who had bled to death.

Clark looked up at the tall young man with the burning eyes. Cold slimy fear put a bony hand on his shoulder. For the first time in his evil life, Clark knew what death looked like.

"You gonna make it quick, ain't you?"

"Not likely," Smoke said, then kicked him on the side of the head, dropping Clark unconscious to the floor.

When Clark came to his senses, he began screaming. He was naked, staked out a mile from the cabin, on the plain. Rawhide held his wrists and ankles to thick stakes driven into the ground. A huge ant mound was just inches from him. And Smoke poured honey all over him.

"I'm a white man," Clark screamed. "You can't do this to me." Slobber sprayed from his mouth. "What are you, half Apache?"

Smoke looked at him, contempt in his eyes. "You will not die well, I believe."

He didn't.*

"Jesus," Swede whispered, sweat appearing on his forehead.

Slaughter shook his head to clear it of the images Mary had implanted in his mind. "What happened to the rest of the men who rode off?" Whitey asked, though he thought he knew the answer.

Mary shook her head. "You don't want to know. Suffice it to say, they all died in horrible ways at Smoke's hand."

*The Last Mountain Man

Slaughter stared at her through narrowed eyes. "So, you think our taking you has made this a personal matter with Jensen, huh?"

A small, sad smile tugged at the corners of Mary's mouth. "Yes, I do. And if I know my neighbors, Smoke Jensen won't be the only man to ride with Monte. I'm very afraid you've bitten off more than you can chew, Mr. Slaughter," she added with a slight nod of her head.

"This is all bullshit, Boss," Whitey growled as he stood up and drank the rest of his coffee. "Ain't no man gonna ride over three hundred miles just 'cause some old bounty hunters once kilt his wife and son."

Slaughter turned to look at the albino, a resigned look on his face. "I'm afraid you're wrong, Whitey. I would, and evidently so would this gunfighter named Smoke Jensen."

Swede sleeved sweat off his forehead, his eyes troubled. "I think we made a big mistake bringin' this woman here, Boss."

Slaughter nodded. "Maybe so, but it can't be helped now. Remember, we're holed up in the best place on earth to defend against any attempt by Monte and his friends to rescue Mrs. Carson. There simply ain't no way they can get in here without us knowin' about it beforehand."

"So what are we gonna do about it?" Swede asked, his face knotted with worry.

Slaughter shrugged. "Nothing, for the moment. I'm sure that if we do no harm to Mrs. Carson, Monte will be more than glad to hand over the money he owes us and take his wife on home. If she tells him we've treated her all right, he won't have no kick comin'. After all, it IS our money he stole."

When Mary smiled, Slaughter whirled on her. "What are you grinnin' about?" he almost screamed.

"I'm afraid you've forgotten what kind of man my husband is, Mr. Slaughter. It doesn't matter whose money it is. Now that you've involved me in this matter, he will never rest until he sees you dead and buried. Even if you get the money in a trade for me, you will have to spend the rest of your lives looking back over your shoulders for Monte Carson. And someday, somehow, when you least expect it, he will be there and you will cease to exist."

Thirteen

Monte Carson was delighted to see Smoke and the others when they arrived at his camp with Muskrat Calhoon. He stepped from behind a tree and let the hammer down on his rifle when he saw them approaching the camp.

"Man, am I glad to see you," he said, leading them to his campfire where he had a pot of coffee brewing.

As the men stood next to the fire warming their hands, he filled coffee mugs from the pot and passed them out. The fall air was just above freezing, and in spite of their heavy coats the men were chilled to the bone from their long ride on horseback.

Muskrat lifted his nose to the air and took a deep whiff. "Smells like snow," he said.

Pearlie glanced at the cloudless sky, then back at the mountain man. "I don't see no clouds," he said. "How do you know it's gonna snow?"

Muskrat sipped at his coffee, making a loud slurping sound. "More'n fifty years in the high lonesome, pup," he answered with a stub-toothed grin. "After a while, ya git to know these things, or ya don't survive yer first blizzard."

Monte was impatient with the small talk. "Smoke, just what did you find out in Jackson Hole? Anything on Mary?"

"No, Monte, no one there mentioned seeing Slaughter

or any of his men with a woman," Smoke said. "But that doesn't mean anything. Slaughter would hardly bring her to town where she might yell for help or attract attention he didn't want."

Louis lit a long cigar and between puffs added, "We did ascertain that he has between twenty and thirty men in the hole-in-the-wall with him, however."

Monte's face sobered. "Them's pretty long odds," he said.

"Is it yer woman he's taken, young man?" Muskrat asked, staring at Monte through narrowed eyes as if taking the lawman's measure.

Monte nodded. "Yes."

"Then, don't go gittin' discouraged 'bout odds nor nothin'. We got right on our side, an' ol' Muskrat gonna show you how to sneak up on the bastards and hit 'em 'fore they know what's happenin'."

Monte's expression lightened. "When can we get movin'?"

Muskrat glanced at the mountain peaks surrounding Monte's camp. "I'd say this here storm gonna blow for a day or two. Won't do no good to take off now an' git caught in it."

Smoke nodded his agreement. "Muskrat's right, Monte. It'll be better to use the time to plan just what we're going to do when we get in position around the hole-in-the-wall, after we see how the place is laid out and how many men he's got on sentry duty."

"Do you think we might fix some supper first?" Pearlie asked, a pained expression on his face. "I think a lot better when my belly's full."

Louis glanced at the cowboy. "I wasn't aware your belly ever got full, Pearlie, since I've never known you not to be hungry."

Cal walked to one of the packhorses and pulled a burlap bag off its back. He carried it to the fire and set it down. "Before we left, I had Aunt Bea fix us up a mess of fried chicken and biscuits and some tinned peaches an' stuff. It ought'a do to put the fire in Pearlie's innards out for a while."

After they'd eaten, they scattered their ground blankets near the fire and sat in a group, discussing how best to attack Slaughter's men without causing Mary to be harmed.

"Muskrat, have you ever been to the hole-in-the-wall?" Monte asked.

Muskrat pulled a pint bottle of whiskey from his coat and pulled the cork before replying. After fortifying himself with a drink that emptied half the bottle, he sleeved off his mouth with his arm.

"Yep. Passed through there on a couple'a occasions a few years back. Place is a deep valley betwixt several peaks. Got its own little stream runnin' through it, so it won't be possible to starve 'em out. They prob'ly got enough provisions to last 'em for weeks."

"If we positioned ourselves on the surrounding mountainsides, what kind of range are we talking about for shooting down into the camp?" Louis asked.

"Dependin' on jest where ya are, anywhere from a couple of hundred yards to a quarter mile or more," the mountain man answered.

Louis pulled a rifle from his pack. "I brought a new Remington Rolling Block rifle with me," he said, wiping the polished walnut stock with a rag. "It's a single-shot, but it's built strong and takes a .44-caliber rifle slug. I figure it's good for up to three hundred yards, shooting downhill."

Smoke nodded. "I have a Sharps .52-caliber, like yours, Muskrat. If I have to, I'm pretty accurate up to fifteen hundred yards."

Muskrat grinned. "Well, since my eyes've gotten a little dim with the passin' years, I can't hit nothin' past a thousand yards with my ol' Fifty," he said, referring to the Sharps Big Fifty.

Pearlie shook his head. "Our Winchesters aren't much good over two hundred yards, Smoke, so I guess Cal and me better be on the short side of the mountain."

Monte looked from one to the other of the men, a worried expression on his face. "Wait just a damned minute here. If we go firin' into those bastards, they're liable to shoot Mary."

Smoke held up his hand. "Hold on, Monte. We're not going to start anything until we know Mary's safe."

"And just how do you plan to do that, young feller?" Muskrat asked, tipping his bottle for another long drink.

Smoke glanced at him. "Why, I plan to go down into the robbers' camp and get her out before we let them know we're there."

Muskrat laughed. "You mean yore gonna just traipse on down there an' tell this Slaughter feller, 'Excuse me, but I'm gonna take yer hostage on outta here'?"

The other men nodded. It was a fair question, and they all wanted to know how Smoke would be able to do it.

"Muskrat, you've been in this country for a lot of years. Do you remember how the Indians used to hunt buffalo, back when all they had were bows and arrows?"

The old man thought for a moment, then grinned. "Shore. They didn't have much range with those old bows, so they'd cover themselves up with an ol' buff'lo skin, smear some buff'lo crap on they skin, and creep right into the middle of the herd."

Smoke nodded. "That's how I plan to do it."

Pearlie looked over at Smoke, his face puzzled. "How's dressin' up like a buffalo gonna fool those men, Smoke?"

All the men around the campfire laughed, and Cal slapped Pearlie on the shoulder. "Sometimes, Pearlie, you're dummer'n dog shit."

Snow began to fall, just as Muskrat had said it would,

so the men built up the fire and wrapped themselves in thick, woolen blankets, trying to get some sleep before tackling the long journey up into the mountain passes toward hole-in-the-wall.

"How long do you figger this snow's gonna last?" Pearlie asked Muskrat.

Muskrat held his hand out and looked at the size of the snowflakes, sniffed the air, and glanced up at the sky. "Oh, prob'ly till tomorrow afternoon. We should be able to be on our way by jest past our noonin'."

Just as Muskrat said it would, the snowfall began to lighten around noon the next day. The men finished off the last of Aunt Bea's fried chicken and packed the horses for their journey up into the mountains.

Muskrat stepped up on a paint pony such as Indians rode and said, "C'mon, horse, git movin'."

Cal spurred Silver up next to the mountain man. "How come you don't give your horse a name, Muskrat?"

Muskrat cut a piece of tobacco off a twist he pulled from his coat and stuck it in his mouth. As he began to chew, he glanced over at Cal. "Ya don't never want to give nuthin' a name ya might have to eat someday, young'un."

Cal's face showed his distaste. "You mean you'd eat your horse?"

Muskrat chuckled, "Hell, pup, I've seen times so bad up here in the winter I'd eat my partner, if'n I ever had one."

"I could never do that," Cal said with some feeling.

Smoke trotted Joker up next to the boy. "Don't never say never, Cal," he advised, a small smile curling his lips.

"That's right, boy," Muskrat added. "After twenty or thirty days of snow up to yer neck and nothin' to eat 'cept bark off'n trees, when yer stomach is pressin' agin yore backbone, you'd eat yer shoes if'n ya didn't need 'em to keep yer feet from freezin' an' fallin' off."

Cal finally smiled. He knew when he was being teased. "Now, I know Pearlie'd eat anything that didn't eat him first, but I just don't know as I could do it."

"Hell, I jest hope ya don't never need to find out jest what you'd do, pup," Muskrat said, and kicked his pony into a trot up the trail.

Smoke rode next to the mountain man, making sure he learned the way up the mountain, just in case he needed to lead the way back down.

He glanced around at the brilliant colors of fall foliage on the mountain slopes. The sugar maples were in full bloom, their leaves bright yellow and red and orange, intermixed with aspen and birch whose leaves were a golden yellow and seemed to glow with an almost iridescent flame in the bright sunlight. The peaks in the background were already covered with a layer of snow, looking like pieces of chocolate cake covered with marshmallow icing.

"You ever get tired of the colors of fall, Muskrat?" Smoke asked.

The mountain man glanced around and smiled, his eyes twinkling in the sunlight. "Nope, cain't say as I do, Smoke. Some say it's what keeps mountain men so young inside, the glories we see ever day up here in the high lonesome."

He shook his head and leaned to the side to spit a brown stream of tobacco juice at a lizard on the side of the trail, making it scamper to hide in a pile of fallen maple leaves.

"I cain't fer the life of me figger why anybody in they right mind would elect to live in a city or town when they got this beautiful country so close at hand."

Smoke grinned. He knew Muskrat was a kindred spirit. "Nor can I, Muskrat, nor can I."

As they followed the twisting, turning trail, which at times became no more than a path between copses of trees and outcroppings of granite boulders, Muskrat would point out to Smoke features to remember along the way . . . a boulder whose cracks and crevices looked like the face of a bear, a particularly old and weathered oak tree that looked to be over a hundred years old, a bubbling mountain stream they passed near a group of rocks that looked like a child's building blocks piled on top of one another.

The higher they climbed, the more the vegetation changed. Maple and birch trees became more and more scarce, and the evergreens such as fir and ponderosa pine began to become more prevalent.

"Are we going to have to climb above the tree line?" Smoke asked.

The old man shook his head. "Nope, but we're gonna come awfully close to it. Air's already gittin' so thin we gonna have to let the horses rest ever little way or they'll founder."

"This is as good a time as any," Smoke said as they came again to a small mountain stream. "We can fill our canteens and make some coffee while the mounts rest up."

After they'd dismounted, Pearlie began to pile some rocks in a circle in the clearing to make a fire.

Muskrat walked over and shook his head. "Not out here in the open, little beaver. They'll be able to see the smoke."

He picked up the rocks and piled them at the base of a large fir tree, whose limbs stretched sixty feet in the air.

"Gather me up some deadfall, the drier the better," he said to Cal and Pearlie.

After they'd piled old branches and twigs under the

tree, Muskrat used a small gathering of dead leaves and his flint to start a fire.

As the smoke curled upward, the branches of the tree dispersed and scattered it so it wasn't visible from more than a couple of hundred feet.

"This way won't nobody know we're here," Muskrat said as he watched Pearlie begin brewing a pot of coffee.

Then Muskrat pulled a package of jerked beef from his saddlebags and handed pieces out to the others. "Better git used to this," he said, " 'cause it's gonna be a while 'fore we have a hot meal again."

"Are we gettin' close?" Monte asked, a hopeful expression on his face.

Muskrat pointed to a ridge about two hundred yards up the slope. "Jest over that ridge an' round a bend in the trail an' we'll be lookin' right down on the hole-in-the-wall."

"What about sentries?" Smoke asked.

Muskrat shook his head. "They all on the other side of the hole, on the downslope side. Nobody'll figger we gonna come at 'em from up the mountain."

It took them until just before dusk to make their way along the narrow mountain trails until they were in a position where they could look down into the hole-in-the-wall without being observed.

The place was laid out just as Muskrat had remembered. There were five crude log cabins arranged along the walls of the canyon, with a small, mountain stream running through the center of the area. In addition, there were ten lean-to-type structures where most of the gunmen bedded down at night. The horses were kept in a large corral at the far end of the canyon, with saddles and blankets arrayed along the wooden fence surrounding the corral.

There was a large fire that seemed to be kept going day and night in the center of the cleared area between the cabins, where most of the men ate and gathered to drink and smoke and socialize during the evening hours.

The main trail into and out of the canyon could be seen winding down the mountainside, with several places where men in groups of two were stationed as sentries.

Muskrat pointed out vantage points around the canyon where Smoke and the others could place themselves so as to get clean shots down into the compound.

"All right, Smoke, I done my part, I got ya here. Now it's yore show from here on out," Muskrat said.

Smoke nodded. "The first thing we have to do is find out which cabin Slaughter has Mary in."

"Then what?" Louis asked as he knelt next to Smoke, cradling his Remington Rolling Block rifle in his arms.

"Then, we watch the sentries to find out what kind of schedule they're on. I'm going to need to intercept one after the sentries change, before he gets back to the camp, and take his place."

"You mean you're going down there amongst them *bandidos?*" Cal asked, his eyes wide.

"I don't see any other way to get Mary to safety before we attack," Smoke answered.

"Wait a minute, Smoke," Monte interjected. "Mary is my responsibility, so it should be me takes the chance on goin' down there."

Smoke shook his head. "You can't do it, Monte. Your wounds aren't healed enough to get the job done. I may have to carry Mary up part of the way on the steeper slopes. Your shoulder would never stand the strain."

"What can we do to help?" Pearlie asked.

"Keep your eyes peeled on those cabins. Mary will probably be in the one that Slaughter goes in and out of. He'll want her close by him in case of trouble."

In less than an hour, Louis saw two women make their

way from the largest cabin toward the outhouse behind the building. One of the women was wide and short, the other tall and thin. They were accompanied by a cowboy, evidently along as a guard to make sure Mary didn't make a run for it.

Louis scrambled over to where Smoke was squatting, watching the sentries. "She's in the big cabin, Smoke, the one closest to the trail out of the canyon, on the north side."

Smoke raised his head up over the bushes he was behind and fixed the location in his mind. He gave a low whistle and the others came to squat next to him.

"All right men, get to your positions. As soon as I'm out of there and Mary is out of the line of fire, I'll give you a signal. When you hear it, let loose with everything you have to cover us until we get up here."

"What if they raise the alarm before your signal?" Monte asked.

Smoke smiled grimly. "Then don't wait. Pour as much lead and dynamite into the camp as fast as you can."

"How are you going to get her out of that cabin?" Louis asked. "Slaughter probably has his best men in there with him."

Smoke's teeth gleamed in the moonlight as he grinned. "Just keep a close eye on the cabin and you'll see," he said. Then he was up in a crouch and moving fast down the trail toward the nearest group of sentries.

Fourteen

It was almost dusk as Smoke made his way down a footpath toward the sentries' post below. When he got close to the two men, he exited the trail and circled around until he was below the men, between their post and the camp in the canyon.

He stationed himself behind an outcropping of boulders and hunkered down to wait for the change of sentries, cupping his hands around his mouth and blowing on them, trying to keep them from stiffening up as the temperature dropped to near freezing.

He figured he wouldn't have long to wait. Most times sentries were changed about the time of the evening meal, so the men coming on duty could eat before taking up their post, and the men relieved of duty could have a hot meal waiting for them on their return.

Smoke climbed up on one of the boulders and peered over the cliff edge at the canyon below. He could see food being prepared at the large campfire in the center of the canyon. He was surprised at the number of women he saw working around the fire, but then realized these weren't the kind of men to deprive themselves of female company for any length of time. He supposed most of the women were prostitutes, as men like these weren't likely to be the marrying kind.

Before long his patience was rewarded with the sound

of two men making their way up the trail toward the sentries on duty.

"Yo, Curly and Mike," one of the newcomers yelled. "Don't go shootin' us. It's just Joe and Charley comin' to relieve you."

"It's 'bout time," the larger of the two sentries called back. "Mike and me are 'bout to freeze our balls off up here."

The man who spoke, evidently named Curly, was just about Smoke's size. He was tall and broad through the shoulders, had a heavy whisker growth that made his jaws look blue in the fading light, and wore a bright red flannel shirt under a thick, black woolen coat and a dark hat pulled low over his forehead.

"He'll do," Smoke thought as he watched the four men talk for a moment before changing places.

"What's fer supper tonight?" Curly asked, rubbing his hands together and hunching his shoulders against the cold.

"What do ya think?" Joe answered. "Elk meat and beans and tortillas."

"Goddammit," Curly growled. "Don't those whores know how to cook anythin' else?"

Joe laughed. "They wasn't brought up here 'cause of their skills with a skillet, Curly."

"Yeah," Mike said. "Leastways they know how to keep a body warm at night."

"Yeah, but I'll bet that little lady the boss has in his cabin is a sight better at it than those whores," Curly said, his teeth showing in a wide grin.

Joe nodded. "Yeah, it's a shame the boss don't share her around some."

Smoke felt his mouth go dry and his heart hammer at the way the men were talking about Mary Carson. His hands clenched as his fury mounted. There would be no mercy shown this night for these bastards, he thought.

"Well, you boys keep your powder dry and try to keep your fingers from freezin' off tonight," Mike said as he and Curly started down the trail, their hands in their coat pockets as they leaned into the frigid wind blowing down the mountain slopes.

Knowing he dared not make a sound, Smoke pulled his Bowie knife from its scabbard on the back of his belt and stood up, moving slowly so his knees wouldn't creak and give his position away.

He pulled his left-hand Colt and held it in one hand and the knife in the other. As the two men passed him, he stepped out and brought the Colt down hard on the back of Curly's head. When he collapsed with a grunt and Mike turned around, his eyes wide, Smoke swung the knife in an upward motion, letting the point of the blade enter his chest just below the left rib cage, the blade continuing up to pierce Mike's heart. He was dead before he hit the ground.

Smoke pulled both bodies off the trail and into the thick brush up the slope a ways. Working fast, he stripped Curly's coat, hat, and shirt off and laid them on the ground. After a moment, Curly began to groan and move his arms and legs.

"Sorry about this, Curly," Smoke said, "but you shouldn't talk in such a manner about a lady like Mrs. Carson."

In a quick movement, Smoke drew the knife across Curly's throat and rolled him over, so the spurting blood wouldn't get his clothes dirty.

As fast as he could, Smoke put on Curly's shirt, coat, and hat, then bent and took a handful of dirt and smeared it on his cheeks and jaws, hoping in the darkness it would look like the man's heavy whisker growth.

Satisfied the bodies couldn't be seen from the trail, Smoke walked down the side of the mountain toward the canyon below, whistling a low tune through lips growing stiff with the cold.

When he reached the canyon floor, he stayed in shadows away from the campfire until most of the other bandits had finished their meal, grabbed their women, and retired to the other cabins or their sleeping bags. He eased up to the pot of meat and beans and piled some on a tin plate, poured himself a cup of coffee, and walked off to the side, as near to Slaughter's cabin as he could get and still not arouse suspicion.

He sat on the ground with his back to a fir tree and ate and drank his coffee, trying to keep his muscles from stiffening up while he waited for his chance to make a move.

A drunken cowboy with one arm around a thickset woman, and a whiskey bottle in the other hand, walked by.

"Howdy, Curly," the man mumbled, glancing at Smoke, who sat with his head lowered as if he were concentrating on his food.

"Ummm," Smoke mumbled back as if his mouth were full of food.

"Cold enough for ya?" the man asked, squeezing his woman closer as he ambled by.

"Uh-huh," Smoke answered without looking up, hoping the man was too drunk to notice it wasn't Curly he was talking to.

After the pair passed, Smoke glanced up and saw the door to Slaughter's cabin open. A tall woman walked out and, followed by a man, proceeded toward the outhouse behind the cabin.

Smoke set his plate and cup on the ground and got to his feet, making his way around behind the outhouse.

The man was leaning away from the wind, trying to light a cigarette when Smoke approached him.

"Got a light?" Smoke asked, making his voice low and guttural.

"Shore, Curly," the man answered, and held out the match.

When the light hit Smoke's face, the man's eyes widened. "Say, you ain't Curly . . ."

Before he could sound an alarm, Smoke's Bowie knife flashed, impaling the man's chest on the twelve-inch blade.

Smoke threw his arms around him and held him up as he died, then eased the body to the ground and pulled it behind the outhouse where it wouldn't easily be seen.

After a moment, the door opened and Mary stepped out, arranging her long dress.

Smoke stepped up to her. "Mary," he whispered, "it's Smoke."

"Oh!" she said, her hand flying to her mouth.

"Come on, we've got to make tracks before they miss you," he said, his voice harsh with urgency.

She nodded and followed him as he moved back into deep shadows near the wall of the canyon. He took her arm and walked as rapidly as he could toward a small footpath he'd seen near the outhouse. It wasn't much more than a clear area running up the slope between fir and pine trees, and was so steep at times that he had to almost carry her up the wall.

They had made it almost a hundred yards up the canyon wall before the door to the cabin opened and a large, broad-shouldered man appeared. He had a cigar in his mouth and stood on the small porch of the cabin for a moment, looking back toward the outhouse.

He must have sensed something was wrong when he didn't see the guard he'd sent with Mary, for he suddenly drew his pistol and ran toward the privy.

"Jack, where are you, Jack?" he hollered.

Smoke and Mary stopped and watched as he suddenly

stiffened when he found Jack's body crumpled on the dirt behind the small structure.

He jerked the outhouse door open, then turned around and held his pistol in the air.

Before he could fire, Smoke cupped his hands around his mouth and screamed like a mountain lion, a harsh and guttural sound that would make the hairs on the back of a man's neck stand up.

Suddenly the night lit up with explosions of gunfire from all sides of the canyon walls. The first to fall were the sentries guarding the mountain passes into and out of the canyon.

Without waiting to see what happened next, Smoke took Mary's arm and propelled her up the slope as fast as they could go.

Behind and below them, the outlaws' camp erupted in a nightmare of dynamite explosions, gunshots, and screams of men hit and dying.

Bandits rushed out of cabins and sleeping bags like ants from a disturbed mound. They ran into the center of the camp, pointed their pistols and rifles at the walls surrounding them, and fired blindly, shooting at the night as if they could somehow stop the death raining down on them.

A stick of dynamite landed square in the center of the main campfire, exploding and blowing burning logs and branches in all directions. Two of the smaller cabins caught fire, sending men and women screaming out into the darkness, their hair and clothes in flames.

Slaughter did his best to rally his men, shouting orders at them, trying to be heard over the explosions of gunfire and dynamite.

"Goddammit, get under cover," he screamed, crouching and firing upward at the barrel-flashes above with his pistol.

Finally, evidently figuring his pistol hadn't the range

to reach their attackers, he ducked back into his cabin and reappeared moments later with a rifle, accompanied by Whitey and Swede, who also had long guns in their arms.

Meanwhile, men outlined by the light of the burning cabins and other fires started by dynamite, were being cut down where they stood. Bodies littered the canyon floor, screams of pain and fear echoed through the night, punctuated by the booming explosions of high-powered rifles from above.

Before long, the outlaws learned to stay hidden, crawling behind fir and pine trees on their bellies, crouching next to dead bodies, and some even made their way to the corral trying to hide among their mounts to escape the withering fire from above.

The shooting slowed as targets became scarce.

Smoke and Mary eventually made it to the cliff tops overlooking the valley below. She stepped up behind Monte, who was crouched behind a boulder pouring shot after shot into the men below.

"Monte," she said quietly.

He dropped his rifle and rose to throw his arms around her, his eyes finding Smoke and glistening in gratitude.

"We don't have a lot of time for a reunion," Smoke said, his voice urgent.

"We won't be able to keep them pinned down for long, so I want you and Mary to get on your horses and get the hell away from here," he added. "Find Muskrat and have him lead you down the mountain the fastest way. Get to Jackson Hole and take the first train out of town."

"What if it's not heading for Colorado?" Monte asked.

Smoke shook his head. "I don't care where it's going, just get her out of here."

As he led Mary toward the horses, Monte said, "What about you and the others?"

"Slaughter doesn't know who attacked him and his

gang," Smoke said. "We'll give it another hour or two then head back to Jackson Hole. We'll get back in the rooming house and act as if we don't know anything about the attack. After a few days, we'll make our way back to Big Rock."

"What do you think Slaughter's gonna do?" Monte asked as he saddled one of the packhorses for Mary.

Smoke shrugged. "If he's smart, he'll cut his losses and figure this was a bad idea."

"And if he's not?"

"Then he'll come looking for us at Big Rock, and we'll be ready for him."

Monte helped Mary up into the saddle, then swung up on his mount.

Smoke pointed off to the left. "Muskrat's over there. Find him and get moving."

Monte leaned down and stuck out his hand. As Smoke took it, he said, "Thanks, Smoke."

Smoke glanced at Mary, whose eyes were moist with gratitude.

"Don't mention it, partner. Just get Mary back to Big Rock. My advice is to take her to Sugarloaf and tell Sally we'll be back in a week or two."

Monte nodded and spurred his horse toward where Muskrat's big Sharps could be heard sending .50-caliber slugs toward the outlaws' camp.

Smoke picked up his Sharps, eared back the hammer, and leaned over a boulder, searching for someone to kill.

Fifteen

Close to midnight, Smoke and his friends fired their final shots at the outlaw camp and jumped on their horses to ride back to Jackson Hole. They left behind them a camp in ruins, with most of the cabins destroyed or severely damaged, the corral torn asunder and the horses scattered and running wild. At least ten men lay dead and many more were wounded.

As they rode back down the mountain, Smoke watching carefully for the landmarks Muskrat had pointed out to him, Louis pulled his bronc up next to Joker.

"You think there's any chance we killed Slaughter and put an end to this entire sorry episode?"

Smoke shook his head. "In all my years out here, Louis, I've trailed lots of men and had some on my trail, and I've never had a problem solved that easily. I think we'd better figure on Slaughter surviving our assault."

"What do you think he's going to do?"

"Well, first off it's going to take him a while to sort out the mess we left back there, at least a day or so. Then, he's going to get to thinking that the only place an attack like that could have come from would be Jackson Hole. I think he's going to come to town loaded for bear, looking for anyone who's new to town or doesn't fit in. He'll want revenge, and I don't think he'll be particularly selective on who he takes his anger out on."

"Perhaps we should pack our gear and get on the trail toward home before he comes looking."

"We can't. We've got to stay here long enough to give Monte and Mary time to get away clean. If we can stall him for a few days, there won't be any way he can catch up to them before they manage to get back to Big Rock."

"And if he and his gang comes to Big Rock looking to get even?"

"I'm going to send Sally a wire tomorrow morning. Monte and Mary have lots of friends back home. I'll tell her to organize the town and to be ready. We may be in for a monumental fight once he rebuilds his gang."

"Do you really think he'll go to all that trouble for a mere fifty thousand dollars?"

Smoke shook his head. "It's gone way beyond the money now, Louis. Slaughter's been dealt a severe defeat, and in his own backyard. It's his reputation he's going to be concerned with now. If word gets around that some country sheriff took Big Jim Slaughter on and kicked his ass, Slaughter won't be able to move without looking back over his shoulder all the time to see if someone else thinks they can do the same thing."

Just as they came down off the mountain slope and pulled onto the main trail headed toward Jackson Hole, a light snowfall began. Smoke and the others pulled their coats tight around them, settled hats low to keep the snow out of their eyes, and spurred their mounts toward town.

For the next two days, Smoke and Louis and Cal and Pearlie were careful to take their meals apart and not to be seen talking to each other. Louis continued to frequent the gaming halls, giving expensive lessons to the cowboys about the dangers of playing poker with an expert. Smoke spent most of his time in various saloons, hanging around and listening to idle talk. Cal and Pearlie made it a point to let everyone think they were miners, working a claim in the nearby mountains, so if Mr. Schultz told anyone they'd bought some dynamite and gunpowder, there wouldn't be any suspicions raised.

Sheriff Walter Pike walked up and stood next to Smoke at the Cattleman's Saloon bar. "Howdy, Mr. West."

Smoke took a drink of his beer before replying. "Hello, Sheriff Pike."

"Well, I've gone through all of my circulars and can't seem to find any recent paper on you, Johnny."

Smoke shrugged, as if it were no concern to him. "I told you, Sheriff. I'm just a law-abiding citizen hanging around until I can find some work."

Pike nodded, his experienced eyes taking in the way Smoke moved and handled himself. "Uh-huh, sure you are."

"What's that supposed to mean, Sheriff?"

"I've seen a lot of men come through here, West, and I've gotten to be a pretty good judge of character. You don't fit in with the rest of the pond scum in this town."

Smoke raised his eyebrows. "Oh?"

"No. Oh, I can see you're handy with a gun, that's evident. But you don't go around trying to impress everyone with how mean and tough you are, even though it's plain you could take just about anyone else in town with those six-killers on your hips."

"Sheriff, I make my living with these pistols. I'm not one to use them unless there's a profit in it for me. That's all."

Pike smiled. "I'm not so sure that's all, Johnny. You don't fit in, so I'm gonna be watchin' you to see just what your game is. All right?"

Smoke shrugged. "Sure, Sheriff. It's your town, you can do anything you want."

Pike tipped his hat. "See you around, Johnny."

"Be seeing you, Sheriff."

* * *

The next day, Smoke was having lunch in Aunt Bea's dining room when he glanced out of the window and saw a group of four men talking to Sheriff Pike on the boardwalk in front of the Cattleman's Saloon. After a moment of conversation, the sheriff inclined his head toward Aunt Bea's boardinghouse and said a few words. The four men looked over, nodded, and began to cross the street toward Bea's place.

Smoke took a deep breath. Unless he missed his guess, it was starting. Across the room Louis was at a table by himself, and Cal and Pearlie were sharing another table. Smoke caught their eyes and nodded slightly, cutting his eyes toward the dining room door. His friends nodded back, and he could see each of them reach down and take the hammer-thongs off their pistols. Louis leaned back and straightened his right leg, allowing him easy access to his pistol.

Smoke pushed his plate away, built himself a cigarette, and concentrated on his coffee cup when the four men entered the room.

A large, broad-shouldered man was the leader, and behind him was a tall, heavyset blond man, a thin, wiry albino, and a young kid in his teens wearing a black vest and twin pearl-handled Colts on his hips.

After standing in the doorway for a moment, surveying the customers, the tall man noticed Smoke and began to walk toward him, his friends fanning out behind him.

He stopped at Smoke's table. "Howdy, mister. Would you be Johnny West?"

Smoke slowly looked up. He took a deep drag of his cigarette and let smoke trail from his nostrils as he replied. "Maybe. Who wants to know?"

"I'm Big Jim Slaughter."

"So?"

The young kid's hand moved next to the butt of his pistol and his face clouded with anger. "So, watch your mouth, cowboy!" he snarled.

Smoke let his unconcerned gaze drift over to the young man. "I ain't no cowboy, sonny, boy, an' if your hand twitches again, I'll kill you where you stand," he said in a low, dangerous voice.

Slaughter put his hand on the Durango Kid's arm. "Hold on, Mr. West, there isn't any need for hostilities. May we join you?"

Smoke shrugged. "It's a free country."

After getting extra chairs from a nearby table, the four men sat down across from Smoke.

Slaughter got right to the point. "I heard you were asking around about me last week," he said, staring at Smoke to see his reaction.

"That's right. I was asking about a lot of people, trying to see if anyone was hiring guns."

"And were they?"

"Nope. For a supposedly wide-open town, it's been quiet as a church around here."

Slaughter leaned back in his chair. "I thought maybe someone had hired you to do a little job out at the hole-in-the-wall the other night."

"Oh?"

"Yeah. My men and I were attacked out there night before last."

Smoke let his lips curl in a nasty smile. "Well, then, it couldn't have been me done the job."

"Why not?" the albino interjected.

" 'Cause if I'd hired out to attack you, Slaughter, you'd all be dead now, not sittin' here askin' me fool questions."

The Durango Kid's face flushed with anger and he dropped his hand to his side, saying, "Why, you . . ."

In the wink of an eye, Smoke's pistol was in his hand and he slapped the barrel backhanded across the kid's face, knocking him backward out of his chair. He landed spread-eagled on his back with his nose bent to the side and a deep gash running across his cheek, leaking blood.

"Goddamn!" Swede said. "I never even saw him draw!"

As the kid shook his head and started to get up, Smoke eared back the hammer and pointed the barrel at the kid's face. "You sure you want some more of this, sonny, boy?" he growled.

The kid's eyes widened and his face paled, fear-sweat breaking out on his forehead. "Uh . . . no . . ."

Before he could answer, Aunt Bea appeared at the table, a long-barreled shotgun cradled in her arms. "We aren't gonna have any trouble in here, are we, boys?" she asked.

"No, ma'am," Slaughter replied, though his eyes remained fixed on Smoke. "Kid, get up and wait for us over at the Cattleman's," he said.

"But . . . but Mr. Slaughter," the kid whined.

Slaughter turned to stare at him, his face showing he would brook no argument. "I said go!"

"Yes, sir," the kid replied, his face flaming as blood spilled down onto his fancy black vest and shirt.

He got to his feet and walked rapidly out of the room without looking back.

Aunt Bea grunted. "If you men are going to stay here, you're gonna eat, not fight."

Slaughter smiled up at her. "Would you bring us three of the house specials, please, and some coffee?"

After she left, Slaughter addressed Smoke. "I thought the Durango Kid was supposed to be fast."

Smoke smiled. "Evidently not fast enough. The Kid ought'a change professions, 'fore he gets killed tryin' to be something he's not."

"You interest me, Mr. West. I might have a place for you in my organization."

"I don't come cheap," Smoke replied, as if he might be interested.

"I'll bet you don't," Slaughter said. "Would you be willing to travel?"

"Depends," Smoke said. "How far, an' what's the pay?"

"Me and my men are going to take a little trip over to Colorado in a few days. The pay's a hundred a month against a cut of what we make when we get there."

Smoke grinned. "A hundred a month, huh? That what you're paying these men?"

Slaughter nodded. "Yeah."

"Then I'm gonna cost you a hundred and a half," Smoke said.

"What?" Slaughter asked.

"And you're lucky I don't ask for two hundred, since I'm at least twice as good as what you got working for you now."

Slaughter laughed, while Swede and Whitey scowled. "All right, Mr. West. If we decide to use you, you'll get a hundred and fifty a month."

Smoke nodded. "Sounds fair."

"Good. I'll let you know in a day or so."

Smoke dropped his cigarette butt in his coffee and stood up. "You know where to find me."

Slaughter nodded. "That I do, Mr. West, that I do."

Sixteen

After Smoke left the room, Whitey glanced at the door to make sure he was gone, then turned back to Slaughter. "What'a you think, Boss?"

Slaughter rubbed the beard stubble on his face, his eyes contemplative. "I don't know yet. Mr. West could'a been one. He's certainly good enough with a six-shooter."

"Why didn't you let the Kid take him on, Jim?" Swede asked.

"We lost over half our men the other night, Swede, an' another third're so scared they ain't gonna be worth spit. West would've killed the Kid as easily as swattin' a fly."

"You think he's that good?"

Slaughter looked at him. "Did you see him draw? He has the fastest hands I've ever seen. He could snatch a double eagle off a snake's head and give him change 'fore he could strike."

"He don't look all that bad to me," Whitey said, his lips curled in a sneer.

Slaughter laughed. "Then you weren't lookin' at the same man I was."

As they ate, the three men looked around at the other customers in the dining room.

"See any other likely suspects?" Swede asked.

Slaughter nodded. "Those two over there in the corner impress me as being right sure of themselves."

Swede glanced over his shoulder at the table containing Cal and Pearlie. "You mean those two boys?"

"They're not exactly boys, Swede," Slaughter said. "Oh, I'll grant you they're young, but look at their eyes. They've seen plenty of action, an' the way they wear their guns shows they ain't no pilgrims."

"You want I should go brace 'em?" Whitey asked.

Slaughter thought for a moment, then shook his head. "No. Let's finish our food, then we'll see what happens."

Cal could see Slaughter and his men watching them out of the corner of his eyes.

"Pearlie," he said, "I think they're talkin' 'bout us."

Pearlie paused a moment from shoveling pancakes into his mouth to glance up at Cal. "I don't doubt it, Cal. I figger they gonna be lookin' at most everbody in town for the next day or so, just like Smoke said. They got to know the men who blasted 'em came from here, so it's only natural to try an' figger out who it was."

"What're we gonna do if'n they come over here askin' a lot of questions?"

Pearlie gave a small shrug. "Just act like Smoke tole us. We're miners, pure an' simple. Don't wanna have no truck with gunfighters an' such."

Sure enough, when Slaughter and his men finished their breakfast, they got up from their table and ambled over to stand in front of Cal and Pearlie.

Slaughter stood there, looking down until the two men glanced up at him.

"Howdy, boys," he said.

Pearlie nodded, his mouth bulging with eggs and pancakes.

Cal just looked and didn't answer.

"I was wondering if you men were interested in hiring on with me and my men," Slaughter asked.

"Doin' what?" Pearlie asked after he washed his food down with a slug of coffee.

Slaughter pointed to the pistol on Pearlie's hip. "Usin' those six-killers on your hip."

Pearlie looked at Cal and grinned. "See, Cal. The man thinks we're gun hawks."

He glanced back up at Slaughter and the two hard-looking men standing with him. "Thanks for the offer, mister, but my brother an' me is miners. We don't hire our guns out."

"Miners, huh?" Slaughter asked. "Doin' any good?"

Pearlie let his face get a suspicious look on it. "Some days're better'n others. Why?"

"Oh, no reason. Just wonderin'."

"Well, we're makin' enough to keep us in beans an' bacon, an' that's all anybody needs to know."

"You two must be the pair that bought some dynamite from Schultz's store the other day."

Pearlie leaned back and wiped his mouth with his napkin. "You been askin' round 'bout us?"

"Well, let's just say we're interested in anybody who bought dynamite."

"Yeah, we bought some. You ever tried to dig through twenty feet of granite, mister?"

"Schultz said these two men also bought a lot of cartridges at the same time."

Pearlie nodded. "Lot of men try to take other people's gold, 'stead of diggin' it out themselves. You got any more fool questions?"

Whitey stepped forward, his hand near his pistol. "I'd watch your mouth, miner man, 'fore somebody shuts it for you."

Pearlie scooted his chair back and let his hand rest on his thigh next to his holster. "You're welcome to try, mister, any time you think you're ready."

Slaughter raised his eyebrows. Not many men stood up to someone as mean-looking as Whitey.

"You're pretty tough for a miner," Slaughter said.

"I've mined in Tombstone, Deadwood, an' lots of other places filled with men who thought they were fast with a gun," Pearlie answered. "I ain't particularly fast, but I generally hit what I aim at an' I'm still alive, so call your dog off, mister, or somebody's gonna get a gut full of lead."

Slaughter grinned, shaking his head at Whitey. "You sure you don't want a job? I could use some men who ain't afraid to use their guns."

Pearlie shook his head. "No, I told you, we're minin' right now." He hesitated a moment. "But you might ask again after the snow fills the passes. If we don't dig out enough to get us through the winter, we might just take you up on your offer."

Slaughter smiled. "I'm afraid that'll be too late." He tipped his hat. "Good luck to you in your hunt for gold," he said, and turned to walk out the door.

"Jimminy," Cal said after they'd left. "I thought for a minute there that albino was gonna draw on you, Pearlie."

Pearlie nodded. "So did I. He's lucky he didn't, or he'd be headed for boot hill by now."

Pearlie rotated his head to loosen neck muscles made tight by the confrontation. Then he looked around the room. "Now where is Aunt Bea? I'm ready for some more pancakes an' coffee."

Louis, who'd been watching the scene with Slaughter and Pearlie, relaxed as the men left. He reached down and eased the hammer-thong back on his Colt, grinning when he saw Pearlie order more food. *Unbelievable how much chow that cowboy can consume,* he thought. *I do believe someday when the Grim Reaper comes for Pearlie, he's going to ask the man with the sickle what kind of food they serve up in heaven, and if he doesn't like the answer, he'll probably ask to be taken to the other place.*

Seventeen

After Smoke left Aunt Bea's dining room, he ambled over to the Cattleman's Saloon. He figured Slaughter and his men would show up there sooner or later, and he wanted to know what they had planned. He knew Slaughter was short of men and the Cattleman's was the logical place for him to go and try to hire new men for his mission of revenge.

When he entered the batwings, he stood for a moment to let his eyes adjust to the gloom. He let his gaze roam the room, and it didn't take him long to see the Durango Kid sitting at a table with some other men, probably also on the payroll of Big Jim Slaughter. The Kid'd evidently stopped off at the doc's office, since he had a piece of white plaster stuck to his cheek where Smoke'd slashed it with his pistol. Most of the blood had been cleaned off his vest and shirt, too.

When Smoke walked to the bar, the Kid stopped whatever he was saying and stared at Smoke with hard eyes, as if he might scare him with the ferocity of his look.

Smoke grinned and nonchalantly tipped his hat at the Kid as he sidled up to the bar. He stood so he could see the men in the room, not wanting to present his back to anyone who might want to put a bullet in it.

"What'll ya have?" the barkeep asked as he wiped down the bar with a dirty rag.

"Shot of whiskey with a beer chaser," Smoke said. He rarely drank whiskey and never this early in the day, but he had an image to project and had to stay in character.

As Smoke downed the whiskey and followed it with a drink of beer, the Kid leaned over and said something in a low voice to the men at the table with him, causing them to stare at Smoke with hate-filled eyes.

He could see the Kid's face getting redder by the minute, and knew it wouldn't be long before the young man who fancied himself a gun hawk would try his hand. There was just no way he could allow Smoke to pistol-whip him and keep his self-image as a gunslick intact.

Jim Slaughter and the albino and Swede walked through the batwings, striding to the center of the room as if they owned the place.

Slaughter nodded at Smoke, then turned to face the many tables where men were sitting and drinking their breakfast. He held up his hands for attention.

"Gentlemen, my name is Jim Slaughter an' I'm hirin' men who aren't afraid of usin' their guns. If anybody's interested, see me at my table and I'll tell you what the job is and what it pays."

When he was finished speaking, he walked over to a table in the corner where two men were sitting. He stood there, looking down at them for a moment until they hurriedly got to their feet and went to another table across the room. Slaughter and Whitey and Swede took their seats, and Slaughter motioned for the bartender to bring him a bottle of whiskey and some glasses.

While he was filling the glasses, the Kid got to his feet and hurried over to his boss's table. He stood there, talking animatedly for a moment, looking over his shoulder at Smoke as he spoke.

Slaughter got a pained look on his face and shook his head. The Kid kept talking, gesturing wildly with his arms. Finally, Slaughter lost his patience and pointed toward the table where the Kid had been sitting, as if he were sending an unruly child to bed without his supper.

The Kid hung his head and slouched back to his table, glaring at Smoke from under the brim of his hat.

In the next fifteen minutes, over twenty cowboys approached Slaughter's table to ask about the job he was offering. Smoke had no way of knowing how many took the outlaw up on his offer, but he supposed with the wages Slaughter was willing to pay, quite a few of them did. He briefly wondered where Slaughter was getting that kind of money, because the fifty thousand he expected to get from Monte wouldn't go far if split among twenty or thirty men.

After the last of the men in the saloon had finished talking with Slaughter, he got to his feet and began to walk toward Smoke, a half grin on his face.

Over his shoulder, Smoke saw the Durango Kid get to his feet, his face a mask of hate and humiliation. When Slaughter was no more than ten feet from Smoke, the Kid made his move, crouching and going for his pistol. As he aimed it at the back of Slaughter's head, Smoke drew in one lightning-fast motion and fired, his bullet passing only inches from Slaughter's ear.

Slaughter whirled and ducked, reaching for his own pistol just as Smoke's slug hit the Kid at the base of his throat, blowing out the back of his neck and almost severing his head from his body. The Kid was catapulted back onto his table, and one of the men there also grabbed iron.

Smoke's second shot took the Kid's friend in the forehead, blowing brains and blood and hair all across the room.

Slaughter came out of his crouch pointing his gun toward Smoke, until Whitey yelled, "Boss, no! He wasn't shootin' at you!"

Slaughter and Smoke stood there for a moment, pistols

pointed at each other, until Smoke's lips curled in a grin. "You want to make it three, Slaughter?" he growled.

Slaughter glanced back over his shoulder at the bodies sprawled spread-eagled on the table and floor. "What happened?" he asked, still holding his gun at waist level.

Smoke shrugged. "Evidently the Kid didn't take kindly to you dressing him down in front of the other men. Looked to me like he was going to plug you in the back."

Whitey and Swede rushed up to stand next to Slaughter. "He's right, Boss," Swede said. "The Kid already had his pistol out and was aimin' at the back of your head."

Slaughter relaxed and holstered his Colt. "And why didn't you do something about it?" he asked his two henchmen, scorn on his face. "Isn't coverin' my back what I pay you for?"

Whitey ducked his head, his eyes unable to meet Slaughter's. "It all happened so fast, Jim. How'd we know the Kid was gonna do somethin' crazy like that?"

Slaughter gave Smoke an appraising glance. "You mean the Kid had his gun out and pointed at me and West was able to draw and fire before he could pull the trigger?"

Swede nodded, his eyes on Smoke. "That's right, Boss. I ain't never seen nothin' like it. One second the Kid was set to shoot you in the back, and the next West's gun was in his hand blowin' the Kid to hell and back."

As they talked, Smoke broke open the loading gate on his Colt and punched out his empties, letting them fall on the floor. He reloaded his pistol and stuck it in his holster.

Slaughter walked up and stuck out his hand. "I guess I owe you my thanks, West," he said with a smile.

Smoke took his hand. "Don't take it personal, Slaughter. I couldn't care less if one of your men shoots you. It's just that I can't abide a backshooter."

Slaughter's eyes narrowed, then he smiled again. "Well, that's still one I owe you."

Smoke shrugged and turned back to his drink on the bar.

Slaughter leaned on the bar next to him and ordered a whiskey. When he picked up his glass, Smoke noticed his hand had a fine tremor. Evidently, the outlaw didn't like having someone try to gun him down.

After he finished his drink, Slaughter said, "I've decided to hire you on, West. I have need of someone who's as good with a gun as you are."

Smoke leaned back, sipping his beer, and stared at Slaughter. "Just where are you planning on going in Colorado?" he asked.

"A little town named Big Rock. There's a man there owes me fifty thousand dollars an' I aim to collect every dollar of it."

Smoke raised his eyebrows. "Big Rock, Colorado?"

"Yeah."

Smoke pursed his lips. "The gent owes you this money wouldn't happen to be Smoke Jensen, would it?"

Slaughter shook his head. "No, but I hear Jensen has thrown in with the man that I'm goin' after."

Smoke shook his head. "Then I'm not interested."

Whitey, who was standing next to his boss, leaned toward Smoke. "You mean you're afraid of that old gunman?"

Smoke smiled. "You might say that. I had a run-in with Jensen a few years back. I made the mistake of drawing down on him."

Slaughter smiled. "Well, what of it? I see you're still alive."

"Only 'cause Jensen was so fast he had the drop on me 'fore I cleared leather. He didn't need to shoot me 'cause I never got my gun out of my holster."

Swede looked as if he couldn't believe it. "That can't be! I ain't never seen nobody as fast as you are, West."

Smoke shrugged. "Jensen is. And you don't have

enough money to cause me to go up against him a second time."

Whitey's face burned red. "Then you're tellin' us you're yellow?"

Smoke glanced at the albino, making his face suddenly pale. "There's a difference between being yellow and knowing when someone's faster'n you are. I feel a man ought'a know his limitations if he's gonna make his living with a gun."

Whitey opened his mouth to speak, but Smoke interrupted him. "Just like you should know yours, sonny. You say one more word, an' Slaughter here's gonna have to hire someone to replace you, 'cause you're gonna have an extra hole in your head."

Whitey's mouth clamped shut with an audible snap.

Slaughter nodded. "All right, West. But what you say don't change my mind. I still aim to get my money."

Smoke shrugged. "Well, good luck to you, Mr. Slaughter. But I'd advise you to take plenty of shovels with you to Colorado, 'cause if you go up against Smoke Jensen you're gonna have a lot of graves to dig."

Slaughter grinned. "I guess that won't be all bad. It just means there'll be fewer men to split the money with after I've put Jensen and his friends in the ground."

Eighteen

After supper that night, Smoke met with his friends in his room to plan their next move. They'd just settled down when a knock came at the door.

Four pistols were drawn and aimed as Smoke stepped to the door. "Who is it?" he called, standing to the side so a bullet fired through the wood wouldn't hit him.

"It's me, Muskrat Calhoon."

Smoke pulled the door open and stepped back to let the mountain man enter. Muskrat took off his coonskin hat and grinned. "Howdy, boys."

Smoke peered out in the corridor to make sure no one had followed the old man up the stairs, then closed and locked the door.

After everyone told Muskrat hello, he glanced around the room. "What kind'a meetin' is this? I don't see no nectar around."

Louis smiled, pulled a bottle of whiskey from the bureau drawer, and flipped it to the mountaineer.

Muskrat pulled the cork and took a deep swig. "Ah, that'll git the chill of winter outta my bones," he groaned with pleasure.

Smoke sat on the bed and leaned back against the headboard, motioning for Muskrat to take his chair. "What can we do for you, Muskrat? I thought you were headed up into the high lonesome for your wintering."

As the old man took his seat, Pearlie moved quietly to the window and opened it a crack, hoping the night breeze would remove some of the smell.

"Well," Muskrat said, taking another sip of whiskey and smacking his lips, "I was on my way up the mountain when I got to thinkin' 'bout our little fracas the other night." He glanced around at the men watching him. "I ain't had so much fun since back in '42 when Preacher and Bear Tooth an' me blowed hell outta some Injuns down in Arizona."

His eyes opened wide. "I plumb forgot how good it feels to put some lead in folks that sorely need it. Hell," he continued, "it made me feel like I'se a young buck again 'stead of an old fart waitin' round to die."

Smoke nodded. "I know the feeling, Muskrat. Combat surely does get the juices flowing."

Muskrat shook his head. "No, Smoke, 'twas more'n that. It was that I'se doin' somethin' useful agin."

Louis spoke up. "Well, we certainly couldn't've done it without your help, Muskrat. We never could have found our way up to the hole-in-the-wall without your showing us the way."

Muskrat nodded. "That's why I decided to circle around and take me 'nother look at the hole-in-the-wall."

Smoke leaned forward, suddenly interested in what the mountain man had seen. After the battle the other night, they'd left so quickly they hadn't had time to fully assess the damage they'd done.

"What'd you see, Muskrat?"

"The place was a mess. All of the cabins was pret' near destroyed. A couple'a walls was still standin', but they ain't in no shape to keep nobody warm in the winter."

"What about the outlaws?" Pearlie asked.

"They had a pile of bodies all stacked up over near one corner of the valley, an' some of the men were diggin' a big hole." He shrugged. "I guess they gonna pile 'em all in there together 'fore they start to stink."

"How many men were left?" Smoke asked.

"I counted ten or twelve that was motivatin' on they own, an' four or five that was laid out on the ground blankets with bandages an' such like they was wounded pretty bad."

Smoke looked at the others. "Slaughter had four men with him in town today, and it looked like he managed to hire another fifteen or twenty."

"That gives him close to thirty hard cases to take with him to Colorado when he goes after Monte," Louis said, a worried look on his face.

"I noticed he had one of his men hangin' around the telegraph office," Cal said. "I guess he don't want nobody to send a wire warnin' Monte he's comin'."

"He knows at least some of the men who attacked his camp are still around," Smoke said, a thoughtful look on his face.

"How are we gonna get word to Miss Sally about his plans?" Pearlie asked.

Smoke shook his head. "I don't think we need to worry about that. Monte knows what kind of man we're up against. He'll be ready for whatever Slaughter decides to do."

"Do you think we ought to hightail it to Colorado and be waiting there for him when he shows up?" Louis asked Smoke.

Smoke shook his head. "No. I think a much better plan will be to see if we can slow him down along the way."

Muskrat smiled. "You mean you want to do like the Comanches did when they was fightin' the cavalry?"

Smoke gave a slow smile. "Exactly."

Cal gave Smoke a puzzled look. "What do you mean?"

"The Comanches were badly outnumbered by the Army, but they were much better horsemen and fighters.

So, they'd hit and run, attacking at night and other times when the Army was least expecting it. They never stood their ground, but would ride in, kill a few men, and ride out again . . . over and over. Soon, the cavalry men couldn't get any sleep for worrying about when the next attack was coming."

Pearlie grinned. "We gonna wear war paint an' such too?"

"No," Smoke said, "but we're going to hit them fast and hard and ride away to fight another day. That'll serve two purposes. It'll slow them down and give Monte more time to get ready for them, and if we're lucky, we'll be able to cut their numbers down a mite before the final battle in Colorado."

Louis grinned. "Not to mention what it will do to their morale."

Smoke nodded. "Exactly."

Muskrat took a deep drink from his bottle and sleeved his lips off with the back of his arm. "You fellers want some company on this little jaunt?"

"You think you're up to it, Muskrat? We're going to be riding fast and hard."

Muskrat sat up straight in his chair and puffed out his chest. "Hell, sonny," he said to Smoke, "I been sittin' a saddle for more years than you been walkin'. The day I can't outride some mangy ol' gun hawks is the day I lay down and die."

"All right, here's what we're going to do," Smoke said, sitting forward, his elbows on his knees. "Louis and Muskrat and I will take our pack animals and equipment out of town and camp a half day's ride toward Colorado. Cal, you and Pearlie will hang around and keep an eye on Slaughter and his men. As soon as they mass up for the ride, you'll hightail it on down the road and we'll be waiting for them when they make their first camp."

"How'll we find your campsite?" Pearlie asked.

Muskrat laughed. "Don't you worry none, little beaver. You boys jest head on out the eastern trail toward Colorad'a, an' we'll see ya comin'."

In Big Rock, Monte and Sally Jensen were getting the town ready for whatever Slaughter had in mind. Mary had suffered no lasting ill effects from her abduction.

Monte called a town meeting, and he and Sally explained that Big Jim Slaughter was most probably on the way to seek vengeance for what Monte and Smoke and the others had done to him.

The townfolks, after hearing the story of the stolen Army payroll and how Monte had returned the money, were standing behind their popular sheriff and his wife. Not a single person in the entire town voted against helping the couple out.

Monte supervised getting the town fortified and ready for the anticipated onslaught. Barricades were erected at each end of the town, rifles were handed out, and men assigned to rooftops and high points as both lookouts and assault teams. Men were sent to station themselves miles from the town on the trails leading toward Wyoming, so they could return and give ample warning of Slaughter's approach, when and if it happened.

Sally took charge of the women in town, helping them cook large amounts of food to have ready in case there was an extended siege. The children were put to work helping build the barricades and fences at the entrances to the town. Everyone pitched in and worked as fast as they could to make Big Rock ready for the attack.

Nineteen

Big Jim Slaughter stood in the center of the valley at the hole-in-the-wall with his hands on his hips and surveyed the damage.

Several men were rolling bodies into a large, common grave and shoveling dirt and rocks over them. Another group of men, the outlaws who planned to stay in the hole-in-the-wall through the winter, were cutting logs and sawing limbs, working feverishly to repair the cabins destroyed in the fight.

Slaughter shook his head. "Damn! I'd give a hundred dollars to find out who Carson found up here to help him do this," he said.

Whitey, standing next to him, scowled. "My money's still on that gunny Johnny West."

Slaughter cut his eyes to his second in command. "I don't know, Whitey. It'd take a man with powerful *cojones* to come up here, kill half my men, and then stay in town when he'd have to know we'd come lookin' for whoever did this."

"Man'd have to be a damn fool to hang around after that," Swede said, "an' West don't look like no fool to me."

"Sheriff Pike didn't have no ideas?" Whitey asked.

Slaughter snorted through his nose. "Sheriff Pike ain't exactly on our side in this matter, boys. While he don't bother us none as long as we stay out of his hair, that don't mean he's all that anxious to help us. He did tell me Carson and his wife got on the first train out of Jackson Hole the morning after the attack, headed east. I'm sure they're headed back to that jerkwater town where he's sheriff."

Swede glanced at the group of men standing near a fire in the center of the compound, drinking coffee and warming their hands on the flames. The weather was turning steadily colder and snow flurries were becoming more and more common as the days passed. "You figure these extra men you hired are gonna do us any good?" Swede asked.

Slaughter followed his gaze. "Some of 'em are all right; some of the others are just gonna be cannon fodder."

"How many men we got total now?" Whitey asked.

"Close to thirty, thirty-five," Slaughter answered. "A few will probably drop out along the way to Colorado. It figures to be a hard trip, what with the weather turning so fast."

Swede nodded. "Yeah. It won't be so bad on the flatlands, but gettin' through the passes might be tough if we get a blizzard or two."

"How about supplies?" Slaughter asked Whitey. "You manage to get what we need in town?"

Whitey nodded. "Yes, sir. Every man has a rifle and at least one pistol. We got two wagons of foodstuffs and extra ammunition, along with some dynamite and gunpowder in case we need to blast our way into that town Monte Carson lives in."

Swede's brow furrowed. "You really think we're gonna have to tree Big Rock, Boss? Far as I know, ain't no Western town ever been taken from the outside before."

Slaughter's face got a stubborn look on it. "We'll do whatever it takes to get Carson and get our money, Swede. If it means burning Big Rock to the ground, then we'll put fire to the town an' flush the bastard out."

"You think it'll come to that, Jim?" Whitey asked.

The outlaw shook his head. "No, I doubt it. I don't figure any town's gonna let itself get burned to the ground to protect an ex-outlaw an' his money. Once we let 'em know what's gonna happen if they don't give him up, they'll give us Monte faster'n you can spit."

Swede nodded. "I sure hope so. I don't hanker to kill a bunch of innocent women and children just to get Carson's hide hung on a barn door."

Slaughter turned hard eyes on Swede. "I really don't give a damn what you 'hanker' to do, Swede. When the time comes, you'll do what I tell you to do, is that clear?"

"Sure, Boss," Swede said, his eyes dropping. "I didn't mean nothin' by what I said."

Slaughter shook his head and walked away, toward the men by the fire. "Come on, boys, let's go start gettin' the men ready to ride. We got a long way to go and we need to stay ahead of the weather."

On the ridge overlooking the hole-in-the-wall, Pearlie lay on his stomach behind a large blueberry bush and peered at the activity through binoculars. Cal lay next to him, watching over his shoulder.

"What're they doin', Pearlie?" Cal asked.

"Just standin' there jawin', it looks like."

"I see a couple'a wagons over to the side."

Pearlie shifted his binoculars to take a look. "Uh-huh. It appears they're full of guns an' food an' stuff like that."

"So they are gettin' ready to head to Colorado, just like Smoke said."

"Yeah, looks like Smoke had Slaughter figgered right. He's plannin' on goin' after Monte an' his money, all right."

"You reckon we should head back to Jackson Hole, or stay out here and see what they do?"

Pearlie paused a moment, thinking. "It don't look to me

like they gonna be goin' back to Jackson at all. They already got all their supplies, so I guess we ought'a plan on campin' up here in the woods so's we'll know when they take off."

Cal stepped back from the ledge to where he couldn't be seen from below and glanced at the sky. "Looks like snow in them clouds. It's gonna get mighty chilly up here come nightfall, Pearlie."

Pearlie nodded. "Yeah, an' we won't be able to make no fire neither, or else they'll see it."

Cal gave a halfhearted smile. "I guess that means you're gonna miss a meal, Pearlie. You think yer stomach can take goin' twenty-four hours without being stuffed plumb full?"

Pearlie glanced over his shoulder at his friend. "What makes you say that? 'Fore we left Jackson Hole, I had Aunt Bea fix us up a mess of fried chicken, some sinkers, an' I bought a couple'a cans of sliced peaches. We may freeze our butts off, Cal, boy, but we shore as hell ain't gonna go hungry."

Cal grinned. "I should'a know'd you had some food stashed somewheres or else you'd never of left Jackson Hole."

"Like Smoke always says, Cal, you gotta learn to plan ahead or else you'll git caught with your pants down."

A loud snapping sound from the forest nearby brought both men to their feet.

"What was that?" Cal asked.

Pearlie put a finger to his lips and whispered, "Sounds like we got company comin'."

Just as he finished talking, four men walked out of the brush, axes and saws over their shoulders. Evidently they were part of the crew of men cutting timber to repair the cabins down below.

"What the hell?" the man in the lead said, pulling up short with a surprised look on his face.

The man following him bumped into him, stumbling and dropping his ax.

The six men stared at each other for a moment, all of them too surprised to move at first.

"Take it easy, boys," Pearlie said. "We're just a couple of miners up here looking for gold."

"Bullshit!" the first man said, his hand dropping toward his pistol. "You're the men who shot us up the other night."

Pearlie crouched and filled his hands with iron, while Cal took one step to the side to give the men less of a target to shoot at and drew his Colt Navy .36-caliber pistol.

Pearlie and Cal got off the first shots, taking two of the men in the chest and blowing them backward into the other two, knocking them all to the ground.

Pearlie thumbed off another shot, hitting one of the men on the ground in the forehead, exploding his head in a red mist of brains and blood and bone.

Cal's second shot took the fourth man in the shoulder just as he fired. The force of the blow threw the outlaw's aim off and his bullet tore into Cal's left thigh with a loud smack, spinning the young man around and throwing him to the ground.

As the man eared back his hammer for another shot, Pearlie put lead between his eyes, putting his lights out forever.

Pearlie rushed to Cal's side and leaned over him. "Cal, you all right, boy?"

Cal rolled over and sat up, his face covered with sweat from the shock of being shot. He pulled his leg up and looked at where the bullet had torn a hole in his pants and burned a shallow groove along the outside of his thigh.

His face paled and he looked as if he was about to faint. "Yeah, I guess so. He just winged me."

Pearlie shook his head. "I should'a know'd it. It's been over a month since you got shot the last time. You were past due, boy," he said, grinning with relief and teasing Cal about the number of times he'd been wounded in the past.

Cal's eyes fluttered and he took deep breaths to keep from passing out. "It was just a lucky shot," he moaned.

Pearlie stepped behind him and put his hands under his arms, lifting him to his feet. "Nevertheless, we got to git goin'. Them gunshots is gonna bring Slaughter an' his men up here like bees buzzin' round a nest with a stick poked in it."

Cal gingerly put his weight on his injured leg, grimacing with pain as he took off his bandanna and tied it in a knot to slow the bleeding. "You go get our horses an' I'll be there in a minute."

When Pearlie brought their mounts, Cal walked around and got on from the right side, his left leg unable to pull him into the saddle.

"Come on, Cal," Pearlie said. "We got to make tracks around the mountain to the other side where we can find some cover. They gonna be searchin' for us 'fore long."

Cal nodded, leaning over his saddle horn and holding on for dear life, trying his best to stay in the saddle. He knew if he passed out he was as good as dead.

In the valley below, Slaughter jerked around at the sound of gunshots on the ridge above them, his hand automatically going for his pistol.

When he realized they were not under attack again, he began to shout orders. "Whitey! Get some horses saddled and get some men up on that ridge and find out what the hell's goin' on!"

"Yes, sir!" Whitey shouted back, motioning to several men by the fire to follow him as he ran toward the corral.

"Goddamn!" Slaughter growled, putting his pistol back in its holster. "It's probably the same men who were here the other night."

"Maybe we should'a kept the sentries doubled up, Boss, 'stead of cuttin' 'em back to one man at each station," Swede said, his eyes scanning the mountainside, looking for any movement.

Slaughter glared at him, knowing Swede was right but resenting the implication that he himself had made a mistake. "You know we were short of men after the attack, Swede," he snarled.

Swede, realizing his mistake in questioning his boss's orders, nodded quickly. "That's right, Boss, an' who would'a figgered they'd hit again so soon?"

Mollified a bit by Swede's statement, Slaughter turned and watched as Whitey and five men rode up the narrow trail leading to the ridge where the shots were heard.

In less than thirty minutes, Whitey came back down the trail alone.

He rode over to Slaughter and got down off his horse.

"What happened up there?" Slaughter asked.

"Four of the men cutting timber for the cabins were shot and killed," Whitey said. "From the tracks, it looks like two men were lying up there watching us and were surprised by the other four."

"Four to two and all four of our men were killed?" Slaughter asked, his face doubtful.

"Yes, sir. But it looks like they managed to put lead in one of 'em, 'cause there's blood on the ground where their tracks were."

"Blood but no body?"

Whitey nodded. "I've got the boys tryin' to track 'em down now. With any luck, they'll find 'em and kill 'em."

Slaughter snorted. "Huh, if I had any luck they'd already be dead." He pointed his finger in Whitey's face. "I don't want those men back in camp until they find and kill these bastards. It's probably part of the same bunch who attacked us the other night."

Whitey looked upward at the ridge. "Yeah, it's the

same place they fired from before." He looked back at Slaughter. "What I'm wonderin' is, how'd they get up there without our sentries knowing about it?"

Slaughter's eyes narrowed. "There must be a back way up there that don't go by our sentry posts. That's the only way I can figure it."

"What are we gonna do about it?" Whitey asked.

Slaughter shrugged. "Nothing. It won't matter after tomorrow, 'cause we'll be on our way to Colorado."

Twenty

Halfway down the back side of the mountain, on the opposite side from the hole-in-the-wall, Pearlie found a cave hidden among a group of granite boulders.

He dismounted and pulled his pistol, warily walking into the cave entrance. "Phew," he called to Cal, "smells like a bear crawled in here and died."

From his saddle, Cal said, "Be careful, Pearlie. Now's the time of year fer bears an' such to hibernate. Liable to be a big ol' grizzly in there just settlin' down fer winter."

"If'n there is," Pearlie replied, "it's gonna git awful crowded in here, 'cause we got to find a hole to crawl in 'fore those *bandidos* come after us."

When he disappeared into the black hole of the entrance, Cal shucked his Winchester rifle from its saddle boot and cradled it in his arms, ready to fire if Pearlie came running out of the cave with a bear on his trail.

After a few moments, Pearlie reemerged, taking a deep breath of fresh air. "Nothin' in there but some old bones. Looks like a bear had his dinner in there an' decided it weren't time for the long sleep just yet."

Cal rebooted his rifle and climbed painfully down from his saddle. His leg felt like it was on fire, but at least the bleeding had stopped.

"Come on," Pearlie said as he grabbed the reins to the

horses. "Let's see if we can get these mounts to go in there."

When they smelled the acrid bear-scent, both horses reared back and fought their reins, wanting no part of a dark place that smelled of a carnivore as large as a grizzly.

After some coaching and lots of heavy pulling, the boys finally managed to get the horses into the cave and back to where it opened up at the rear. There was a hat-sized opening in the rocks above that let a little sunlight and some welcome fresh air into the cavern, so the horses calmed down a little, helped some by handfuls of grain handed out by Cal.

"You try to get the broncs settled down and I'll go sweep our tracks and put some deadfall around the entrance," Pearlie said. "With any luck, the outlaws won't find us."

"And if our luck don't hold an' they do?" Cal asked.

"Then we'll blast hell out of 'em an' take as many with us as we can."

While Cal was trying to get the horses completely calmed down, Pearlie took a pine limb and used it like a broom to sweep away all tracks leading to their hiding place. After he was finished, he moved piles of fallen branches and limbs to the front of the cave, hiding the entrance from sight.

In less than an hour, the two men could hear sounds of horses and men outside the cave. Cal stayed in the rear, his hands on the noses of their mounts to try and keep them from whinnying or making any other sounds, while Pearlie took his rifle and lay on his belly just inside the entrance, peering through branches at the outside.

Five outlaws rode down the narrow trail through the piney woods, rifles and shotguns cradled in their arms. Pearlie could hear them joking about what they were going to do to the men who'd killed their friends.

"I jest hope we can catch 'em alive, so's we can string

'em up over a fire and roast their asses off," one of the men growled.

"I don't care if'n we git 'em alive, just so's we git 'em. Slaughter'll have our butts if'n we come back without them bastards," another replied.

"Well," yet another added, "I ain't seen no sign of tracks nor nothin' fer the last hour, an' it shore looks like we gonna git a blizzard 'fore long." He shook his head, glancing at the sky, which was overhung with dark, roiling clouds blocking the sun and causing the temperature to drop rapidly.

"I vote we head on back 'fore we git trapped up here an' freeze our balls off."

The first man nodded. "Yeah. If those men are up here, they gonna die in the blizzard without no cover to git to. We can tell Slaughter there just ain't no way they could survive out here when the snows come."

There was a general mumbling of agreement, and the group of searchers jerked their mounts' heads around and headed back the way they'd come.

Only when they were out of sight and Pearlie couldn't hear them any longer did he let himself breathe a sigh of relief.

He walked back to the rear of the cave, and heard Cal talking in a low voice to Cold and Silver. Pearlie smiled. The boy did have a way with horses, he thought.

"Good work keepin' them animals quiet, Cal," he said. "I think they've given up on findin' us."

"Then we can get out of here an' head on back to town?" Cal asked, a hopeful gleam in his eye.

Pearlie shook his head. "Nope. Looks like there's a helluva storm brewin' out there. It wouldn't do fer us to get caught in it halfway to town, an' we still got to keep an eye on these bastards till they leave so's we can warn Smoke."

Cal wrinkled his nose. "I don't know if'n I can stand

to spend the night in here, Pearlie. I cain't hardly breathe with the bear-stink so strong."

Pearlie shrugged as he walked to his saddlebags and took out a bag of fried chicken and biscuits and canned peaches. "Suit yoreself, Cal, but if'n you go out there tonight, I'm gonna have to build a big fire in the mornin' to thaw yore frozen butt out. It's gettin' mighty cold an' it ain't even dark yet."

Pearlie opened the bag of chicken and pitched a leg to Cal. "Here. I know you likes the legs the best."

Cal took a bite and as he chewed, he asked, "You got enough sinkers fer both of us?"

Pearlie pursed his lips. "I dunno. There might be one or two I can spare."

Slaughter was furious when the search party returned and reported they'd caught no sight of whoever killed the four men on the ridge.

"Goddammit!" he screamed, fire in his eyes. "There ain't no place to hide up there on the mountain. How could you not find any sign of them?"

Billy Bob Justice, the man in charge of the search, hung his head, not wanting to look at Slaughter. "I don't know, Boss. They just seemed to disappear. One minute they's tracks as plain as day leading around the mountain, an' the next they was gone with no trace."

"And you say it looked like there was only two of 'em?"

"We only found tracks of two hosses."

"What about the blood trail?" Slaughter asked.

"It went for about a hundred yards, then it petered out too," Justice said. "We figgered they's gonna freeze to death if they stay up there on the mountain with this blizzard that's comin'."

"Damn! I'm surrounded by fools," Slaughter yelled as

he turned and walked toward the fire. He stood there a moment, warming his hands and thinking.

After a moment, he looked up at the sky as large, wet snowflakes began to fall. "All right, I guess it can't be helped." He turned to Whitey, who was standing next to him.

"Whitey, get the men ready and pack up our gear. I want to leave at first light, if this damned storm is over by then."

"Yes, sir."

"We need to get movin' before those men have a chance to get back to Jackson Hole and get reinforcements to come attack us again." He glanced around at the valley of the hole-in-the-wall. "Right now, we're easy targets down here since our sentries don't seem to be able to stop 'em."

"Yes, sir, I'll get the men ready," Whitey said.

"I just wish I knew who it is that's doggin' us," Slaughter said.

"Once we get on the trail, I'll have men watching our back trail to make sure they don't follow us an' surprise us along the way," Whitey said.

Slaughter nodded. "That's a good idea, Whitey. At least someone around here is thinking besides me."

He turned to Swede. "It might even be a good idea to leave a few men behind to set up an ambush, catch those bastards with their pants down if they try to trail us."

Swede nodded, his face grim.

"Swede, pick five men you think are pretty good with their guns. After we get five or six miles down the trail toward Colorado, you look for a likely spot for an ambush and get those men set up. We'll teach those sons of bitches not to mess with Big Jim Slaughter."

Twenty-one

Unable to start a fire, Pearlie and Cal spent the night in the cave bundled in their ground blankets, and even covered themselves with brush and pine needles to try to keep from freezing. Luckily, the space was small enough that the warmth given off by the two horses helped keep the temperature bearable.

When he awoke, just after dawn, Cal felt as if his leg was on fire. He pulled the blanket off, and was alarmed to find his thigh swollen to almost twice its normal size.

Pearlie rolled over and glanced at Cal, sitting upright, staring at his leg.

"What's goin' on, pardner?" he asked, yawning widely.

Cal quickly covered his limb and said, "Nothin', just tryin' to wake up."

Pearlie climbed stiffly out of his blankets and walked to the cave entrance. Snow had drifted to a depth of three feet, and had almost covered the hole in the rocks.

Pearlie kicked and dug his way out into bright sunshine, grateful for the warmth of the sun, though the temperature was still below freezing.

He clambered back into the cave. "Damn," he said, "the weather is clearin'. I'd kind'a hoped the storm would stay around for a while to give us some cover."

He fished around in his saddlebags and pulled out a

couple of biscuits and one piece of fried chicken left from the night before.

Turning to Cal, he held them up. "Looks like we got to share one lonely piece of chicken an' two sinkers."

Cal tried to get to his feet, but his leg collapsed beneath him and he fell to the ground, his face furrowed with pain.

Pearlie rushed to his side. "What's the matter, Cal?"

"It's my leg, Pearlie. It hurts somethin' fierce an' it's kind'a swollen."

Pearlie, noticing the flushed appearance of Cal's face, put his hand on his friend's cheek. "Damn, boy! Yore burnin' up with fever."

He pulled the blanket down and winced when he saw Cal's swollen thigh.

"Git those pants down an' let me take a look at that wound, Cal."

Cal unbuckled his belt and struggled to get his trousers down over the swollen leg. When it came into view, Pearlie gasped. The thigh was bright red, swollen, and there was pus flowing from the furrow the bullet had dug in Cal's flesh.

"Shit, boy. You done got suppuration in that bullet wound."

Cal laid his head back, breathing through his mouth. "It'll be all right, Pearlie. Just help me get up on my horse so's we can see what the outlaws are doin'."

"I'll get you up on your hoss, Cal, but we ain't gonna bother with no outlaws this mornin'. We gotta git you back to Jackson Hole so the doc can fix that leg."

Cal shook his head. "We cain't, Pearlie. We gotta keep an eye on them so we can warn Smoke when they leave."

"Bullshit, Cal," Pearlie said as he helped pull Cal's pants up. "If'n we don't git you some doctorin', yore gonna end up losing that leg."

Cal's head lolled back, and he almost fainted from the pain when his trousers moved against his swollen flesh.

Pearlie quickly moved to their horses and began to lead them from the cave. "I'll git the hosses saddled an' then I'll come back for you. You stay still now, you hear?"

It took the boys until almost noon to make their way down the mountain through the heavy drifts of snow. Several times Pearlie had to grab Cal's shoulder to keep him from passing out and falling off his horse.

By the time they reached Jackson Hole, Cal was almost unconscious from the pain in his leg and Pearlie was having to support his full weight to keep him in the saddle. He reined the horses in when they got to the doctor's office, and let Cal fall off Silver into his arms. He had to carry him into the doctor's waiting room.

Doctor Josiah Curry glanced up from his position in front of a cowboy with a swollen red jaw. The doc had a pair of dental pliers in his hand, and was fixing to pull an infected tooth.

"Doc," Pearlie said as he stood there with Cal cradled in his arms, "my friend's got a bullet wound that needs takin' care of."

"Take him in the other room and I'll be there directly," Dr. Curry said. He turned back to the cowboy, stuck the pliers in his mouth, and yanked a bloody tooth out of his gums.

"Yeow-w-w," the cowboy wailed, grabbing his jaw with both hands.

The doc stood up, threw the tooth into a wastebasket, and said, "That'll be twenty-five cents, Joey."

Joey released his jaw long enough to fish in his pocket and hand the doctor some change, then bolted from the room.

"You might want to wash that mouth out with some good whiskey," Dr. Curry called to his retreating back.

A muffled retort came from the cowboy. "Goddamned right!" he said, heading straight for the Cattleman's Saloon down the street.

Curry wiped his bloody hands on his coat and strolled over to look down at Cal on the table.

"When did this happen?" he asked as he pulled Cal's trousers down over the swollen thigh.

"Yesterday afternoon," Pearlie answered. "It 'tweren't much more'n a scratch so we didn't think nothin' of it till it started to swell up."

"How did it happen?" Curry asked, probing the area around the bullet wound gently with his fingers.

Pearlie scowled, wondering what the hell that had to do with fixing the leg. "He was shot," he answered in a tone of voice that indicated to the doctor that foolish questions weren't going to be tolerated.

The doctor raised his eyebrows, looked at the expression on Pearlie's face, and decided not to ask anything else.

He placed the back of his hand on Cal's forehead and whistled softly under his breath. "This boy's burning up with fever. The wound is seriously infected."

Pearlie nodded. Even he knew that much. "Is there anything you can do fer him, Doc?"

Curry probed the area of the wound again, shaking his head. "Well, I can drain some of the suppuration from the muscle. The latest medical books say that helps some, an' there's a new medicine out called aspirin that's supposed to be good for fever and such. That and some laudanum for the pain should do the trick."

"You think he'll get better?" Pearlie asked, not liking the paleness of Cal's skin.

The doctor shrugged. "If he doesn't respond within twenty-four hours, I may have to take the leg off."

Pearlie gritted his teeth. "He's young and he's strong, Doc, an' he's been shot plenty of times before. He'll do just fine."

Curry pursed his lips. "I hope so, 'cause if I have to take his leg off that high, he probably won't survive the surgery."

He turned to a metal tray of instruments and pulled out a long shining scalpel. "Now, why don't you go get some breakfast while I do my work. This is not something you want to watch."

Pearlie put his hand on Cal's shoulder, squeezed it, then picked up his hat and walked out of the room. He headed toward Aunt Bea's boardinghouse, uttering a silent prayer that Cal would be all right.

Pearlie was on his second helping of flapjacks, eggs, and sausage when Sheriff Walter Pike sat down at his table.

"Howdy, son," Pike said, motioning to Aunt Bea to bring him some coffee.

He built himself a cigarette while he waited, not saying anything, but staring at Pearlie as if he might frighten him into confessing to some crime.

Pearlie ignored the sheriff, concentrating on finishing his food so he could get back to the doctor's office to see how Cal was doing.

After Pike got his cigarette going and sampled his coffee, he leaned back in his chair and crossed his legs, still staring at Pearlie.

"A cowboy over at the Cattleman's said you brought in your friend with a gunshot wound."

Pearlie took the last bite from his plate, put his fork down, and picked up his coffee cup. He glanced at the sheriff over the rim.

"That's right," he said, offering no more information.

"How did that happen to occur?" the sheriff asked.

"It didn't happen in town, Sheriff, so I can't see as it's any of yore business how it happened," Pearlie answered, staring back at Pike.

Pike nodded. "You sure you want to play it that way, son?"

Pearlie shrugged.

Pike took a deep drag of his cigarette and let the smoke trail from his nostrils as he talked. "A man came into town yesterday evening from the hole-in-the-wall. He said a couple of men had attacked some cowboys up there and killed four men. He also said one of the killers had been wounded."

"That so?" Pearlie said.

"You boys wouldn't happen to have been up near the hole-in-the-wall yesterday, would you?"

"Like I said, Sheriff, this didn't happen in town. Are you sheriff of the hole-in-the-wall, too?" Pearlie asked. "From what I hear, there ain't nothin' but outlaws and men ridin' the owlhoot trail up that way. Are you paid to watch out for them galoots?"

"No, son, I'm not paid to bother with the hole-in-the-wall. But Big Jim Slaughter has offered a five-hundred-dollar reward for any information on the men who've been attacking him up there."

Pearlie nodded. "Five hundred dollars, huh? That's a right sizable chunk of change."

"More'n I make here in a year," Pike answered.

Pearlie stood up and threw some money on the table. "Maybe you ought to think about changing jobs then, Sheriff, if money means that much to you."

"Goddammit, son, I don't give a shit about the money!" Pike answered, standing up also. "But Slaughter has a couple of hard cases here in town who are gonna be awfully interested in anybody with a bullet wound."

Pearlie shrugged. "Let 'em come, Sheriff. I can take care of myself."

Pike stuck his finger in Pearlie's face. "I told you, I'm paid to keep the peace here in Jackson. I don't want any gunplay where innocent citizens might get hurt."

Pearlie gave a slow grin. "Don't worry none, Sheriff. If'n I'm forced to draw iron, won't no innocent people get kilt."

"Your name's Pearlie, isn't it?"

Pearlie nodded.

"I want you to get your friend and get the hell out of my town as soon as he's able to travel."

"You got my word on that, Sheriff," Pearlie said as he walked out of the boardinghouse dining room without looking back.

When he got to the doctor's office, he found the doctor washing off his instruments.

"How's Cal, Doc?" he asked.

"I got about two cups of pus out of that leg," the doctor answered, "and the swelling's gone down quite a bit. I've given him some laudanum, so he's resting quietly for now."

Pearlie stepped over to stand next to the table on which Cal lay. The boy's face was covered with sweat and he was mumbling in his sleep, turning his head from side to side.

"I've got a room in the back where you can keep him," the doctor said. "You need to keep feeding him beef broth and soup and keep his strength up if he's going to fight off the infection."

Pearlie nodded. "I can do that," he said.

"The next twenty-four hours should tell us if he's going to make it or not."

The doctor and Pearlie picked Cal up and carried him into the back room, placing him on a bed.

After the doctor left, Cal's eyes flicked open and he stared at Pearlie, his pupils pinpoints from the laudanum. "Howdy, Pearlie," he mumbled through dry, cracked lips.

"Hello, Cal. How're you feelin'?" Pearlie asked, sitting on the edge of the bed.

Cal's lips curled in a half grin. "I been shot, you fool," he answered. "How do you think I feel?"

Pearlie forced himself to grin back, though he felt more like crying seeing his friend so sick. "Well, hell, Cal. You been shot so many times before, I'd've thought you'd gotten used to it by now."

He reached down and wiped sweat off Cal's forehead. "I guess we gonna have to paint a big ol' bull's-eye on your carcass, make it easier for the outlaws to hit next time."

"Hell, pardner," Cal answered, "they don't seem to have no trouble hittin' me as it is."

"I done tole you, boy, you a magnet fer lead," Pearlie said.

"Pearlie, I want you to leave me here an' go warn Smoke about Slaughter. He needs to know what's goin' on."

"Don't you worry none 'bout Smoke, Cal. He's got Louis an' Muskrat with him. They can take care of theyselves."

"But . . ."

"No buts, Cal. You rest now while I go over to Aunt Bea's an' git you some grub. The doc says you got to eat so's you can git over this wound."

"All right, Pearlie," Cal said, letting his eyes close. "I am a mite tired . . ."

When he lapsed into unconsciousness, Pearlie stood up and walked out to the doctor's front room.

"You take care of my friend, Doc, money's no object," Pearlie said.

Dr. Curry smiled. "It's not a question of money, mister. It's in God's hands now. All we can do is wait to see what He's decided to do with your friend."

"Well, while God makes up His mind, I'm gonna go over to Aunt Bea's an' git him some grub so's he can get better," Pearlie said, his face grim.

Twenty-two

Smoke stood on a promontory overlooking the trail leading from the hole-in-the-wall toward Colorado, his binoculars to his eyes.

Muskrat Calhoon stirred the small fire they'd built under the overhang of a group of boulders. The temperature was rising after the freezing chill of the snowstorm last night, but the air was still cold enough to freeze water in a canteen. "You see anythin', Smoke?" he asked.

Smoke shook his head. "No, but I figure Slaughter will be getting his men moving before too long, else he's going to have some heavy winter storms to deal with on his way to Colorado."

Louis poured himself another cup of coffee and leaned back on his ground blanket, lighting a long, black cheroot off a burning twig from the campfire. "I'm a little concerned that we haven't heard from Cal and Pearlie, Smoke."

Smoke nodded. They'd all heard what they took to be distant gunfire from the direction of the hole-in-the-wall the night before, and were worried that perhaps Cal and Pearlie had been discovered watching the outlaws' hideout. "Me, too, Louis. If anything's happened to those boys, I don't know what I'd do."

Muskrat cut a piece of tobacco off a twist he pulled from his coat pocket. "Don't you worry none 'bout those two young'uns, Smoke. 'Pears to me they got enough hair to look out for theyselves."

"That's the trouble, Muskrat," Smoke answered, stepping down from his perch on a boulder. "They're too brave for their own good. I just don't want them to get hurt because of their loyalty to me."

Louis drained his cup. "This isn't just about you, Smoke," he said. "Both Cal and Pearlie are doing this for Monte and Mary. They hate an injustice as much as we do, and taking a man's wife to settle an old score just isn't done."

"I understand that, Louis, but would you want to try and explain it to Sally if either one of them is shot? She thinks of them as our sons."

Muskrat grinned. "It ain't never easy to 'splain nothin' to a woman, Smoke, 'specially if'n it concerns one of her pups."

Smoke smiled. Mountain men had a way of getting right to the heart of the matter, he thought. They were men of little or no formal education, but their years in the high lonesome seemed to endow them with knowledge of life and death that far outstripped men with college degrees.

"Sally's as tough as any man I know, Smoke," Louis said. "If worse comes to worst, she'll understand."

Smoke took a biscuit out of the frying pan sitting on red-hot embers and popped it into his mouth. "Well, let's hope it doesn't come to that. Cal and Pearlie are both too brave for their own good sometimes, but they're also smart and crafty. I believe it'll take someone smarter than Jim Slaughter to get the drop on them."

Back in Jackson Hole, Pearlie was staying out of sight as much as he could to keep from running into the men Slaughter had sent to look for them. Other than his frequent trips to Aunt Bea's for food for himself and Cal, he spent all his time sitting by Cal's bed, talking to him and forcing him to eat the beef soup and broth so he could heal properly.

Doctor Curry was encouraged that the swelling in Cal's leg had gone down and not returned. The redness of the surrounding tissues was getting better hour by hour and his temperature had returned to normal, both good signs according to the doctor.

By the morning after his surgery, Cal was feeling fit enough to try to walk around the room on his injured leg, though the doctor forbade any longer journeys.

"Walking short distances will help get rid of the stiffness," he'd said, "but don't overdo it and undo what healing is going on."

As Pearlie watched Cal's appetite return, he began to have hope there would be no long-lasting effects from the wound and infection in his leg.

On the morning of the second day, Doctor Curry said it would be all right for Cal to mount a horse and ride, as long as he took frequent breaks and stopped if the swelling or redness returned.

"I've done all I can, boys," Doc Curry said. "Now it's just gonna take some time for the final healing to occur. You take it easy on that leg for the next couple of weeks, young man," he said to Cal.

"Yes, sir," Cal answered, glad to finally be given permission to ride out of town. Like Pearlie, he was concerned that Slaughter and his men would be on the move before they both could leave the area.

"C'mon, Cal. Let's go git a final breakfast at Aunt Bea's, then we can hit the trail," Pearlie said.

Cal nodded. "Good, I'm 'bout ready for some eggs and flapjacks 'stead of that damned beef soup you been forcin' down my gullet."

Pearlie grinned. "Forcin', hell! You sucked that stuff down like it was honey."

Pearlie forced a handful of greenbacks into the doctor's hand, thanked him again, and they set out for Aunt Bea's place.

An hour and a half later, they were just finishing their final cups of coffee when Sheriff Walter Pike stepped through the rear door of the dining room.

He made his way toward their table, a worried look on his face.

"Uh-oh," Pearlie said. "I don't like the way Sheriff Pike's lookin' at us, Cal."

"Me neither," Cal said, unconsciously unhooking the hammer-thong on his Colt Navy.

Pike stopped in front of their table. "Boys, I got some bad news for you."

"I kind'a figgered that from the sour look on yore face," Pearlie drawled, taking a drink of his coffee.

"Slaughter's men talked to Doc Curry. They found out about your bullet wound and they're waiting in front of the Cattleman's Saloon for you to try and leave town."

"How many of them are they?" Cal asked.

"Four."

Pearlie grinned. "Sounds like fair odds to me."

Pike shook his head. "You don't understand. These are hard men, hired killers every one." He hesitated, looking over his shoulder out the window. "Why don't you let me sneak you out of town the back way?"

Pearlie pursed his lips. "I don't know. What do you think, Cal?"

Cal shrugged, pulling his Navy out and flipping open the loading gate to check his loads. "Seems to me if we take care of 'em now, it'll be four less men Smoke will have to worry about later."

Pearlie nodded and stood up from the table. He put his hat on, pulling it down tight on his head. "Thanks for the offer, Sheriff, but I think we'll go out the front door after all."

"You boys are crazy!"

Cal grinned. "We've been told that before, Sheriff."

They walked out the front door. A slight limp in Cal's gait was the only sign of his injury.

As they stood next to their horses, four men stepped off the boardwalk in front of the Cattleman's Saloon and spread out in the street.

"Hey, you there," one of the men called, his hand hanging next to his pistol. "We want a word with you."

Cal and Pearlie squared around, facing the men. "I got the two on the left," Pearlie said under his breath.

Cal nodded, not speaking, his eyes watching the eyes of the men in the street. Smoke had taught him not to look at the hands, for the eyes would give the first signal a man was about to draw.

Sheriff Pike stepped out of the dining room door. "I don't want no trouble in town, boys," he called to the men.

"It's too late for that, Sheriff," one of the men said. "Slaughter offered to pay you for your help, an' you should'a taken him up on it. Now it's our play."

As the outlaw's eyes narrowed, Cal and Pearlie crouched and stepped apart, to give less of a target, then filled their hands with iron.

Pearlie fired a fraction of a second faster than Cal, but the two shots were so close together they sounded as one.

Two of the men across the street grabbed their chests as they were blown backward, one landing in a water trough, staining the water red with the blood that spurted from a fist-sized hole in his chest. Neither had managed to clear leather before they were dead.

"Goddamn!" one of the remaining bandits yelled as he clawed at his pistol.

Pearlie's second shot took him in the throat, blowing out the back of his spine and almost taking his head off as he spun and flopped on the ground like a chicken with its neck wrung.

The fourth man was a mite faster on the draw, managing to get off a shot that missed Cal's head by inches and splintered the wooden post next to him.

Cal thumbed back the hammer on the Navy and without consciously aiming put a bullet between the man's eyes, snapping his head back and dropping him like he'd been poleaxed.

Sheriff Pike had his gun only half out of his holster when it was all over.

"Jesus, Mary Mother of God," he exclaimed at the sight of four men blown to hell in less than three seconds.

Pearlie and Cal looked around, still holding their pistols out in front of them, making sure there were no more outlaws who wanted to ante up in this hand.

Bystanders on the street, who'd ducked for cover at the sound of gunfire, returned from their hiding places to gather around the outlaws' bodies, staring over at Cal and Pearlie as if they'd never seen anything like them.

Pearlie holstered his pistol and turned to the sheriff. "Sheriff Pike, if you have no further need of us, we'll git on our way," he drawled, as if shooting down four men was an everyday occurrence in his life.

Pike removed his hat and sleeved sweat off his forehead with the back of his arm. "Uh . . . no, I don't think you need to stay around."

He glanced at the bodies lying sprawled on the dusty street. "In fact, I'd be obliged if you'd get out of my town and not return," he said with a sickly grin. "You're givin' boot hill too much business to hang around."

Pearlie swung into the saddle. He tipped his hat at Pike. "From what you say, Slaughter pays pretty good. There ought to be enough money in their pants to pay for their burials."

Pike nodded.

Cal inclined his head toward Aunt Bea's dining room as he stepped into his stirrups. "Give what's left over to Aunt Bea an' tell her we 'preciate the good grub."

As they rode slowly out of town, the mayor of Jackson Hole walked up to Sheriff Pike.

"Who the hell were those men, Sheriff?" he asked.

Pike shook his head. "I don't rightly know, an' I didn't ask. But I'm sure glad I'm not the one they're after."

"You mean Jim Slaughter?"

Pike nodded. "Yeah, an' I'd be willin' to bet we won't be seein' Big Jim Slaughter and his Marauders back here next year, not if those two are any indication of what he's gonna be facin' in Colorado."

Twenty-three

Jim Slaughter rode at the head of a procession of thirty-four of the hardest men he could find. There wasn't one of them who wasn't wanted by the law in one place or another, most for murder, armed robbery, or rape.

He glanced at the man riding next to him. "Whitey, you got those men watching our back trail like I told you?"

"Yes, sir," the albino answered, looking back over his shoulder. "I've got two groups of four men each. One group is about five miles back and the other is two miles back. That way, if the first group gets into trouble, the second group can ride up here and warn us."

Slaughter nodded. "That's good. I don't know who the hell is bent on causin' me trouble up here, but whoever they are, they're sure persistent about it."

Swede, riding on the other side of Slaughter, glanced at him. "Yeah, two attacks in a couple of weeks that cost us fifteen men dead and another six wounded so bad they cain't fight no more."

"You don't think Monte Carson could have spent some of that fifty thousand to hire gunnies to come after us, do you?" Whitey asked.

Slaughter shook his head. "Naw, Monte's not that smart, an' besides, he knew if I suspected he had anything to do with this I'd've killed his wife pronto."

Swede agreed. "He's right, Whitey. I asked all around an' nobody'd been approached for a job like that."

"Maybe he hired them someplace else," the albino continued, still not convinced. "Hell, maybe it was that Smoke Jensen everbody's jawin' about."

Slaughter jerked his head toward Whitey. "You know, that's not too unlikely. Maybe Monte brought the old gunman up here with him an' a few of his friends. That might explain why nobody in Jackson knew anything about it."

"But if Jensen was involved, why didn't he finish the job?" Whitey asked. "From what I hear about the old man, it ain't like him to leave a job half done."

"What do you mean, half done?" Swede asked, leaning over in his saddle to glare at Whitey. "He got Monte's wife back and Monte an' the rest of whoever helped him out free an' clear. What more did he need to do?"

Whitey shook his head. "It still don't sound like Smoke Jensen to me. I think he would'a come into the hole-in-the-wall with his guns blazin' till he was sure Jim was dead."

Slaughter shook his head. "No, I don't agree, Whitey. With odds of twenty to one, he'd have to be a fool to press his attack any more than he did." Slaughter hesitated. "And from what I hear, Smoke Jensen ain't no fool, else he wouldn't have survived as long as he has. He got what he came for an' he left a winner, like Swede says."

Whitey gritted his teeth until his jaw muscles bulged. "Well, he sure as hell ain't gonna stay no winner. When we git to Colorado, I'm gonna blow his damned head off."

Slaughter smiled, shaking his head. "You think you're that good, Whitey?"

Whitey glared at him, his eyes narrowed. "Don't you?"

Slaughter shrugged. "Well, I know I'd hate to go up against you." After a moment he added, "Course, if I did,

I'd kill you, but that don't mean this old gunny Jensen can."

"What'a you think, Swede?" Whitey asked, his tone indicating he was itching for a fight.

Swede laughed. "I don't know, Whitey. You and Big Jim are the fast draws around here. I know I could beat the bastard to death with my fists if it came to that, but I wouldn't want to go up against no quick-draw artist with a handgun."

One of the men from the rear of the column came galloping up to them. "Hey, Boss, we been ridin' without stoppin' since dawn. You think we might stop fer a noonin' soon?"

Slaughter grinned. "Yeah, there's no big hurry. Let's stop and build a fire, cook some vittles, and rest our backsides. It's been a long time since I spent all day in a saddle and my bacon is achin'."

From a ridge halfway up the slope of a nearby mountain, Smoke, Louis, and Muskrat Calhoon watched the procession as it stopped and men began to build a fire and cook their food.

Smoke glanced back over his shoulder. "I'm getting a mite worried, Louis. We've been tracking those bastards since ten o'clock this morning and we still haven't heard from Cal or Pearlie."

Louis's face showed his concern. "Me too, Smoke. Those boys would have been here by now if they were able to travel."

Smoke's hands unconsciously formed into fists at his side. "I just hope Slaughter and his men haven't managed to put lead into the boys," he growled. " 'Cause if they have . . ." He let the sentence hang in the air unfinished, but Louis shivered at the tone of his friend's voice. *God help them if they've killed Cal or Pearlie,* he thought, *because there's no telling what Smoke would do.*

Louis had heard the story of Smoke scalping and skinning men who'd harmed his family in the past, and he knew Slaughter could expect nothing less if he'd hurt Cal or Pearlie.

Smoke turned to the mountain man. "Muskrat, will you backtrack for a few miles and see if you can find any trace of Cal or Pearlie? I need to know they're safe before we start our attacks on Slaughter."

Muskrat nodded. "Sure thang, Smoke. You an' Louis fix you somthin' to eat an' I'll head on back down the trail a piece an' see what's goin' on back there."

Smoke and Louis stepped out of their saddles and pulled the horses back into the brush so there was no chance of them being seen if Slaughter posted lookouts.

"I guess we'll have to have a cold nooning," Smoke said. "No way to build a fire with the outlaws so close."

"That's true, but all is not lost," Louis said with a grin. "I took the trouble to acquire some provisions before we left Jackson Hole for just such an eventuality."

He pulled two cans of potted meat, a can of sliced peaches, and a can of sliced pears from his saddlebags. "We may have to eat it cold, but that doesn't mean it has to taste bad."

"Louis," Smoke said, licking his lips, "I always knew there was something about you I liked."

Barely an hour had passed before Muskrat returned. He jumped out of the saddle and squatted next to Louis and Smoke, smiling as they handed him his share of the food. He didn't bother with knives or forks, just shoveled the food into his mouth with his fingers, hardly bothering to chew before he swallowed.

"What'd you find out?" Smoke asked.

The mountain man glanced up from his plate with a sly look on his face. "Slaughter ain't as dumb as I thought he was," he began. "He's left two parties of men behind to guard his back trail. One is hunkered down four or five mile back, an' the other two mile back."

Smoke thought about it for a moment, then looked over at Louis. "That means if Cal and Pearlie were delayed for some reason and try to catch up with us, they're liable to be ambushed by those bastards."

Muskrat nodded, as did Louis.

"So, we've got to take out the rear guard first, before we do anything else," Smoke finished.

"An', we got to do it quiet-like, so's the others don't know nothin' 'bout it," Muskrat added.

After Slaughter's main body of men finished lunch and packed up their gear and moved on, Smoke crossed to the other side of the trail, leaving Muskrat and Louis where they were. They set up an ambush not far from the edge of the road, and waited for the two groups of rear guards to come.

It took the first party of four men an hour and a half to appear. They were moving slowly down the trail, keeping their eyes to the rear.

As they came abreast of the ambush site, Smoke stood up, signaled to Muskrat and Louis, and broke from cover.

He had the tomahawk he always carried in his right hand and his Bowie knife in his left. As the first man turned and caught sight of Smoke, he let fly with the tomahawk. It turned over in the air three times and embedded itself in the cowboy's chest, knocking him backward off his horse with a harsh grunt.

The second man turned just in time to see Smoke fling himself through the air. Then the man was knocked off his horse. Seconds after they landed with Smoke on top, Smoke buried his knife to the hilt in the outlaw's abdomen and jerked upward as hard as he could, filleting the man like a fish where he lay.

Smoke rolled off the body in time to see Louis and Muskrat take out the other two. Louis with a long, wicked-looking stiletto, Muskrat by the simple expedient of swinging his long-barreled Sharp's Big Fifty like a baseball bat and caving in the side of his opponent's head, which made a sound like a pumpkin being dropped from a second-story window onto hardpan.

"Let's get these bodies out of sight and wait for the others," Smoke said.

Cal and Pearlie were riding along, keeping their mounts at an easy, ground-eating lope.

"We gotta be careful, Pearlie," Cal said. "We don't want'a ride up Slaughter's rear 'fore we see 'em."

"Don't you worry none, pup," Pearlie said, using the same term for Cal that Muskrat had, knowing it irritated his young friend. "I got my eyes an' ears open. We'll see them 'fore they see us, I guarantee it."

The words were barely out of his mouth when four men stepped from the bushes next to the trail.

"Hands up, gents," the lead man called, a shotgun cradled in his arms, its barrel pointed at Cal's chest.

"Shit, Pearlie," Cal mumbled under his breath, "I thought you was watchin'."

"I was watchin' the trail, Cal, not the bushes alongside it," Pearlie answered, his face flaming red at being caught with his pants down.

As they raised their hands and climbed down from their horses, the head man pointed his shotgun at Pearlie. "What the hell are you two galoots doin' followin' us?" he asked.

Pearlie raised his eyebrows in puzzlement. "Followin' you? We weren't followin' nobody."

"Oh, yeah?" the man asked, his suspicion evident. "Then what were you doin' on this trail today?"

Pearlie decided to take a chance. "They tole us in Jackson Hole Big Jim Slaughter an' his men were headed out this way."

"So you two decided to ride up behind us an' bushwhack us, huh?"

Pearlie shook his head. "No, you got it all wrong, pardner. Mr. Slaughter asked us to join his gang last week an' we decided to take him up on his offer."

"Why'd you change yore minds?"

Cal grinned. "That blizzard changed our minds, that's what. We 'bout near froze our butts off up in the mountains lookin' fer gold."

Pearlie nodded. "Yeah, an' diggin' in that frozen ground in the winter's like tryin' to dig granite." He gave an elaborate shrug. "So, we decided to take a job with Mr. Slaughter until next spring when the weather's a bit more to our likin'."

The man didn't look convinced. "Still sounds suspicious to me," he said. "I'll tell you what. You hand down those pistols an' we'll take you on up to see Big Jim." He nodded. "We'll let the boss decide what to do with you."

Cal and Pearlie handed the man their pistols and the four men followed them down the trail.

After a couple of miles, Cal noticed a series of dark stains ahead of them in the dirt of the road. He nudged Pearlie with his arm and inclined his head toward the bloodstains.

Pearlie grinned and gave his head a slight nod. When they pulled abreast of the stains, Pearlie and Cal reined in their horses, jerking their heads around toward the men behind them.

The leader raised his shotgun. "Hey, what the hell's the matter with you two?" he yelled.

"We got to pee," Pearlie said, making sure all the men's eyes were on him and Cal.

Seconds later, Louis, Muskrat, and Smoke stepped from the bushes. "Drop your guns or we'll kill you where you sit," Smoke called in a loud voice.

The four men raised their hands, eyes wide at the sight of men stepping from the bushes to capture them.

After Cal and Pearlie retrieved their pistols, they made the men get down off their horses. "Now," Smoke asked, "how can we make sure these men don't join up with Slaughter later?"

Muskrat grinned and drew his finger across his throat, his tongue sticking out. "I say kill 'em an' scalp 'em as a warnin' to that bastard Slaughter."

One of the outlaws gave a nervous laugh, until he looked into Muskrat's eyes and knew he was seconds away from death. The laughter died in his throat.

Smoke nodded, his face serious. "That's one way. Any other suggestions?"

Louis walked over to the men and held out his hands. "Give me your boots," he said.

"Are you crazy?" the leader of the bandits asked. "Our feet'll freeze out here. We'll lose all our toes."

Louis shrugged. "I'll give each of you a couple of shirts from your saddlebags to wrap around your feet. That should protect your toes long enough to get back to Jackson."

The man looked at his partners and shook his head. "No way, mister."

Louis shrugged and pulled out his Arkansas Toothpick. "All right, it's your choice. I guess I'm going to have to cut your Achilles tendons," he said, motioning to the back of his ankles with the knife, "and let you crawl all the way back to Jackson."

"Hold on, stranger," the man said, hurriedly pulling off

his boots and handing them to Louis, as did his companions.

Cal and Pearlie rounded up the men's horses and the group rode away, while the outlaws began the long walk back toward Jackson Hole.

"Why didn't ya let me scalp 'em?" Muskrat asked Louis.

"This way's better. By the time those men get to Jackson, their feet will be in such bad shape they won't be able to walk for weeks, and by then this will all be over."

Muskrat shook his head and spat a brown stream of tobacco juice onto the ground. "Damn it all, man, I hadn't scalped anybody in a couple of years. I'm gonna git outta practice."

Twenty-four

Slaughter sat by the campfire as dusk closed in on his group of hired killers. He'd sent Whitey back along their back trail to tell the men he'd posted there to come in for supper and to get some sleep.

As he scraped the last of his beans and fried fatback off his plate, Whitey rode up in a cloud of dust, his face carrying a worried look on it.

Damn, looks like more bad news, Slaughter thought as he built himself a cigarette and lit it off an ember from the fire.

"Boss," Whitey said, squatting next to Slaughter, looking over his shoulder as if he was afraid someone was behind him.

"Yeah?"

"I rode at least six miles back, an' I searched both sides of the trail goin' an' comin'."

"And?" Slaughter said, letting smoke trickle from his nostrils in his impatience.

"There was no sight of any of our men . . . not a trace."

"You see any blood on the trail?"

Whitey shook his head. "Nothin'—no tracks, no blood, just an empty trail."

"Damn!" Slaughter said, slamming his hand on his

thigh. "I told you someone was out to get me, make me look bad."

Whitey stared at his boss, an unbelieving expression on his face. "Takin' out eight men without leaving a trace or firin' a shot goes way beyond tryin' to make you look bad, Jim."

Slaughter dipped his head, wiped his face with both hands, and took a deep breath. "Yeah, I guess you're right."

"What are we gonna do about it, Boss?" Swede, who was sitting next to Slaughter, asked.

"You don't dare post any more men away from the main group," Whitey said. "We can't afford to lose any more guns."

Slaughter waved a dismissive hand. "I can always hire more guns, that's not the problem. I just don't want the men to get the idea we're fighting a losing battle here."

Swede cleared his throat. "Uh, you ever think that maybe we'd be better off just forgittin' 'bout that money Monte Carson owes us an' goin' on down the trail, Boss?"

Without warning, Slaughter backhanded the big man across the face, knocking him backward onto his back, his head stirring up coals and embers in the fire.

Swede jumped to his feet, frantically brushing small fires out of his hair, his face a mask of hate and fury as he glared at Slaughter.

Slaughter's lips curled in a slow grin, his fingers wrapped around the butt of a Colt Peacemaker. "Go on, keep talking like that, Swede, and I'll put one in your gizzard."

Swede's face slowly relaxed and his fists unclenched. "I didn't mean nothin' by it, Boss. It was just a suggestion."

Slaughter pointed his finger at Swede. "Just be sure you don't ever say anything like that in front of the men."

Swede hung his head. "I won't."

"Good, now you and Whitey go get some shut-eye. We're gonna need to keep a sharp lookout tomorrow."

The outlaws' campfire had almost died out when Smoke waved his hand at Muskrat, pointing to the men sitting guard at regular intervals around the camp.

Muskrat nodded, the stubs of his teeth glowing in reflected moonlight as he grinned. Seconds later, he was gone from sight, moving as silently as a cloud.

Smoke hunkered down, moving on his toes and placing his feet carefully so as not to make a sound. He moved from shadow to shadow, never letting the guard he was stalking get a glimpse of his movement.

It took Smoke twenty minutes to cover the thirty yards to the guard. He came up behind him, put his hand over his mouth, and slit his throat with one quick slash of his Bowie knife.

He eased the man back and laid him flat on the ground, then he moved the knife blade in a semi-circle around the man's head. He hooked his fingers in the slit and gripped and pulled, yanking a bloody scalp off in one piece.

Smoke got no enjoyment from desecrating the dead man's body, but he wanted to sow seeds of doubt and fear into the men riding with him, and nothing did that quite like a bloody corpse, killed with no sounds.

Muskrat, at the same time, was doing exactly the same to the other guard at the opposite end of the camp, but he was enjoying it considerably more.

Louis, Cal, and Pearlie had been waiting for almost an hour by the time Smoke and Muskrat returned, hands bloody from their grisly task. Smoke was carrying a pot in one hand.

Cal took one look at their hands and made a face. "Did you have to do that, Smoke?" he asked.

Smoke gave him a serious look. "Cal, once you kill a

man, it doesn't make any difference to him what you do to his body, it's just a piece of meat. If scalping those men makes a few of the outlaws think better of this journey and they take off, then we've saved some lives by what we did."

Cal shook his head. "No matter what you call it, I don't think I could do it."

Smoke put his hand on the young man's shoulder. "That's why I didn't ask you to do it, Cal."

"Did you scalp your man too?" Pearlie asked Muskrat.

The old mountain man nodded, grinning. "Yeah, but that's not all I did."

Smoke cut his eyes at the old man. "What else did you do?"

"I cut some chunks outta his arm an' leg, and made a couple of slashes over his liver, like I was takin' some home to eat."

"Oh, no . . ." Cal said, covering his mouth.

"Aw, come on, pup. I ain't gonna eat it. I jest wanted some of the men back there to git the idea that somebody was."

Smoke grinned. "Good move, Muskrat. Wish I'd thought to do the same."

Louis shook his head with a low laugh. "I don't know about those fellows over there, Smoke, but you and Muskrat are sure scaring the hell out of me!"

Pearlie sniffed the air, looking pointedly at the pot Smoke was carrying. "Uh, do I smell grub?"

Smoke nodded. "Yeah. Since we can't build a fire, I stole some of their beans and fatback. It's still warm, so help yourselves."

As Pearlie grabbed for the pot, Cal knocked his hand away. "Uh-uh, Pearlie. You go last. That way there's a chance the rest of us will get something to eat too."

* * *

Slaughter rolled over, brushing a light coating of snow off his ground blanket and sleeping bag. Covering a wide yawn with his hand, he grabbed the coffee cup lying next to his saddle and began to move toward what was left of the campfire.

That's strange, he thought, eyeing the mound of coals and embers that were almost died out. *The guards are supposed to keep the fire going through the night.*

Sensing something was not right, he glanced at the sky. There was as yet no sign of dawn, so it was still very early. He bent over and felt the coffeepot sitting on the edge of the fire. It was barely warm. Now he knew something was seriously out of kilter. The one thing men on guard duty made sure of was hot coffee to keep them awake during the long, quiet nights.

Slaughter went back to his sleeping bag and pulled his Colt pistol from his holster. He eared back the hammer and moved quickly over to Whitey and Swede, who were sleeping next to each other.

He shook Whitey's shoulder. "Whitey, wake up," he whispered. "Something's goin' on."

Whitey came awake with a start, his hand automatically grabbing for his gun. "What . . . ?" he said sleepily.

"Get up, and wake Swede up too. I'm going to check on the guards," Slaughter said as he moved away into the darkness.

Whitey and Swede got out of their blankets and followed Slaughter toward the guard posts.

Just as they caught up to him, they heard Slaughter gasp. "Jesus!" he said, stepping back, a match flaring in his hand.

By the light of the match, Swede and Whitey could see what was left of the guard. Bare white skull gleamed, reflecting the light, and chunks of both arms were missing and deep cuts had been made over the man's liver.

Swede bent to the side and vomited in the grass, his

gasping heaves loud in the stillness of the pre-dawn hours.

"Shut up, you fool," Slaughter whispered urgently.

"But . . . but that's Joe Lacy," Swede said. "Him an' me used to be saddle partners."

"He's just dead meat now," Slaughter said. "You and Whitey drag him off into the bushes over there. I don't want any of the other men to see this."

"But, Boss, it looks like somebody ate on him," Swede said, dry heaving again.

Slaughter slapped him across the face, gently so as not to make too much noise. "Shut the hell up, I said. You got to get a hold on yourself, Swede, or you ain't gonna be any use to me."

Swede sleeved off his face and nodded. "All right, Jim, I'll try."

"Now, do like I said and get Joe's body out of sight. I'm gonna go take a look at the other guard. I have a feeling he's gonna be in a similar shape or we'd've heard something from him by now."

"But, Boss, who could've done this?" Whitey asked, looking around at the darkness surrounding them, a worried expression on his face.

"The same ones who attacked us at the hole-in-the-wall an' the same ones who killed or ran off our guards yesterday," Slaughter said. "Now get movin', we ain't got all night."

As dawn began to lighten the sky, the men in the gang began to move out of their sleeping blankets and stand and stretch and make their way to the campfire. Slaughter had gotten it going again and had several large pots of coffee brewing and beans and bacon cooking in large cast-iron skillets.

"Gather around here, men," he called. "I got some bad news for you."

As the outlaws crowded near the fire, warming their

hands and getting mugs of coffee, Slaughter stood in front of them. "It seems some of the men I hired to go to Colorado with us have turned yellow and deserted us during the night."

The men began to mumble and talk to one another, but no one questioned Big Jim Slaughter to his face.

He held up both hands. "No need to worry, though. We pass through several towns on the way to our destination, and I'm sure I can hire suitable replacements for the yellow-bellies that took off."

Whitey, at a nod from Slaughter, joined in. "Yeah, an' I'll bet they'll be better to have by our sides in a fight than the cowardly dogs that left."

"How many of us are there left now?" Billy Bob Justice called from the rear of the crowd.

"We still have over twenty-five hands, all good men with a gun," Slaughter answered. "And with the extras I'm gonna pick up along the way, we'll have plenty of men to do the job I have planned."

"By the way, Mr. Slaughter," called out Jimmy Silber, "just what is the job we're headed for?"

Slaughter smiled and shook his head. "You'll find out when we get there, Jimmy. Until then, you're all being paid damn good wages to go for a ride in the country, so enjoy it."

"Damn good wages don't do much good if'n we don't live to spend 'em," Jimmy muttered, turning his back and walking toward his horse.

Sensing he was losing some of the men, Slaughter held up his hands. "And just to make things interesting, there's gonna be a thousand-dollar bonus in it for every man who stays the course until we're done. That's in addition to the hundred-dollars-a-month wages," he added.

Jimmy Silber slowed, thought about it for a minute, then walked back to the fire, holding out his cup for more coffee. "I can always use an extra thousand or so dollars," he said with a grin.

Swede and Whitey accompanied Slaughter back to his sleeping blankets.

"How the hell are we gonna give ever'body an extra thousand, Boss?" Whitey asked. "That won't leave diddly for us."

Slaughter grinned. "Just how many men do you think are gonna survive this little expedition, Whitey? You know with Monte waitin' for us, he's gonna be loaded for bear."

He struck a lucifer on his pants and lit a cigarette. "I figure we're gonna lose two out of three of these men just getting our hands on the payroll, and as for the rest"—he shrugged—"they may not survive to get their share either."

Whitey grinned. "I getcha, Boss."

Slaughter nodded. "Yeah, once we get our hands on that money, I may just retire and settle down someplace. I may even give up the owlhoot trail."

Swede grinned. "That'll be the day."

Twenty-five

Smoke eased back on his hands and knees from the bushes he was lying behind, until he could get to his feet and return to his friends without being seen by Slaughter's men. He'd been watching the efficient way Slaughter dealt with the dead men he and Muskrat had left for him to find.

"What'd you hear, Smoke?" Pearlie asked.

Smoke shook his head, reluctant admiration on his face. "Slaughter is a smooth operator. He hid the guards' bodies, and told his men they deserted the gang. He didn't say anything about them being killed."

"So all that was for nothin'?" Cal asked, remembering the sight of Smoke and Muskrat's bloody hands.

Smoke shook his head. "Not for nothing, Cal. We cut the number of outlaws down by ten men, over a third of their strength. And more importantly, we showed Slaughter we can get to him any time we want to, which has got to be eating on him inside." Smoke took a long drink from his canteen, wishing they were far enough away to build a fire so he could have some hot coffee.

Louis stepped over to Cal. "You don't realize how important that is, Cal. Once you break a man's confidence, make him know in his heart he is vulnerable, you are only a step away from breaking his spirit. And when a man's spirit is broken, it shows to those around him, making it tougher for him to be an effective leader."

Muskrat nodded from where he sat on his haunches,

and bit off a chaw of tobacco from the twist he always carried. "That's right, young'un. Men won't hardly foller nobody they don't have confidence in, 'specially if'n it means puttin' their butts in a wringer like a gunfight."

Cal held up his hands, "All right, I understand," he said with a grin.

Pearlie laughed. "Smoke, you know ol' Cal's like that mule we got back at Sugarloaf, the one we call Jezebel. Sometimes you have to hit her in the head with a two-by-four to git her attention, then she MIGHT do what you want her to."

"Speakin' of gittin' somebody's attention, what do you plan to do now, Smoke?" Muskrat asked as he leaned over to spit a glob of brown juice at a ground squirrel nearby.

Smoke hesitated, looking back over his shoulder toward Slaughter's camp. "Well, I figure we're wasting our time here, and sooner or later we're going to make a mistake and I don't like the odds for a head-to-head fight with twenty hard cases."

"Does that mean we're going to return to Big Rock?" Louis asked with a hopeful expression. He was getting awfully tired of cold food and missed Andre's kitchen magic back at his saloon.

Smoke nodded. "Yeah. Eventually. We need to get home and make sure Monte has the town ready for Slaughter and his men's attack."

Louis looked at Smoke suspiciously. "I don't know as I particularly like that word 'eventually.' "

Smoke grinned. "Well, I don't think we should leave without a little good-bye party first, do you?"

Pearlie slapped his thigh. "Hot damn! Now yore talkin', Smoke. I'm sure gittin' tired of all this pussy-footin' around."

Cal nodded his agreement. "Let's strike up the band and call the dance, Smoke. Those hombres'll never know what hit 'em."

Smoke gave Cal a hard look. "You sure you're up to this, Cal? Your leg is going to take quite a beating if we ride into that camp with our six-guns blazing."

Cal felt of his thigh. "It's a mite sore, I won't lie to you, Smoke. But it'll be all right, an' the wound's pretty near all healed up."

"I thought you didn't like the odds of a head-to-head fight," Louis said.

Smoke shook his head. "I don't plan on a siege, Louis. What I want to do is hit 'em hard, bust up and wound or kill as many as we can in one lightning strike, then high-tail it toward Big Rock as fast as we can."

"They'll come after us," Louis cautioned.

"Sure, but it'll take them a while to get organized, and by then we'll be so far ahead of them they'll never catch us."

"What 'bout me?" Muskrat asked.

Smoke looked at the old man. "Are you willing to continue to help us for another week or so?"

"I ain't never quit no job a'fore, young'un, an' I don't intend to now."

Smoke grinned. "Then, what I need you to do is follow Slaughter's gang after our attack, but stay out of sight and don't do anything that might get you killed."

Muskrat arched an eyebrow, as if the very thought that Slaughter and his men were good enough to kill him was an insult. "And jest what do you want me to do, 'sides foller them?"

"If we do this right, we're gonna kill another ten or so of his men, so he's going to have to hire more gun hawks in the towns between here and Big Rock. I need you to let us know just how many men we're going to be facing when he gets to Big Rock. You'll have to stay back out of sight and every time he leaves a town send me a wire telling me if he's managed to get any more men."

"You think we'll have enough time to get ready, Smoke?" Pearlie asked.

"Sure. It's going to take Slaughter twice as long to make the trip with all those men, especially since they're going to want to spend a few nights in the towns along the way getting liquored up and whored up."

Muskrat got to his feet, brushed the seat of his pants off, and stuck out his hand. "Then you best be on your way, little beaver," he said to Smoke.

Smoke took his hand and gripped it hard. "Thanks for all you've done, Muskrat. We couldn't have done this without you."

The mountain man nodded, a grin on his lips. "I know. But I been hankerin' to make a trip down Colorader way fer some years now. I figger it's 'bout time I looked ol' Bear Tooth up an' seen how he's doin'."

Smoke turned to the others. "Let's saddle up and shag our mounts, boys. We're burning daylight."

Louis, Cal, and Pearlie all pulled out their pistols and began to check their loads. Dawn was just breaking and they wanted to hit the outlaws' camp before the hard cases were up and functioning with clear heads.

As they got on their mounts, Muskrat said, "I'll give you boys a little coverin' fire from up here with my ol' Sharps. I ought'a be able to put lead in a couple of those bastards 'fore the fight's over."

Smoke grinned and pulled his hat down low as he put the spurs to Joker, the reins in his teeth and both hands filled with iron.

Sally Jensen and Mary Carson strolled down the boardwalk of the main street of Big Rock, Colorado, watching the construction going on around town.

"I haven't seen this much activity since Smoke and I founded the town some years ago," Sally said.

"That was during the Tilden Franklin affair, wasn't it?" Mary asked.

"Yes, about six months before you and Monte became engaged. He'd taken control of the town called No-Name, and we wanted decent folks to have a place to live and raise their children without having gunmen running the town."*

"Well, you've certainly succeeded."

Sally glanced at her companion. "In a large part, that's due to Monte's influence, Mary. He manages to keep the riffraff out of town while letting men be men and not overly regulating their natural horseplay."

Mary nodded. "Big Rock is a good town, Sally, and Monte is a good man. I'm so happy we have so many friends here that have pledged to help us in our fight with Jim Slaughter."

Judge Proctor passed by the ladies on the boardwalk, tipping his hat in greeting.

"Good morning, ladies."

"Good morning, Judge," they both replied.

The portly man looked around at the men on nearby roofs, nailing up railings and walls with gun ports in them. "Looks like a fine day for construction," he said.

Both ladies smiled. "Yes it does, Judge," Sally replied.

As they were talking, the town preacher, Ralph Morrow, and his wife, Bountiful, approached.

Morrow tipped his hat to Sally and Mary, and Bountiful walked over to take Mary's hand. "Oh, Mary, I'm so glad you are all right after your ordeal."

Mary smiled, winking at Sally. They both knew Bountiful. While she was a lovely young woman who cared deeply about her husband's congregation, she was inclined to be a bit theatrical at times.

"Oh, it wasn't so bad," Mary replied. "Actually, Mr.

Trail of the Mountain Man

Slaughter treated me quite well and made sure the other men did the same."

Sally, while listening to Mary tell the men and Bountiful something of her journey with Jim Slaughter, noticed Ralph was wearing a gun tied down low on his hip. While he'd never actually been a gun hawk, Ralph was a tough man who knew his way around a six-killer and wasn't afraid to mix it up when duty or honor called for action.

"Ralph, I notice you're wearing a pistol," Sally said.

"Yes, I am. And Bountiful and I have set up the church at the end of the street with cots and bedding and huge pots of soup and other food we're going to keep ready in case of a long siege. We intend to do our part to help protect Monte and Big Rock from the depredations of men like Big Jim Slaughter and his henchmen."

Over Ralph's shoulder, Sally saw Johnny North and his wife, Belle, riding into town, a packhorse behind them with a suitcase strapped on it. North, an ex-gunslick, had married the Widow Colby after the Tilden Franklin affair, and lived about twenty miles outside of Big Rock on a ranch next to the Sugarloaf. Evidently a lot of people who liked and admired Monte Carson were coming into town to stay until the fight was over.

"Hello, Johnny, Belle," Sally called, waving to the Norths as they rode by.

"Mornin' Sally," Johnny replied, a grin on his face. "Good day for a gunfight, ain't it?"

Sally nodded, her right hand unconsciously falling to check the short-barreled .32-caliber pistol she was wearing in a holster on her right hip. The people of Big Rock were used to seeing Mrs. Jensen wearing men's trousers and a tucked-in shirt with a pistol on a belt around her waist. Sally was very practical in her dress and didn't give a hang what the conventions said about what young ladies of refinement should wear. If she was going to ride a horse or engage in gunplay, she believed in dressing accordingly, and to hell with what anyone thought about it.

Sally and Mary said good-bye to the judge and the Morrows and continued their walk. When they came to the general store they had to step out into the street to avoid the crowd of men and women going in and out.

Peg Jackson, the owner's wife, was behind the counter, a curl of hair down over her forehead as she worked to get people's orders ready. Ed, her husband, was busy nailing boards across the big front window of his store. He stopped to tip his hat to Sally and Mary.

"Hello, Ed," Sally said.

"Howdy, Sally, Mary," he replied, sleeving sweat off his face.

"Business looks like it's booming," Sally said.

He smiled. "Yes, it is. However, in view of the nature of this . . . emergency, I'm selling ammunition and building supplies at my cost." He shook his head. "I wouldn't want to profit off the Carsons' troubles."

"That's awfully nice of you, Ed," Mary said.

"Heck," he answered, blushing, "it ain't nothin'. Everybody's pitchin' in. That's what friends are for."

They were interrupted by the approach of Haywood Arden, the editor of the *Big Rock Guardian,* the town newspaper. He was gray-haired with ink stains on both hands, and wore a white shirt with the sleeves rolled up and a plaid vest.

"Mary, do you have time for a quick interview?" he asked.

"Why, what do you need to know, Haywood?" she asked.

He pulled out a pad and pencil. "I know the leader of the gang is Jim Slaughter, but I don't know the names of any of his cohorts."

Sally put her hand on Mary's shoulder. "I can see you're going to be busy for a while, so I'll just go on up

to Monte's office and see how the preparations for the
attack are going."

Mary nodded as she turned back to Haywood. "There
was this albino named Whitey Jones, and this very tall
man called Swede Johanson . . ."

Sally walked to the sheriff's office and knocked on the
door.

"Come in," Monte called.

She entered to find him leaning over his desk, staring
at a sketch of the town.

"Oh, hello, Sally."

"Hello, Monte. I just came by to see how you're doing
with the fortification of the town."

"Here," he said, "let me show you."

She stepped to the desk and watched as he pointed out
where the citizens of the town were building blockades
and fortifications in preparation for Slaughter's attack.

When he finished, he stood back. "So you can see,
Sally, once the outlaws come into town, the blockades
will funnel them down to the center of Main Street."

She glanced again at the drawing. "Where you have
both sides of the street covered by men on rooftops and
in buildings along the way."

He nodded. "That's right. We'll have maximum firepower and minimum chance of any citizens getting shot."

Suddenly, his face fell and he leaned forward, both
hands on his desk.

"What is it, Monte?" Sally asked, sensing his discom-
fort.

He shook his head. "I just don't feel right, letting the
town get in the middle of my problems," he said. "There's
bound to be someone that takes lead 'cause of me and
what I did years ago. It just isn't right."

Sally smiled. "This is our town, Monte, and you are our
sheriff and our friend. There is not one person in Big Rock
who, even if they know they are going to be shot, will not

stand next to you in your time of need. Like Ed Jackson said to Mary a while ago, that's what friends are for."

Monte looked up at her. "I know, I just don't want anyone hurt on account of me."

She nodded. "Then work as hard as you can to make our defenses as good as you can. That's all anyone here expects."

Twenty-six

Jim Slaughter was in the process of folding up his ground blanket and sleeping bag when he heard what sounded like hoofbeats coming from the mountain slope on the east side of the camp.

He straightened up, his hand going to the butt of his pistol, and looked toward the sound. He could see nothing through the heavy morning mist, which hung close to the ground like dense fog. Though the sun was peeking over the horizon, it shed little warmth and even less light through the haze.

He glanced over his shoulder toward the campfire and saw that most of his men were still milling around, grabbing biscuits and beans and coffee, most of them still half asleep at this early hour.

Damn, he thought, *we're all targets out here with no sentries left to stand guard.* "Whitey," he called, pulling his pistol and grabbing his rifle from his saddle boot on the ground.

"Yeah, Boss?" Whitey answered from over near the fire.

Before he could reply, four shapes materialized out of the fog like crazed ghosts on a fierce rampage, orange blossoms of flame exploding from the guns they held in their hands.

Their faces were covered with bandannas and their hats

were pulled low over their faces as they rode straight into the knot of men around the campfire, shooting as fast as they could pull the triggers.

David Payne, a gunny from Missouri who'd ridden with Quantrill's Raiders, drew his pistol and got off one shot before a bullet took him in the throat and flung him backward into the fire, scattering embers and ashes into the air.

Jim Harris, a tough from Texas who'd fought in the Lincoln County War, had his gun half out of his holster when two slugs tore through his chest, blowing blood and pieces of lung on the men next to him. He only had time for a surprised grunt before he hit the ground, dead.

Slaughter's men scattered as fast as their legs could carry them, some diving to the ground, others trying to hide behind trees or saddles on the ground as the marauders galloped through camp.

An ex-Indian scout called Joe Scarface managed to get his rifle cocked, and was aiming it at one of the riders when an explosion from the direction of the mountainside was followed by a large-caliber bullet plowing into his back between his shoulder blades, which lifted him off the ground like a giant hand and threw him facedown in the dirt, a hole you could put your fist through in his chest.

"Goddamn!" Slaughter yelled, glancing over his shoulder. They were under attack from all sides, it seemed. He dove to the ground behind his saddle as one of the riders, a big man with broad shoulders on a big, roan-colored horse with snow-white hips, rode right at him.

He buried his face in the soft loam of the ground, and felt rather than saw the bullets from the big man's pistols tear into his saddle and the ground around him as the giant Palouse jumped over him. Miraculously, he was unhit.

"Shit!" he said, spitting dirt and leaves out of his

mouth. He recognized that horse. It was the one Johnny West had been riding in Jackson Hole. So he was one of the bastards who'd been killing his men all along. The son of a bitch had played him for a fool.

Whitey Jones ran for his saddle, hunched over, expecting a bullet in his back the whole way. As he bent to grab his Greener shotgun, one of the raiders rode by, his pistol pointing at the albino.

Whitey whirled, pointing his express gun just as the rider fired. The bullet grazed Whitey's cheek and tore a chunk out of his left ear, spinning him around and snapping his head back, blood spurting into his eyes and blinding him momentarily.

Ike Mayhew, one of the men who'd joined Slaughter's gang in Jackson Hole, snapped off two quick shots and saw one of the riders flinch as one of his slugs hit home. He grinned, and had eared back the hammer for another shot when the man he'd hit leaned to the side and fired point-blank into his face. Mayhew's head exploded in a fine, red mist as the .44-caliber bullet blew his brains into his hat.

Two more explosions from the distant mountainside sent two more men to the ground, one dead and one with his left arm dangling from a shattered bone. Milt Burnett screamed in pain as he grabbed his flopping arm and went to his knees, just as a gray-and-white Palouse rode directly over him, its hooves pounding his chest to pulp. He died choking on bloody froth from a ruptured lung.

Whitey sleeved blood out of his eyes and rolled onto his stomach, pointing his ten-gauge at the back of a raider and letting go with both barrels. Just as he fired, Ben Brown, one of the men who'd been with Slaughter for several years, stepped between them, his arm outstretched as he aimed his pistol.

Whitey's double load of buckshot hit Brown square in

the back, blowing him almost in half as he spun around, dead before he hit the ground.

Swede, too far from his saddle to get his gun, pulled his long knife out and stood there, waiting as a rider rode down on him. He bared his teeth and screamed a defiant yell, holding the knife out in front of him.

The rider's eyes grew wide as he saw the man had no gun and he held his fire, lashing out with his leg and catching Swede in the mouth with a pointed boot as he raced by, knocking out several of his teeth and putting out Swede's lights as his head snapped back and he somersaulted backward, unconscious.

Jimmy Silber, thoughts of his thousand-dollar bonus still in his mind, fired pistols with both hands, crouched near the fire. When his guns were empty, he bent over to punch out his empties. Then a sound made him turn his head.

He looked up just as a young man on a gray horse rode toward him. The last thing Jimmy saw was a tongue of orange from the man's pistol as the slug tore the left side of his face off and left him standing there, dead on his feet.

The entire firefight lasted only four or five minutes, but to the men of Slaughter's command it seemed like hours before the four riders rode off into the mist, disappearing as quickly and as silently as they'd arrived, leaving bodies lying all over the Wyoming countryside.

Slaughter got to his feet, brushing dirt and leaves and sweat off his face. Whitey was twenty feet away, squatting over the prone body of Swede, shaking his shoulder to see if he was alive.

Slaughter looked around him as he walked toward his two lieutenants. He counted five or six dead and several more so severely wounded he knew they'd either be dead soon or of no use to him in his quest for the fifty thousand dollars.

"Whitey, how's Swede?" he asked, standing over the two.

Whitey turned his head, and Slaughter saw a bleeding furrow along his left cheek and most of his ear missing. Blood was streaming down Whitey's face, but it wasn't spurting, so Slaughter figured he'd be all right, though quite a bit uglier than he was before.

"Looks like he's lost most of his front teeth and he may have a broken jaw," Whitey said, shaking Swede's shoulder.

The big man finally opened his eyes, wincing at the pain the movement caused him. He rolled to the side and spat out pieces of teeth along with blood and mucus. "Goddamn," he mumbled, barely understandable, "what the hell hit me?"

"One of those bastards kicked you in the face," Whitey said. "I saw the whole thing. He had you dead in his sights and instead of blowing your head off, he tried to kick it off when he seen you didn't have no gun."

Swede mumbled something else, but Slaughter couldn't quite get it. "What'd he say?" he asked.

Whitey grinned. "He said the son of a bitch is gonna wish he'd shot him if he ever sees him again."

Slaughter walked to the campfire and poured himself a cup of coffee, looking around him at the mess the attackers had made of his command. "Well, from the looks of things, we'll probably be seein' more of 'em than we want to. It don't look like they have any intention of leaving us alone on our way to Colorado."

Whitey helped Swede to his feet and poured him some water from a canteen. As the big man washed blood and more bits of teeth from his mouth, groaning in pain as he did so, Whitey glanced at Slaughter.

"So, you haven't had enough yet, huh?"

Slaughter pulled his makin's out and began to build himself a cigarette. "Hell, no! This has gone too far for me to quit now. I'm gonna get that money, kill Carson and everybody helping him, and then I'm gonna kill his wife an' his friends an' his dog if he has one. I'm gonna make the sumbitch wish he'd never laid eyes on me."

Swede looked up, blood dripping from his ruined mouth. "You can count me in on that, Boss. Nobody gets away with doin' this to me, nobody!"

"How about you, Whitey? You in or out?" Slaughter asked.

Whitey shrugged. "Hell, Boss, you know I'm in. I been with you through good times and bad, an' damned if this ain't one of the worst so far . . . but I'm in."

"Good. Then let's check the men out and see how many we've got left who are able to go on."

"What are we gonna do about the wounded?" Whitey asked.

"Those that can ride we'll take with us to the next town. Those that can't . . ." He shrugged, as if their fate held little interest for him.

"The other boys may not like that much," Swede mumbled through swollen lips.

Slaughter whirled on him. "I don't give a good goddamn what the boys like or don't like," he growled. "They'd better learn to like what I tell them to like or they'll end up just like those other suckers out there, facedown in the dirt as dinner for the worms."

Swede glanced at Whitey, as if wondering whether Slaughter would show as little concern for *him* if he were seriously wounded.

Whitey gave his head a little shake, letting him know not to pursue the matter any further, and began to wander among the men lying on the ground, looking to see if any were capable of riding.

He rolled Jimmy Silber over, wincing when he saw

what was left of his face and head. "Jesus, I guess he won't be seein' any of that thousand-dollar bonus," Whitey murmured to himself, letting the body fall back to the ground.

After he'd made the rounds and salvaged what wounded men he thought might be able to make the trip, Whitey approached Slaughter, who was still standing by the campfire, drinking coffee, lost in his own thoughts.

"You want me to have the men make up a burial party?" he asked.

Slaughter looked at him like he thought he was crazy. "Hell, no. We're gonna mount up and head on down the trail. Stayin' here is just inviting another attack by West and his cohorts."

Swede looked up, his eyebrows raised. "West? You mean that big fellow was Johnny West?"

Slaughter nodded. "Yeah. I recognized that big roan Palouse he was ridin'. It was the same one he had in Jackson Hole."

"I never trusted that son of a bitch," Whitey said. "I knew he was a ringer from the get-go."

"Well, he fooled me," Slaughter said, a wry expression on his face. "Hell, I even tried to hire him."

"You were right as rain about one thing," Swede said.

"What's that?"

"He was damn sure a killer. He went through us like grain through a goose an' never got a scratch on him."

Whitey slapped his pistol in its holster. "He won't be that lucky the next time I see him."

"If you don't get these men mounted up, we might not live long enough to see that," Slaughter said, throwing the remainder of his coffee on the fire and turning to saddle up his horse.

Twenty-seven

Two days later, Slaughter and his men rode toward the outskirts of Pueblo, Colorado. They'd lost two of the wounded on the trail already when Roscoe Archer, known throughout Arkansas as "The Butcher," fell sideways off his horse. He'd taken a bullet in the left arm, which Whitey had bandaged with the outlaw's own bandanna. The arm had since swollen to three times its normal size and was almost black.

Archer screamed when he hit the ground and sat hunched over, holding his injured arm tight against his body. Tears streamed down his face.

Blackjack Tony McCurdy, his partner for the past three years, jumped off his horse and squatted next to his friend.

"Hey, Roscoe," he said, watching as the other men continued to ride on by. "You got to git up, or they're gonna leave your sorry butt here for sure."

Roscoe shook his head, rocking back and forth, cradling his arm as if it were a newborn baby he had to protect. "I don't care," he said, looking at his riding partner through eyes reddened and bloodshot from fever. "I can't stand this pain no longer, Blackjack. You got to help me."

"Help you? I ain't no doctor, Roscoe. Maybe they got one in that town up yonder that'll fix you up."

Roscoe shook his head. "Uh-uh, I ain't fixin' to let no sawbones cut my arm off. I can't face going the rest of my life with only one arm." He hesitated. "You got to put one in me, Blackjack . . . put me outta my misery."

"I can't do that."

Roscoe grabbed Blackjack's arm. "I'd do it for you, pal."

Blackjack gritted his teeth, then suddenly drew his pistol and shot Roscoe in the heart, knocking the big man flat on his back, ending his pain forever.

After a moment of quiet consideration, Blackjack removed Roscoe's boots and tooled leather gun belt, and took all the money he had in his pockets. He took off his own boots and slipped on Roscoe's. "I always did like these handmade boots you got in Del Rio, partner," he said to the dead man as he hurried to get back on his horse and join the others.

Slaughter glanced back over his shoulder at the men riding behind him. "Damn, we're down to fifteen men. We need to see if we can pick up a few here," he said, tilting his head at the sign that read, "Pueblo, Colorado."

Whitey looked around at the town as they entered the city limits. "It looks pretty promising," he said. "Most mining towns like this have their fair share of hard cases and men who fancy themselves gun hawks."

"Take the men to the biggest saloon in town. I'm going to have a word with the sheriff."

"The sheriff?" Swede asked, able to talk a little better now that the swelling had gone down in his face and jaw. He still couldn't eat anything solid and was living on mashed-up beans and biscuits soaked in coffee.

"Yeah. I'm gonna make him an offer that he'll have a hard time turning down."

While the men proceeded to the nearest saloon, Slaughter reined in before a wooden building with a hand-lettered sign on it reading "JAIL."

He walked through the door and found a tall, heavyset man with a huge potbelly leaning back in a chair with his feet up on two planks, which were stretched across a couple of beer barrels and evidently served as his desk.

The man spoke around a toothpick in the corner of his mouth. "Yeah? What can I do for you, mister?"

"You the sheriff?" Slaughter asked.

The man looked pointedly at a tin star on his shirt. "You think I'm wearin' this for decoration?" he asked sarcastically.

Slaughter grinned, then slapped the man's feet off the desk and when he started to get to his feet, backhanded him, knocking him spinning back into his chair. As the sheriff grabbed for his gun, Slaughter drew his pistol and stuck the barrel against the sheriff's nose.

"I doubt if they pay you enough to try what you're thinkin' of tryin'," Slaughter growled.

"What . . . what do you want?" the sheriff said, his eyes crossed, fixed on the hole in the end of Slaughter's gun against his face.

"What's your name?"

"Will, Will Durant."

"Well, Will, I'm here to help you out."

Durant took his eyes off Slaughter's pistol long enough to give him a disbelieving stare.

"I'm gonna start by putting this back in my holster, but don't even think about tryin' to outdraw me, Will. Men a lot better an' faster'n you have tried an' they're all forked end up now."

"Who ARE you, mister?"

"My name is Jim Slaughter."

"Big Jim Slaughter?" the sheriff asked, sweat breaking out on his forehead.

"There's some that calls me that," Slaughter answered.

"What can I do for ya, Mr. Slaughter?" Durant asked,

his face regaining some of its color as Slaughter holstered his Colt.

"It's what we can do for each other, Will. I'm going to give you a hundred dollars, an' you're gonna point out the baddest men in town to me. The ones who give you bad dreams at night. The kind you don't want to run into on a dark night."

"Why would you want . . ."

Slaughter held up his hand. "Will, don't ask foolish questions. All you have to know is you're gonna be a hundred dollars richer, an' you're gonna have a lot less men you have to worry about in a couple of days."

Durant grinned weakly. "All right, Mr. Slaughter. Let's take a walk around town an' I'll show you the bad asses, an' this stinkin' town's got plenty of 'em."

By just after dusk, Slaughter and Sheriff Durant had picked out twenty men who were known to make their living using their guns instead of their wits. As the men were pointed out to him on his rounds with Durant, Slaughter approached each of them and told them to meet him after dark at the Lucky Lady Saloon on the edge of town.

As he walked through the batwings, followed by Whitey and Swede, Slaughter looked around at the saloon, which was little more than a large tent with planks for a bar and whiskey bottles with no labels on them lining the shelves. He shook his head. "What a name for this place." He laughed. "There isn't a lady in sight, and if there was, no one in their right mind would call her lucky."

"You got that right, Boss," Swede said, looking around at the motley crew of men assembled. "I've seen better places than this in ghost towns."

Slaughter walked to the bar and motioned for the barman to give him a bottle. He took it and banged it on the wood to get the attention of the men sitting around the room so they'd quiet down enough for him to be heard.

"My name's Jim Slaughter," he said, smiling at the murmur of voices as the men recognized the name. "I've got a little job planned a few miles from here, an' I need to hire some men who know their way around a six-gun, and ain't afraid of usin' it."

"What kind'a job?" asked a portly man with a full beard.

"The kind where you do what you're told an' you make a lot of money," Slaughter replied.

"That ain't good enough for me," the man said belligerently.

Slaughter shook his head, an almost sad look in his eyes. "What's your name, mister?" he asked in a pleasant tone of voice.

"Augustus Skinner. Why do you want to know?"

"So they'll know what to put on the cross over your grave on boot hill," Slaughter replied, drawing his pistol and pulling the trigger.

The gun exploded, sending an ounce of molten lead hurtling into Augustus Skinner's chest, knocking him backward off his chair to land in the lap of a man sitting behind him.

The men in the room all jumped at the sound of the gunshot, some reaching for pistols, until they saw Whitey ear back the hammers on his ten-gauge Greener and grin at them over the sights.

"Somebody drag that carcass out of here so we can get down to business without it stinkin' up the place," Slaughter said, holstering his pistol and pulling the cork from his whiskey bottle.

As he took a deep drink, two men grabbed what was left of Augustus Skinner by the heels of his boots and dragged him through the batwings, leaving a trail of blood on the floor. The barman scurried from behind the bar and quickly covered the mess with sawdust.

"Now, are there any other questions?" Slaughter asked.

A man in the back of the room stood up, holding his hands out from his sides so Whitey wouldn't mistake his intentions. "If it wouldn't piss you off too bad, I'd kind'a like to know what the job pays 'fore I sign on," he said.

Slaughter laughed, as did most of the men in the room. "No, that's perfectly all right. I'm payin' a hundred a month or any part thereof, and there's a bonus of a thousand dollars a man when the job's over."

"I got one more question," the man added.

Slaughter frowned impatiently. "Yeah?"

The man grinned. "Where do I sign up?"

As the others in the room laughed, Slaughter held up his hands. "Let me warn you before you all rush up here to join our little group. This is no cakewalk. The men we're goin' up against are tough and are also good with their guns. A lot of you won't be coming back OR collecting the money. It's a dangerous job and that's why the pay is so high."

"Mr. Slaughter," another man across the room said, "livin' in this town is dangerous, an' we ain't exactly gettin' paid for it. I'm ready for damn near anything that'll get me a stake so I can get outta here 'fore winter sets in."

"All right, those of you who are interested, the drinks are on me. The rest of you can leave with no hard feelings."

Not one of the men left the room. The pay Slaughter was offering was three times what they could earn doing anything else other than mining, and these were not the sort of men to break their backs digging in the mountains around Pueblo hoping to find enough gold or silver for beans and bacon.

Slaughter turned to the bartender. "Set 'em up an' keep 'em comin' till I say enough."

"Yes, sir!" the barman answered, taking several bottles of amber-colored liquid off the shelves behind him.

None of the men noticed the rather seedy-looking man dressed in buckskins standing outside the batwings, leaning back against the wall and whittling on a stick as if he had nothing better to do with his time.

As Smoke led his friends toward Big Rock, Louis twisted in his saddle and spoke to Pearlie, riding behind him. "How are you doing with that wound? Is it showing any signs or symptoms of suppuration?"

Pearlie stretched his neck and moved his left arm around in a circle to see if there was any pain or soreness. He'd taken a bullet that skimmed along the skin over his left shoulder blade, burning a furrow half an inch deep but not penetrating any deeper. Though the wound wasn't serious, Smoke and the others were worried about infection.

"No, Louis, it seems to be healin' up right nice. A tad stiff, but no more'n you'd expect."

As he spoke, Pearlie noticed Cal had a wide grin on his face.

"What'a you find so funny, Cal?" he asked suspiciously.

"Oh, a thought just sort'a occurred to me," the boy answered.

"Since when did you start thinkin', Cal?" Pearlie asked. "You ain't got a brain in that empty head of your'n."

"Well, it just seemed kind'a funny to me," he answered. "The four of us rode through them outlaws, guns blazin' and goin' off all around us, an' you the onliest one got shot."

"So?"

"So . . . maybe I ain't the only lead magnet around now. It might just be that you're gonna take my place as the one always seems to take a bullet ever time we git in a fight."

Smoke and Louis looked at each other, smiling. It was good to see the boys back to normal, bitching and arguing with each other as only the best of friends could.

"I don't see it that way, Cal," Pearlie said.

"Why not?"

"Way I see it, this here bullet I took was probably headed for you, sure as hell, an' I just sort'a got in the way."

"You sayin' you took lead that was meant for me?"

Pearlie nodded. "Yeah, so that means you owe me for savin' you the misery of gittin' shot again."

Cal stared at Pearlie through narrowed eyes. "If'n that's so, an' I ain't sayin' it is, mind you, I bet I know what you think I ought'a give you for savin' me."

"What's that, Cal?"

"I bet lettin' you have my share of the first batch of bear sign Miss Sally makes when we git home would square things."

Pearlie pursed his lips as he considered this. "Well, now, that just might make things right between us."

Cal shook his head, grinning. "Forgit it, Pearlie. I been thinkin' on those bear sign for the past hundred miles. The worst thing 'bout bein' away from home all these weeks has been missin' Miss Sally's cookin', so you ain't gittin' none of MY bear sign, no, sirree!"

As he listened to the boys banter back and forth, Smoke thought, *I miss you too, Sally, but it's not your cooking I miss the most!*

Twenty-eight

Jim Slaughter lay in bed next to the whore he'd bought for the night and listened to her snore softly. Finally, unable to sleep, he sat up in bed, poured himself a glass of whiskey, and lit a cigarette.

He leaned back against the headboard, smoking and drinking and thinking about Monte Carson. He realized he should have known there was something not quite right about the man the day they'd robbed the Army payroll, years ago . . .

Jim Slaughter sat on his dun stud in the early morning hour, hoping the fog that was just lessening with the coming of dawn wouldn't mess up his plans.

He had ten men with him, some still wearing remnants of the gray uniforms of the Confederacy and some wearing the blue of the Union. His gang wasn't made up of men who had any political ideals. Most were men who had been on the owlhoot trail long before the North and South decided to settle their differences on the battlefield.

He pulled out a battered gold pocket watch and checked the time. The special train carrying the Army payroll was scheduled to be in Fort Smith, Arkansas, at ten in the morning. It was now half past eight, so it should be along any minute now. He didn't like planning the robbery so close to the fort, but it was the only suitable location for miles, so he'd have to chance having the fort send out a posse after them. Of course, if there were no guards from the train left to spread an alarm, he didn't have much to fear from any pursuit.

He grabbed his binoculars and looked down the sloping hillside at the twisted, blackened metal of the tracks where they'd dynamited them just before dawn. The section was at the end of a sharp curve in the tracks, and should be invisible to the engineer of the train until it was too late to stop the speeding locomotive.

His informant at Fort Smith had said this payroll, meant for the troops stationed at nearby forts guarding the Indian Nations, should total forty or fifty thousand dollars. The information had cost Slaughter fifty dollars, but was well worth it if true. The informant, a sergeant in the supply division, had also said there would be no more than eight guards on the train.

Slaughter glanced over his shoulder at the men sitting in their saddles, waiting his command. They were all experienced gunmen, some who hired out to various ranches involved in range wars, some stagecoach robbers, and a couple who'd had experience robbing trains in the past. It was a mixed bunch, men he'd hired with the promise of a big score and lots of money to split up afterward.

He looked to the east and could just make out through the morning mist what looked like smoke from an engine over the horizon.

"Get ready, men," he called. "Load 'em up six and six an' don't worry none if some blue-belly gets in front of one of your bullets. We're gonna get that payroll no matter how many guards they have guarding it. In fact, I wouldn't be too concerned if none of the guards live through the robbery."

One of his men eased a flea-bitten gray horse up next to Slaughter. "You didn't say nothin' about killing a bunch of guards when you talked about this," the man said.

"What's your name again?" Slaughter asked.

"Monte. Monte Carson," the man replied, his eyes meeting Slaughter's directly. The outlaw sensed there was no backing down in this man.

"What did you expect, Carson? You think we were gonna ride down there to that train and hold out our hands and them guards were gonna just hand over the Army's money without a fight?"

Carson hesitated. "No, but I figured if we got the drop on 'em there wouldn't be no need of killin' 'em."

Slaughter turned back to his binoculars. "You let me worry about leadin' this here gang, Carson. You just fill your hands with iron and follow me, all right?"

Carson nodded and reined his horse back to the rear of the group of men, a worried look on his face.

Minutes later, a steam locomotive pulling a passenger car, boxcar, and caboose pulled into view. Slaughter pulled his bandanna up over his nose and motioned for his men to get ready. The dance was about to begin.

The train raced around the curve in the tracks, steam and smoke pouring from its smokestack as if the engineer was intent on making up lost time. *Hell,* Slaughter thought, *he must be doing twenty-five miles an hour!*

Suddenly the engineer must have seen the ruptured tracks, for the screech of metal on metal as he applied full brakes could be heard even from where Slaughter and his men sat.

"Shag your mounts, boys," Slaughter cried, holding his reins in his left hand and a Colt Army .44 in his right as he put the spurs to his horse and galloped toward the slowing train.

The engine was still speeding when it hit the torn tracks, veered sharply to the left, and tipped over. It plowed up thirty feet of Arkansas soil before it finally stopped with the engineer and fireman's bodies hanging unconscious in the broken and twisted engine compartment.

The passenger car just behind the engine was also on its side with several bodies strewn along the furrow in the dirt where it'd been dragged. Four or five men dressed in Army blue were staggering from the wreckage, wobbly on their legs as they tried to figure out what had happened.

Slaughter's men rode down on them, guns blazing. The soldiers quickly scattered and took cover behind the wrecked car. A man in the boxcar eased open the door, poked the barrel of a rifle out, and began to return the outlaws' fire.

One of Slaughter's men went down hard, a bullet having torn his throat out. His name was Johnny Rodriguez and he was from somewhere in Mexico. He'd been real proud of the long handlebar mustache that was now soaked in blood.

As bullets from Slaughter's men peppered the wall of the boxcar, the man inside pulled the door shut with a clang. Two of the soldiers behind the passenger car fell backward, wounded by gunfire, while another of Slaughter's men tumbled from his horse to be trampled by the men racing behind him. His broken, twisted body was thrown around like a child's rag doll before it came to rest in the dirt.

As the gang separated and rode around the train, circling behind the defending soldiers, the men realized their position was hopeless and they threw down their guns, raising their hands in the air.

Slaughter reined in his horse in front of them. "Keep them hands reachin' for the sky, boys," he called, motioning for one of his men to keep the soldiers covered.

He took his remaining eight men and stood in front of the boxcar containing the payroll.

"Open up that door and come out with your hands up an' you won't be hurt," he yelled.

"You go to hell!" a muffled voice from inside the car yelled back.

Slaughter went to his saddlebags and took out four sticks of dynamite tied together with string. He walked to the boxcar and placed the dynamite on the ground underneath the door. Pulling out a long black cigar, he struck a lucifer on his pants leg, lit the stogie, then lit the fuse to the dynamite.

"Get back, boys," he called, running from the car.

Seconds later, the boxcar, which had remained upright after the wreck, was lifted off its wheels as the dynamite exploded and blew wooden boards and framework all to hell.

After the smoke cleared, Slaughter could see the car lying on its side, a strongbox among the wreckage lying next to the wounded guard, who was covered with soot and grime. He was holding his shattered right arm and glaring at the outlaws. His rifle lay nearby but was out of his reach.

Slaughter grinned at his men, pulled his Colt from its holster, and climbed up into what was left of the boxcar.

"I told you to come out," he said.

"You'll pay for this," the man said. "The Army will track you down and you'll spend the rest of your lives in the Yuma prison."

"I don't think so," Slaughter said calmly, and pointed his pistol at the man and shot him between the eyes, blowing the back of his head off and sending blood and brains all over the strongbox lying next to him.

"Goddammit! You didn't have to do that!" yelled the man who'd called himself Monte Carson.

Slaughter looked over his shoulder, smiled, and said, "I know I didn't HAVE to. I wanted to."

He bent, picked up the box, and heaved it off the car

to the ground in front of his men. "Get that lock off and let's see what we have, boys," he called.

Carson, who was nearest to the box, jumped down off his horse and grabbed the box. He pulled out his pistol and shot the lock off, opening the top of the box.

He pulled several canvas bags out and laid them on the ground. Using a knife, he slit the top of one of the sacks and held it up to view. It was filled to the brim with fresh, new greenbacks.

The men nearby all cheered and shot their guns in the air when they saw how much money was in the bags.

"Gather up those bags," Slaughter said as he climbed down from the car. "We still got some work to do."

He walked around the passenger car toward the soldiers who were still standing with their hands in the air.

"All right, boys, get on your knees and face the car," he said, drawing his pistol.

The soldiers looked at him with fear-widened eyes as they kneeled and faced away from him.

He stepped behind the men, eared back the hammer of his pistol, and pointed it at the back of their heads.

"Hold on," called Monte Carson. "There ain't no need of that."

Slaughter glanced over his shoulder. "I told you once, we ain't gonna leave no witnesses."

Carson drew his pistol in a lightning-quick move and pointed it at Slaughter. "And I told you, we ain't gonna kill no defenseless men."

Slaughter's face paled as he looked down the barrel of Carson's gun. "Listen, Carson. If we leave these men behind, they'll warn the Army post at Fort Smith an' we'll have a platoon of soldiers on our trail 'fore we can git away."

"How they gonna warn 'em? Fly?" Carson asked, still holding his pistol pointed at Slaughter. "It's more'n fifteen miles to the fort. By the time these soldiers walk that far, we'll be in the next county, an' they ain't none of 'em seen our faces."

Slaughter hesitated, then shrugged. "What the hell. I guess you're right." He holstered his side arm and walked to his horse. "Stick that money in your saddlebags and let's burn dust an' get outta here," he said, relieved when Carson put his gun away and began to stuff the canvas sacks in his saddlebags.

They'd been riding hard for twelve hours when one of the men shouted, "Hey, look behind us!"

As the gang reined to a halt, they could see trail dust rising from a patrol of Army men less than five miles behind them.

"How the hell did they get on our trail so fast?" one of the gang asked.

"One of them soldiers must've rounded up Rodriguez's or Benning's hoss," another of the bandits replied, referring to the men who'd been killed in the battle. "He must've near rode him to death to get to the fort that fast."

"Now look what you've done," Slaughter growled at Carson. "You might've killed us all by lettin' those men go. I ought'a shoot you down right here."

Carson turned his eyes on Slaughter and let his hand fall to hang next to his pistol. "You're welcome to try, Slaughter. Any time."

Slaughter got a cold feeling in the pit of his stomach when he looked into Carson's eyes, and he remembered how quick he'd been on the draw back at the train tracks.

"Well, it can't be helped now," Slaughter said sullenly. "We gotta split up. Ever'body scatter, an' we'll meet in two weeks down in Del Rio."

"What about the money?" an albino named Whitey asked.

Slaughter thought a moment, then said, "There's no time to split it up now. That posse's gonna be on us like ticks on a dog 'fore long. Carson, you keep the money with you an' we'll divide it up in Del Rio, then head down into Mexico."

As a couple of men started to protest, distant gunshots could be heard as the Army patrol got closer, ending the argument and causing the men to spur their horses in different directions to get away from the patrol.

Slaughter took a final drag on his cigarette and stubbed the butt out angrily. *Yeah,* he thought, *I should'a known a do-gooder like Carson wasn't to be trusted with the money.*

He drained his whiskey, turned to the whore, and slapped her on the butt. "Wake up," he snarled, "I ain't payin' you to sleep."

Twenty-nine

Smoke glanced around at the changes to Big Rock since his last visit there as the group rode into town. They'd been greeted several miles from town by the sentry team stationed there, and he was glad the citizens of Big Rock were taking the threat posed by Slaughter seriously.

As they traveled down Main Street, he could see new construction on many of the rooftops, small wooden walls with gun ports built in, behind which men could kneel and have a clear field of fire to the street below. When he looked down the side streets they passed, he could see barricades at the end of the streets, constructed so men on horses couldn't pass. Windows of many of the storefronts were boarded up to protect the expensive glass panes that had had to be brought in from Denver by wagon.

"Wonder where ever'body is," Cal said, looking around at the almost deserted streets.

"Inside, I suspect," Louis said, "watching us pass by. It seems the town is exceptionally well prepared for the upcoming onslaught by Slaughter and his minions."

Pearlie glanced at Louis. "I wish you'd speak English, Louis. That way a body could understand what you're sayin'."

Louis's suspicions were confirmed when several men,

some holding Winchesters and others shotguns, stepped from doorways to wave and shout hello to the returning heroes.

"Golly, they're treatin' us like we did somethin' special," Cal observed.

"You did, Cal," Smoke said, smiling and nodding at the townspeople. "You went out of your way and put yourself at some risk to help out a friend, all with no expectation of reward." He glanced back over his shoulder at his young friend. "There aren't many people who'd do something like that, and that's why the citizens are treating you special."

"Hell, it weren't all that much," Pearlie said.

Louis looked at Smoke and grinned. Both knew it was indeed a brave and noble thing to do and that not many men had such friends as Monte Carson and his wife, Mary, had.

As they drew abreast of the sheriff's office, Monte walked out the door, a wide grin on his face and a long-barreled shotgun cradled in his arms.

"Damn but it's good to see you made it back safe and sound," he said. "Come on over to Louis's place an' I'll treat you all to some lunch."

"Yes, sir," Pearlie said before anyone else could speak, and he spurred his horse into a canter toward Louis's saloon and restaurant down the street, leaving the others to eat his dust.

Smoke laughed. "Monte, you should know how dangerous it is to mention food to Pearlie when he's astride a horse. You're liable to get run over in the rush to the table."

They all gathered around a table in Louis's place and watched as Louis had an emotional greeting from his employees, especially his chef Andre, who actually wept with joy at seeing his old friend and boss back safely.

"Andre, cook us up some steaks, fried potatoes, sliced

tomatoes and peaches, and some of your special coffee,"
Louis requested. "It's been so long since we had a hot
meal I can hardly remember what good food tastes like."

"Uh, Andre," Pearlie said, "could I have some sarsa-
parilla instead of coffee? My mouth's been waterin' all
mornin' just thinkin' 'bout gittin' some more of that
stuff."

Andre nodded. "For you, Monsieur Pearlie, anything
you want for bringing my friend back alive."

Once they had coffee in front of them, Smoke asked
Monte about the preparations he'd made for Slaughter's
raid.

The sheriff put a match to his pipe, took a sip of coffee,
and began to talk. "We've fortified most of the buildings,
both on the roofs and the doors. Double-backed the doors
with two inches of wood to stop any bullets from pene-
tratin' and covered most of the windows where people
are gonna be stationed."

"I noticed you've barricaded some of the side streets
but not Main Street," Louis said.

Monte nodded, smiling. "That was Sally's idea. The
entire town is now a giant trap. The outlaws can get in
on the main street, but once they're in town they're gonna
play hell gettin' out again."

"But," Cal said with a puzzled look on his face,
"what's to keep 'em from jest turnin' around and headin'
back the way they came?"

Monte grinned. "We've got a couple of wagons loaded
high with hay and boards in a circle in their beds. Once
those bastards get past the city limits, I have some men
ready to station the wagons blocking the street, and then
they're gonna crawl up into the hay and defend the entrance just in case Slaughter's men try to get back out
that way."

"So, the entire town will be like a giant mousetrap,"

Pearlie said. "The rats can get in, but they cain't get out again."

"You got it, Pearlie," Monte said, grinning around the stem of his pipe, sending blue clouds of foul-smelling smoke toward the ceiling.

"How about the citizens?" Smoke asked. "Are they all behind us?"

Monte nodded. "To a man. And that really surprised me. Even some of the men I've had to arrest on more than one occasion are standing firm with us."

Louis smiled and shook his head. "It does not surprise me, my friend. The people of this town know you're the best sheriff we could ever hope to have, and the men you've incarcerated know it as well. I don't believe you realized just how many friends you have in Big Rock, Monte."

Monte nodded. "You're certainly right there, Louis. Mary and I both thank our lucky stars we decided to settle here."

Just then, Andre appeared with two kitchen helpers following behind him bearing platters heaped high with delicious-smelling food for the hungry men.

Pearlie reached down and fiddled with his belt.

"What are you doin', Pearlie?" Cal asked.

Pearlie looked up, his eyebrows raised. "Why, I'm loosenin' my belt to make room for all that food. If the sheriff is buyin', then I plan to eat my fill."

Smoke laughed. "That I've got to see. I've never known you to quit eating because you're full, Pearlie. It's always been because you ran out of food."

Louis glanced at Monte. "If the look on Pearlie's face is any indication, Monte, you may have to get an advance on your paycheck to pay for his meal."

After they'd finished eating, Smoke and Cal and Pearlie headed out toward the Sugarloaf. As he passed the general store, Smoke saw Preacher Morrow and his wife,

Bountiful, talking to Haywood and Dana Arden. Just as Smoke drew abreast of the foursome, they were joined by Ed and Peg Jackson, the proprietors of the store. When they saw him, the group all waved and shouted hello.

Seeing them together reminded Smoke of the time they'd all arrived from back East, hoping to make a life out West. They were the greenest pilgrims he'd ever seen, and before the day was out, he'd had to save their bacon . . .

Ever since gold had been discovered in the area, wagons had rolled and rumbled, bringing their human cargo toward No-Name Town. The line of wagons and buggies and riders and walkers was now several miles long. Gamblers and would-be shopkeepers and whores and gunfighters and snake-oil salesmen and pimps and troublemakers and murderers and good solid family people . . . all of them heading for No-Name with but one thought in their minds. Gold.

At the end of the line of gold-seekers, not a part of them but yet with the same destination if not sharing the same motives, came the pilgrims on a half-dozen wagons. Ed Jackson was new to the raw West—a shopkeeper from Illinois with his wife, Peg. They were both young and very idealistic, and had no working knowledge of the real West. They were looking for a place to settle. This No-Name Town sounded good to them. Ed's brother Paul drove the heavily laden supply wagon, containing part of what they just knew would make them respected and secure citizens. Paul was as naive as his brother and sister-in-law concerning the West.

In the third wagon came Ralph Morrow and his wife, Bountiful. They were missionaries, sent into the godless West by their church, to save souls and soothe the sinful spirits of those who had not yet accepted Christ into their lives. They had been looking for a place to settle when they hooked up with Ed and Peg and Paul. This was the first time Ralph and Bountiful had been west of eastern Ohio. It was exciting. A challenge.

They thought.

In the fourth wagon rode another young couple, married only a few years. Hunt and Willow Brook. Hunt was a lawyer, looking for a place to practice all he'd just been taught back East. This new gold rush town seemed just the place to start.

In the fifth wagon rode Cotton and Mona Spalding. A doctor and nurse, respectively. They had both graduated only last year, mulled matters over, and decided to head West. They were young and handsome and pretty. And like the others in their little caravan, they had absolutely no idea what they were riding into.

In the last wagon, a huge, solidly built vehicle with six mules pulling it, came Haywood and Dana Arden. Like the others, they were young and full of grand ideas. Haywood had inherited a failing newspaper from his father back in Pennsylvania and decided to pull out and head West to seek their fortune.

"Oh, Haywood!" Dana said, her eyes shining with excitement. "It's all so wonderful."

"Yes," Haywood agreed, just as the right rear wheel of their wagon fell off.

Smoke was up long before dawn spread her shimmering rays of light over the land. He slipped out of his blankets and put his hat on, then pulled on his boots and strapped on his guns. He checked to see how Horse was doing, then washed his face with water from his canteen. He built a small, hand-sized fire and boiled coffee. He munched on a thick piece of bread and sipped his coffee, sitting with his back to a tree, his eyes taking in the first silver streaks of a new day in the high-up country of Colorado.

He had spotted a fire down below him, near the winding road. A very large fire. Much too large unless those who built it were roasting an entire deer—head, horns, and all. He finished the small, blackened pot of coffee, carefully doused his fire, and saddled Horse, stowing his gear in the saddlebags.

He swung into the saddle, and made his way slowly and quietly down from the high terrain toward the road miles away using the twisting, winding trails. Smoke uncased his U.S. Army binoculars and studied the situation.

Five, no—six wagons. One of them down with a busted back wheel. Six men, five women. All young, in their early twenties, Smoke guessed. The women were all very pretty, the men all handsome and apparently—at least to Smoke—helpless.

He used his knees to signal Horse, and the animal moved out, taking its head, picking the route. Stopping after a few hundred twisting yards, Smoke once more surveyed the situation. His binoculars picked up movement coming from the direction of No-Name. Four riders. He studied the men, watching them approach the wagons. Drifters, from the look of them. Probably spent the night in No-Name gambling and whoring and were heading out to stake a gold claim. They looked like trouble.

Staying in the deep and lush timber, Smoke edged closer still. Several hundred yards from the wagon, Smoke halted and held back, wanting to see how these pilgrims would handle the approach of the riders.

He could not hear all that was said, but he could get most of it from his hidden location.

He had pegged the riders accurately. They were trouble.

They reined up and sat their horses, grinning at the men and women. Especially the women.

"You folks look like you got a mite of trouble," one rider said.

"A bit," a friendly looking man responded. "We're just getting ready to fulcrum the wagon."

"You're gonna do *what* to it?" another rider blurted.

"Raise it up," a pilgrim said.

"Oh. You folks headin' to Fontana?"

The wagon people looked at each other.

Fontana! Smoke thought. *Where in the hell is Fontana?*

"I'm sorry," one of the women said. "We're not familiar with that place."

"That's what they just named the town up yonder," a rider said, jerking his thumb in the direction of No-Name. "Stuck up a big sign last night."

So No-Name has a name, Smoke thought. *Wonder whose idea that was.*

But he thought he knew. Tilden Franklin.

Smoke looked at the women of the wagons. They were, to a woman, all very pretty and built up nice. Very shapely. The men with them didn't look like much to Smoke; but then, he thought, they were Easterners. Probably good men back there. But out here, they were out of their element.

And Smoke didn't much like the look in the eyes of the riders. One kept glancing up and down the road. As yet, no traffic had appeared. But Smoke knew the stream of gold-hunters would soon appear. If the drifters were going to start something—the women being what they wanted, he was sure—they would make their move pretty quick.

At some unspoken signal, the riders dismounted.

"Oh, say!" the weakest-jawed pilgrim said. "It's good of you men to help."

"Huh?" a rider said, then grinned. "Oh, yeah. We're regular do-gooders. You folks nesters?"

"I beg your pardon, sir?"

"Farmers." He ended that, and summed up his feelings concerning farmers by spitting a stream of brown tobacco juice onto the ground, just missing the pilgrim's feet.

The pilgrim laughed and said, "Oh, no. My name is Ed Jackson, this is my wife, Peg. We plan to open a store in the gold town."

"Ain't that nice," the rider mumbled.

Smoke kneed Horse a bit closer.

"My name is Ralph Morrow," another pilgrim said. "I'm a minister. This is my wife, Bountiful. We plan to start a church in the gold town."

The rider looked at Bountiful and licked his lips.

Ralph said, "And this is Paul Jackson. Ed's brother. Over there is Hunt and Willow Brook. Hunt is a lawyer. That's Cotton and Mona Spalding. Cotton is a physician. And last, but certainly not least, is Haywood and Dana Arden. Haywood is planning to start a newspaper in town. Now you know us."

"Not as much as I'd like to," a rider said, speaking for the first time. He was looking at Bountiful.

To complicate matters, Bountiful was looking square at the rider.

The woman is flirting with him, Smoke noticed. He silently cursed. This Bountiful might be a preacher's wife, but what she really was was a hot handful of trouble. The preacher was not taking care of business at home.

Bountiful was blond with hot blue eyes. She was staring at the rider.

All the newcomers to the West began to sense something was not as it should be. But none knew what, and if they did, Smoke thought, they wouldn't know how to handle it. For none of the men were armed.

One of the drifters, the one who had been staring at

Bountiful, brushed past the preacher. He walked by Bountiful, his right arm brushing the woman's jutting breasts. She did not back up. The rider stopped and grinned at her.

The newspaperman's wife stepped in just in time, stepping between the rider and the woman. She glared at Bountiful. "Let's you and I start breakfast, Bountiful," she suggested. "While the men fix the wheel."

"What you got in your wagon, shopkeeper?" a drifter asked. "Anything in there we might like?"

Ed narrowed his eyes. "I'll set up shop very soon. Feel free to browse when we're open for business."

The rider laughed. "Talks real nice, don't he, boys?"

His friends laughed.

The riders were big men, tough-looking and seemingly very capable. Smoke had no doubt but what they were all that and more. The more being troublemakers.

Always something, Smoke thought with a silent sigh. People wander into an unknown territory without first checking out all the ramifications. He edged Horse forward.

A rider jerked at a tie-rope over the bed of one wagon. "I don't wanna browse none. I wanna see what you got now."

"Now see here!" Ed protested, stepping toward the man.

Ed's head exploded in pain as the rider's big fist hit the shopkeeper's jaw. Ed's butt hit the ground. Still, Smoke waited.

None of the drifters had drawn a gun. No law, written or otherwise, had as yet been broken. These pilgrims were in the process of learning a hard lesson of the West: You broke your own horses and killed your own snakes. And Smoke recalled a sentiment from some book he had slowly and laboriously studied. When you are in Rome, live in the Roman style; when you are elsewhere, live as they live elsewhere.

He couldn't remember who wrote it, but it was pretty fair advice.

The riders laughed at the ineptness of the newcomers to the West. One jerked Bountiful to him and began fondling her breasts.

Bountiful finally got it through her head that this was deadly serious, not a mild flirtation.

She began struggling just as the other pilgrims surged forward. Their butts hit the ground as quickly and as hard as Ed's had.

Smoke put the spurs to Horse and the big horse broke out of the timber. Smoke was out of the saddle before Horse was still. He dropped the reins to the ground and faced the group.

"That's it!" Smoke said quietly. He slipped the thongs from the hammers of his .44s.

Smoke glanced at Bountiful. Her bodice was torn, exposing the creamy skin of her breasts. "Cover yourself," Smoke told her.

She pulled away from the rider and ran, sobbing, to Dana.

A rider said, "I don't know who you are, boy. But I'm gonna teach you a hard lesson."

"Oh? And what might that be?"

"To keep your goddamned nose out of other folks' business."

"If the woman had been willing," Smoke said, "I would not have interfered. Even though it takes a low-life bastard to steal another man's woman."

"Why, you . . . pup!" the rider shouted. "You callin' me a bastard?"

"Are you deaf?"

"I'll kill you!"

"I doubt it."

Bountiful was crying. Her husband was holding a handkerchief to a bloody nose, his eyes staring in disbelief at what was taking place.

Hunt Brook was sitting on the ground, his mouth bloody. Cotton's head was ringing and his ear hurt where he'd been struck. Haywood was wondering if his eye was going to turn black. Paul was holding a hurting stomach, the hurt caused by a hard fist. The preacher looked as if he wished his wife would cover herself.

One drifter shoved Dana and Bountiful out of the way, stepping over to join his friend, facing Smoke. The other two drifters hung back, being careful to keep their hands away from their guns. The two who hung back were older and wiser to the ways of gunslicks. And they did not like the looks of this young man with the twin Colts. There was something very familiar about him. Something calm and cold and very deadly.

"Back off, Ford," one finally said. "Let's ride."

"Hell with you!" the rider named Ford said, not taking his eyes from Smoke. "I'm gonna kill this punk!"

"Something tells me you ain't neither," the other drifter who hanging back said.

"Better listen to him," Smoke advised Ford.

"Now see here, gentlemen!" Hunt said.

"Shut your gawddamned mouth!" he was told by Ford.

Hunt closed his mouth. *Heavens!* he thought. *This just simply was not done back in Boston.*

"You gonna draw, punk?" Ford asked.

"After you," Smoke said quietly.

"Jesus, Ford!" one of the riders who'd hung back said. "I know who that is."

"He's dead, that's who he is," Ford said, and reached for his gun.

His friend drew at the same time.

Smoke let them clear leather before he began his lightning draw. His Colts belched fire and smoke, the slugs taking them in the chest, flinging them backward. They had not gotten off a shot.

"Smoke Jensen!" one of the other drifters said.

"Right," Smoke said. "Now, ride!"*

Smoke grinned at the memory of just how green the now upright and solid citizens of Big Rock had been when they first arrived out West. Even so, he'd recognized their inner strength and worth, and they'd been among the first people he invited to live in Big Rock when he and Sally founded it later that year.

"What're you grinnin' at, Smoke?" Cal asked.

"Oh, nothing, Cal. Just thinking back on old times."

Pearlie laughed. "You mean back in the old days before we became civilized?"

Smoke threw back his head and laughed with the boys. It was true. The more things changed, the more they remained the same.

*Trail of the Mountain Man

Thirty

Smoke felt his heart swell inside his chest at the sight of his cabin on the Sugarloaf. He looked at Cal and Pearlie. "Why don't you boys clean some of the trail dust off in the bunkhouse while I tell Sally hello?"

Cal and Pearlie glanced at each other and grinned. "You mean you don't want us to stick around a while and tell Miss Sally hello, too?" Pearlie asked, an innocent look on his face.

"I've been gone from home for more'n a month. What do you think?"

"Yes, sir, we understand," Cal said, elbowing Pearlie in the side to make him shut his mouth.

The boys peeled off at the bunkhouse, while Smoke rode on up to the main cabin.

By the time he got down off Joker, Sally was running from the porch toward him. She threw her arms around his neck and gave him a very solid, very long kiss.

Smoke leaned back and stared at her, his love evident in his eyes. "What? Don't a man get some breakfast when he comes home from work?"

Sally took him by the hand and marched toward the cabin. "How about we have some dessert first?"

"But you always say that'll ruin my appetite," he teased.

She looked back over her shoulder at him, her eyes

twinkling. "That's not all I'm going to ruin if you don't hurry up."

"But don't you want to hear about my trip?"

"Later!" she growled.

"Yes, ma'am," he said, quickening his steps.

A while later, Sally fixed breakfast and Smoke invited Cal and Pearlie to join them. Pearlie went straight for the bear sign cooling on a windowsill.

Sally slapped his hand when he reached for one. "Not now, Pearlie. AFTER breakfast."

She cut her eyes at Smoke and winked. "You'll ruin your appetite."

"Aw, Miss Sally," Pearlie protested, "I've never known anything to ruin my appetite."

"Nevertheless, sit down and eat," she commanded, her hands on her hips.

"Boy, I ain't never heard nobody have to tell Pearlie that," Cal observed, digging into thick slices of fried ham, scrambled hen's eggs, and flapjacks so light he thought they were going to float off the plate.

While they ate, the men took turns filling Sally in on the happenings on their journey to and from Jackson Hole, Wyoming.

Her eyes widened on hearing of Cal's and Pearlie's wounds. "We need to have Dr. Spalding take a look at those, Smoke."

He held up his hands. "Already done, dear. He gave them both a clean bill of health, though he did say Cal didn't have too much room left on his body without bullet scars on it."

"I tole the doc I guess he'd have to start over again on the same ol' scars," Pearlie said around a mouthful of ham, " 'Cause he dang sure ain't gonna quit gittin' shot."

Smoke cocked his head. "I hear hoofbeats," he said,

rising from his chair, his Colt appearing in his hand as if by magic.

He opened the door and looked out, then holstered his pistol.

"Better set another place, dear," he said. "We've got company."

After a few moments, Muskrat Calhoon stepped through the door. "Howdy, young'uns," he said. When he caught sight of Sally, he removed his coonskin cap and gave a slight bow. "Mornin', ma'am."

"Good morning, Mr. Calhoon," Sally replied. "My husband has told me how much you helped him and I want to thank you."

Muskrat cut his eyes to the bear sign on the windowsill. "A couple of those'd do jest fine as thanks, ma'am."

Sally shook her head. "No, you have to join us for breakfast first. Then we'll have the bear sign."

Muskrat glanced at Smoke. "That's why I never married. Dang women are always denyin' a man his pleasures."

"She's a hardheaded woman all right," Smoke said with a smile, "but she's the only one I have."

Muskrat sat at the table and piled his plate so high with food he could barely be seen behind it. "I will say one thing, ma'am, this is the best food I've had in many a year," he declared, as he stuffed ham and eggs and pancake in his mouth all at one time.

Sally caught Smoke's eye and wrinkled her nose. "I'll go prepare a bath for Mr. Calhoon. I'm sure he'd like to . . . freshen up after he eats."

Muskrat turned fear-widened eyes on Sally. "I got to bathe too 'fore I git any bear sign?"

She smiled. "No, you can have the bear sign first, but the bath comes second."

He glared at Smoke. "You're right, son, she is a hard woman!"

* * *

After Muskrat had his bath and Sally had thrown his clothes in a tub of hot water with lye soap in it, Smoke gave him some of his older buckskins to wear while the mountain man's dried.

"What news do you have of Slaughter, Muskrat?" Smoke asked while they were having smokes and coffee on the porch.

"He managed to hire hisself another twenty or twenty-five gunnies," Muskrat replied. "Some of the worst pond scum in Pueblo from what I could gather."

"That figures," Pearlie said, still chewing on a bear sign doughnut in his hand.

"That means he must have more'n thirty men with him, Smoke," Cal said.

Smoke nodded. "Yes. We're certainly going to have our work cut out for us in Big Rock."

"I figger with the way they're travelin', they'll be here in two or three days at the outside," Muskrat said, taking a deep puff off a stogie Smoke had given him.

"Sally, we'd better get moved into town. Have all the surrounding ranchers been warned?"

"Yes, dear," she said from the kitchen where she was washing dishes. "The Norths are already there, and the others in the area have been put on guard."

"You got room in that there town fer an ol' beaver like me?" Muskrat asked.

Smoke grinned. "Hell, yes. We can sure use that Sharps Big Fifty of yours."

Muskrat nodded. "Good, 'cause I ain't had so much fun since Bear Tooth and me went to war agin the Pawnee."

"You went to war against the Pawnee tribes?" Cal asked, his eyes wide.

"Shore did, boy. It happened like this, me an' Bear

Tooth was trappin' beaver up in the high lonesome near the Pawnee's main camp, an' a couple 'a right pretty young squaws happened by one mornin'." The old mountain man waggled his eyebrows. "Well, we was jest young bucks ourselves at the time, an' one thing led to another an' 'fore we knew it, we got to showin' them pretty young thangs the difference 'tween a white man an' an Injun when it came to . . ."

Smoke groaned. There was no stopping a mountain man once he'd started on one of his tall tales.

Thirty-one

Slaughter held up his hand to halt the column of men riding behind him when he came to the sign saying, "Big Rock, Colorado."

He twisted in the saddle. "Men, load 'em up six and six, and watch your butts. I don't know if Monte Carson is in this town or not, but if he isn't, we're gonna raise hell until they tell us where he's hiding."

Behind him, men pulled Winchesters and shotguns out of saddle boots and cradled them in their arms. They were ready to go to war, and each one felt there wasn't a town in the West that could stand up to a group such as theirs. Shopkeepers and pilgrims and cowboys were simply no match for men trained to use their guns to make war, and the sooner these citizens realized that, the sooner Slaughter would pay them their money.

"What do you think, boys?" Slaughter said to Whitey and Swede as they rode into town.

Swede shook his head. "I just hope it's gonna be as easy as you think it is, Boss. Treein' a Western town ain't never been done before."

"There is a first time for everything, Swede," Slaughter said. "This is the roughest bunch of men I've ever had the pleasure to ride with. There ain't a one of them that hadn't killed more men than they can count. Hell, with this band of desperadoes, I could take Dodge City itself."

Whitey pulled his Greener express gun from his saddle boot and broke it open, checking his loads. "I just want a chance at that Johnny West, or whatever he's callin' himself today." He snapped the gun closed with a savage grin. "I'm gonna spread his guts all over Main Street if he's in town."

Slaughter glanced at the albino. "A piece of advice, Whitey. I've seen West draw, so don't give him a chance to go for his gun. He's snake-quick and that shotgun won't do you no good if he feeds you a lead pill first."

"He won't even have time to blink before I blow him all to hell," Whitey growled, his eyes fierce.

"Hey, Boss," Swede said, his head swiveling back and forth as he looked at buildings on either side of the street.

"What is it now, Swede?" Slaughter said, impatient with Swede's constant whining.

"There's something wrong here."

"What'a you mean?"

"There ain't nobody on the street. It looks like the town's deserted."

Slaughter looked around. For once, Swede was making some sense. Something was out of kilter here, all right. There wasn't a citizen in sight, not even a dog or a chicken. Something was going on, and Slaughter began to worry that perhaps he'd underestimated the ease with which they would take the town.

"Uh-oh," Whitey mumbled.

"What is it?" Slaughter asked.

"Look over yonder," Whitey said, pointing ahead down Main Street.

There was a large sign stuck on a post in the center of the street. Painted on it in large red letters was, "Slaughter's Marauders . . . Welcome to HELL!"

"Shit!" Slaughter exclaimed, pulling his Colt, the hairs on the back of his neck stirring with the warning. Now he knew they were in deep trouble.

He jerked the reins of his horse's head around, getting ready to make a quick exit of the town. Then he saw three wagons blocking the street out of town.

"Damn! They've got us blocked in," he said. He noticed his men were looking around, suddenly worried expressions on their faces, though most were too stupid to realize the trap they were in.

"Jim Slaughter," a voice called from the roof of the Big Rock Hotel just up the street.

Slaughter turned to look up, putting a hand up to shield his eyes from the sun.

The man he knew as Johnny West was standing there, next to Monte Carson. Carson had a long-barreled shotgun in his arms, while West had his hands empty.

"Yeah, what do you want?" Slaughter called back.

Monte Carson said in a loud voice, "If you and your men drop your weapons, your men can leave peacefully. You, however, will be arrested, and in all probability, hanged."

"My men and I haven't broken any laws," Slaughter called back. "We just came into town to have a drink and be on our way."

"I AM the law here, Slaughter," Monte said, earing back the hammers on his shotgun. "You got one last chance to come out of this alive. Drop your guns, NOW!"

"That one's mine!" Whitey growled, swinging his Greener toward Smoke.

Almost quicker than the eye could follow, Smoke drew and fired, his Colt exploding and belching fire and gun smoke toward the albino.

Whitey twisted in the saddle, a hole in his right chest pumping scarlet blood onto the back of his horse's head. "Uh!" he groaned with the impact, looking down at the wound in his chest in disbelief.

His lips pulled back over his teeth in a snarl and with a mighty effort, he tried to raise the barrel of his shotgun toward Smoke, until a second shot punched a neat hole in the center of his forehead, exiting out the back of his skull and striking a man behind him in the chest. Both men toppled off their horses as Slaughter's men all aimed and opened fire.

Jensen and Carson dove behind a wooden wall that'd been erected on the rooftop just as bullets began to pock-mark the boards.

Without warning, gun barrels appeared in many of the windows of the buildings along Main Street, and all began to fire into the heaving mass of men and horses that was Slaughter's gang. The horses reared and stampeded and crow-hopped, throwing some men to the ground, while others hung on for dear life as they galloped down streets and alleys trying to find a way out of the hell that Big Rock had suddenly become.

Slaughter leaned over his horse's neck, saving his life as a slug meant for him took the animal in the throat and threw them both to the ground.

The outlaw scrabbled on his hands and knees through clouds of cordite and gun smoke toward the entrance to the hotel. Maybe he could survive long enough to kill Monte Carson, whose treachery had caused this whole mess.

Swede leaned down in the saddle, spurring his horse forward and firing blindly at windows and doors as he rode down the middle of Main Street, desperately looking for a hole to crawl into.

Juan Garcia and Chuck Clute, two outlaws from Texas who'd come to Wyoming to escape the Texas Rangers, wheeled their mounts around and raced back down Main Street, trying to get out of town the way they'd come in. *To hell with Slaughter and his thousand dollars,* Garcia thought as he emptied his gun at fleeting shadows in windows.

They were twenty yards from the wagons blocking the entrance to town when four men stood up from behind haystacks in the wagons, all leveling shotguns at the bandits.

"Oh, shit!" Chuck Clute yelled when he saw the shotguns explode in his direction. Those were to be his last words on earth, as several hundred molten slugs of 00-buckshot shredded his chest and blew out his spine.

Garcia was stopped as suddenly as if he'd run into a brick wall by the express-gun loads, which catapulted him backward out of the saddle to land on his back in the dirt. His last view was of white clouds in a blue sky overhead before he began his journey to Hell.

Boone Marlow, who'd raped and killed more women than he had fingers, jumped off his horse and jerked open the door under the sign saying, "General Store."

He stopped short at the sight of a man with a Winchester in his arms. "Welcome to Big Rock," Ed Jackson said as he pulled the trigger.

His slug hit Marlow in the upper stomach, doubling him over just as Peg Jackson pulled the trigger on the small .32-caliber pistol she held in her hand. The bullet, though small, made quite a mess of the top of Marlow's head when it blew out his brains.

Dusty Rhodes, a footpad and burglar from Memphis, Tennessee, who'd left that state after killing an entire family when caught robbing their house, made it to the end of Main without being shot. He jumped off his horse, gun in hand, and burst through the doors of the church, his eyes wide and sweat dripping from his face.

A man wearing a minister's collar was stirring some soup at a table loaded with food and blankets.

Rhodes aimed his pistol, a grin appearing on his face. "Hands up, preacher man. You're gonna be my ticket outta here."

Pain exploded in Dusty Rhodes's head as Bountiful Morrow swung a two-by-four piece of wood into the back of his skull, crushing the bone and scrambling his brains.

As he fell forward, blood spurting from his eyes and ears, she said, "Welcome to our church. Would you like to kneel and pray?"

Sam Fleetfoot, on the run from the Indian Nations for murdering three Indian marshals, tried to jump his pony through a window in a boardinghouse to escape the murderous fire from the buildings all around him.

He made it through the window, shattering the glass, but was knocked off his horse to land on his back on the wooden floor. A large piece of glass fell straight down. Sam Fleetfoot held up his hands, getting his fingers sliced off as the sheet of window pane neatly severed his neck. His eyes were still open as his head rolled away from his body, but it was doubtful they could see the blood spurting from his neck.

Muskrat Calhoon calmly took a twist of tobacco out of his shirt pocket as bullets thunked into the wooden wall he was standing behind on the roof of the *Big Rock Guardian.* He bit off a sizable chunk of tobacco, then raised up and leaned his Sharps over the wall. It took but a second for him to spot and aim at a man riding down the street over three hundred yards away. He put the sight six inches over the man's head and slowly caressed the trigger. He was spun half around by the recoil as the big rifle belched two ounces of lead toward the outlaw.

Ernest Melton, noted murderer from Montgomery, Alabama, who'd killed two deputies and a family he took hostage in an escape before heading to Wyoming, never felt the slug that penetrated his spine between his shoulder blades and blew him over his horse's head, broken almost in half by the power of the Sharps cartridge.

Muskrat jacked another shell into the chamber and fired again, this time at a man running toward a dressmaker's shop. As the slug hit Happy Jack Morco in the shoulder and blew his right arm clean off, Muskrat mumbled, "Ya don't need no dresses nohow where yore goin', sonny." Evidently Happy Jack didn't think so either, for he fell squirming to the ground, where his screams of pain could be heard even over the noise of the gunfight, until he bled to death.

Haywood Arden stood in the doorway of his newspaper office, a shotgun in his arms, shouting, "Extra, extra, read all about it! Murderers killed in fatal attempt to take over town!" He punctuated his shouts by firing both barrels of the American Arms twelve-gauge and blowing Frank Broadwell and Chester Hughes out of their saddles as they rode hell-bent for leather down the street.

Dana Arden calmly handed him another shotgun and began to reload his, saying, "Nice shot, Haywood."

Marty Prembook, a stone killer who hired his gun out to anyone with the money to pay for it, decided he wasn't being offered enough for this job and jerked his horse's head around and galloped toward an alleyway. James Hunt, rapist, mugger, and pederast, saw Prembook making a getaway and followed as fast as his horse would run.

As they entered the alley, two figures stepped from the darkness of shadows along the buildings on either side.

Pearlie and Cal raised their Colts and fired as one. Two outlaws twisted and bent and fell out of their saddles to the ground. Hunt was killed instantly. Prembook, severely wounded, held up his hand. "Mercy . . . mercy," he cried.

Pearlie hesitated, then jumped as Cal fired from behind him and punched a hole just above Prembook's nose.

Pearlie looked at Cal, his eyebrows raised, until Cal pointed and he could see the gun in Prembook's other hand, hammer still cocked. Pearlie grinned and held up a finger, showing he owed Cal one.

Smoke saw Swede riding down the street toward the livery from his vantage point on the roof of the hotel. He took two quick steps, jumped to the roof next door, and hurriedly climbed down the stairs on the side wall. Weaving through the alley, he entered the livery stable through the rear door.

Swede was trying to burrow under some hay in the corner when Smoke stepped out into the light.

"You got two choices, outlaw," Smoke growled, his hands hanging at his sides, relaxed.

Swede jerked around at the sound of Smoke's voice, a pistol in his right hand, barrel pointed down at the ground.

"What're those?"

"You can drop that gun and give yourself up and hang."

Swede smiled sadly. "Not acceptable. What's the other choice?"

"I can kill you right here."

"I got a pistol in my hand. Not even you are that fast."

Smoke gave a small shrug. "I have a feeling we're fixing to find out. Right?"

"Goddamned right!" Swede said, and jerked the barrel of his Colt upward.

In one lightning-fast movement, Smoke drew and fired from the hip without aiming. His gun exploded a split second before Swede's did, his slug hitting the big man in the chest.

Swede's bullet grazed Smoke's throat, drawing a fine line across his neck that began to slowly ooze blood.

Swede stood there, a surprised look on his face. Then he looked down at the hole in his chest and the spreading red stain on his shirt.

"You've killed me."

Smoke nodded. "It appears that way."

Swede grinned, then coughed, blood trickling down the corners of his mouth. "Then I'll see you in Hell."

Smoke nodded. "Maybe, but not today."

Swede's grin faded and he fell forward onto his face.

Monte Carson stood up from behind the wooden barrier on the roof and aimed his shotgun down. Ike Black and James Blaine, both men who'd ridden with Quantrill's Raiders and were used to firefights, had dismounted and were standing behind their horses, firing over the saddles at the window to the general store.

Monte pulled the triggers on his shotgun and reeled back as both barrels exploded buckshot at the men. Both men and both horses were knocked off their feet by the force of the blast. When Ike Black struggled to his feet, Monte dropped the shotgun and drew his pistol, shooting the man in the top of his head and driving him to his knees, where he stayed, as if in supplication, though he was dead as a stone.

Otis Andarko, Charley Adams, and Joe Belcham ran their horses up on the boardwalk and made it as far as Longmont's Saloon. They dove off their mounts and scrambled through the batwings, huffing and out of breath from the exertion.

The three men had been *Comancheros* in the past, making their living selling whiskey to the Indians, and guns that were then used to kill innocent settlers.

As they straightened up, they saw two men standing at the bar. One was dressed in a black coat, with starched white shirt and knee-high, highly polished black boots. The other wore a red checked shirt and Levi's jeans and looked like a cowboy.

"Well, looky what we got here, boys," Otis said as he dusted off his pants. "A tinhorn cardsharp and a sodbuster."

Louis Longmont picked up a shot glass and drained the whiskey in one draft. "Johnny," he said to Johnny North, standing next to him.

"Yeah, Louis?"

"Should we kill them now, or have another drink first?"

Johnny pursed his lips. "Gosh, I don't know, Louis. What do you boys think?" he asked the three men standing in the doorway.

Joe Belcham couldn't believe his ears. He looked at his two friends, then back at the two men at the bar. "But we got you outnumbered three to two," he said, his hand moving toward his gun.

Louis shrugged. "I know the odds aren't fair, but we don't have time for you to go get more men."

"What?" Otis asked.

It was to be his last question as Louis and Johnny filled their hands with iron and blew the three men back out through the batwings. None of the three managed to clear leather, much less get off a shot, before they were dead.

"Louis, let me buy you a drink this time," Johnny said.

"Don't mind if I do," Louis said as Johnny poured.

Blackjack Tony McCurdy managed to get through Dr. Spalding's office door with only two minor flesh wounds. As he burst into the room, the doctor looked up and said, "I'll be with you in a minute, sir, as soon as I finish removing a bullet from this arm."

Haywood Arden lay on the table with his wife, Dana, holding his hand. "I told you not to stand in the doorway like that," she said. "I told you you'd get shot."

Haywood nodded, his face covered with sweat. "I know, dear, but what can I say? It was my first shootout."

Blackjack, who'd shot his first man when he was thirteen years old, and hadn't minded that it was his father he'd killed, stepped over to grab Dr. Spalding by the arm.

"Shut the hell up. What's wrong with you people? Can't you see I have a gun?" he said, sticking out his hand with the Colt in it toward Dana.

"Oh, that," Spalding said casually. Then in one quick motion and with a flick of his wrist, he slashed the extensor tendons of Blackjack's right hand with the scalpel he was holding.

The pistol dropped to the floor as Blackjack screamed and grabbed his bleeding right hand with his left. He looked down and saw scarlet stains covering the boots he'd taken from Roscoe Archer's body. His face paled and he fainted, falling to the floor.

"That's right, have a seat and I'll see to that nasty wound as soon as I'm finished here," Spalding said, turning back to Haywood.

Monte Carson climbed through the rooftop door and let himself down to the top floor of the hotel. He'd just finished punching out his empties and reloading his Colt when he heard a sound behind him.

He turned and found Big Jim Slaughter pointing a pistol at him.

"You're the cause of all this," Slaughter said, a crazed look in his eye.

Monte smiled. "No, I'm not, Jim. It's your greed and your stupidity that's brought you here."

"I'm gonna kill you, Carson."

"I don't think so, Jim. Not now, not ever."

As Slaughter eared back the hammer on his Colt, Monte dropped to one knee and raised his pistol, firing twice in rapid succession.

The first bullet hit Slaughter in the right chest and spun him around, while the second entered the back of his head and knocked him to the floor, where he landed facedown in a pool of his own blood.

Monte got up, walked over to him, and rolled him over. Slaughter's face was gone, blown away by the exiting slug from Monte's .44.

Big Jim, you don't look so big now, Monte thought.

Monte stepped to the window and looked at the carnage below. All of the outlaws were either dead or wounded and out of action.

Slaughter's Marauders were as dead as their founder, and dead too was the past of Monte Carson, respected sheriff in Big Rock, Colorado.

Epilogue

Smoke and the acrid smell of cordite hung like an early morning fog over Big Rock, Colorado. The odors and sounds of men wounded and dying and dead assailed the townspeople, who were going about the grisly task of piling corpses in the back of buckboards for the short trip to boot hill, separating out the wounded, who would be first cared for by Doc Spalding, then jailed by Monte Carson, the man they'd come to kill.

Smoke Jensen walked from the livery stable, blood oozing from a close call on his neck. He looked up and down the street, his ears still ringing from the sound of his Colts when he blew Swede to Hell and gone, his pistol hanging at his side.

He took a deep breath, and realized with a start how much he loved the smell and feel and gut-wrenching excitement of a fight. It was not something he was proud of, but he was a pragmatic man, and he knew that one's basic nature could be suppressed, but never changed. He guessed it was something he was going to have to work on.

"Hey, Smoke," Louis called from over by his saloon. "You all right?"

Smoke came out of his reverie and fingered the wound on his neck. "Yeah, Louis, I'm all right," he answered, and moved to join his friend.

Louis and Johnny North picked up the three dead men

in front of the saloon and heaved them in the back of the buckboard Ralph Morrow was driving down the middle of Main Street.

"Looks like you boys had your share of action," Smoke observed.

Louis shrugged. "These men had the gall to interrupt our conversation over two glasses of Napoleon brandy. What else could we do but shoot them for their impertinence?"

Cal and Pearlie sauntered up to join them, Pearlie still reloading his pistol.

"You boys all right?" Smoke asked, relieved to see them walking and know they had no serious wounds. Sally would have his skin if anything ever happened to either one of them.

Pearlie was about to reply when a door slammed from across the street and a man staggered onto the boardwalk, his right hand bleeding and his left filled with iron. As he raised his pistol and fired, Pearlie shoved Cal to the side and stepped in front of him.

Blackjack Tony McCurdy's bullet hit Pearlie in the side, punching through the thin layer of fat on his flank half an inch under the skin and exiting out the back.

As Pearlie doubled over, four pistols were drawn and fired almost simultaneously by Smoke, Cal, Louis, and Johnny. The bullets all hit Blackjack, lifting him off his feet and flinging him back against the wall next to Doc Spalding's office just as the doc came bursting out of the door.

Spalding held out his hands, "I'm sorry, Smoke," he said as he ran to take a look at Pearlie. "He was unconscious and I was removing a bullet from Haywood. He must've woken up and sneaked out the door."

"That's all right, Cotton," Smoke said from where he was squatted next to Pearlie, who was moaning and groaning and holding his side.

The doctor kneeled down and moved Pearlie's hand, checking his wound. Then he looked up and smiled. "I think all this cowboy needs is a small bandage and something to eat."

"Did somebody mention food?" Pearlie said, sitting up and grinning.

"Why'd you do that, Pearlie?" Cal said. "Why'd you take that bullet for me?"

"Hell, boy," Pearlie said as he struggled to his feet. "We done got a record goin' here. You been through two gunfights without gittin' wounded." He shook his head. "I jest didn't want'a spoil your streak."

"Go on in, Pearlie, and have Andre fire up the stove. Tell him I said to fix you anything you want," Louis offered.

Pearlie put his arm over Cal's shoulder and began to hobble into the saloon.

Cal looked at him. "Now, I done thanked you fer takin' that bullet. Don't go tryin' to make it more'n it is."

Pearlie straightened up and quit limping. "Can't blame a feller for tryin', can you?"

Monte Carson stepped through the door to the hotel and made his way across the street. His shoulders were slumped with fatigue and he looked dead tired, but he had a smile on his face.

"Well," he said, "it's finally over."

Smoke nodded. "Yes, I believe it is. Did you finish Slaughter?"

Monte nodded. "His raiding days are over."

Smoke looked up and glanced around the town, watching his friends and neighbors emerge from their stores and offices and homes to begin cleaning up the town. "Then it was worth all this."

Two weeks later, Smoke and Sally stood in front of boot hill. A light snow was falling and the white blanket over the graves and markers almost made the place look pretty.

Smoke nodded at the marker in front of them that said simply, "Jim Slaughter."

He put his arm around Sally. "You know, sweetheart, if it wasn't for you, I could've ended up like that."

She stared at him. "What do you mean, Smoke?"

"I realized during the fight in town that I love the feeling of putting everything you are and everything you own on the line in a fight to the death."

She shook her head. "I know you do, dear, and that is why I've never tried to change you, or to keep you from doing what you know you have to do. But you are as far different from the man lying there as day is from night. You may enjoy the contest of a fight, but you never start a fight or pick on someone who is weaker than you are."

She put her hand on his cheek. "You have a wonderful soul, Smoke, and in the final analysis, that is what separates you from men like Jim Slaughter."

They walked up the street away from the cemetery, arm in arm.

"What are your plans now, Smoke?" Sally asked.

He thought for a moment, then smiled. "After the snow season's over, I thought I might take Cal and Pearlie on a little trip down Texas way."

She looked at him. "You're going to the King Ranch and get some Santa Gertrudis cattle like I wanted to, aren't you?"

He nodded. "That idea of yours to cross them with our shorthorns is a good one. Besides, there's nothing much going on down Texas way right now, no range wars or Indians left to fight, so it'll be a nice quiet trip and I need the rest."

SMOKE'S BROTHER LUKE:
THE JENSEN LEGEND CONTINUES . . .

The last days of the Civil War.
With Richmond under siege, Confederate soldier
Luke Jensen is assigned the task of smuggling gold
out of the city before the Yankees get their hands on it—
when he is ambushed and robbed by four deserters,
shot in the back, and left for dead. Taken in by a
Georgia farmer and his beautiful daughter, Luke is
nursed back to health. Though crippled, he hopes
to reunite with his long-lost brother Smoke,
but a growing romance keeps him on the farm.
Then fate takes a tragic turn. Ruthless carpetbaggers
arrive and—in a storm of bullets and bloodshed—
Luke is forced to strike out on his own. Searching for
a new life. Hunting down the baddest of the bad . . .
to become the greatest bounty hunter who ever lived.

LUKE JENSEN, BOUNTY HUNTER

The Explosive New Series
by the Authors of *The Family Jensen*

Available wherever Kensington Books are sold.

Prologue

A rifle bullet smacked off the top of the log and sprayed splinters toward Luke Smith's face. He dropped his head quickly so that the brim of his battered black hat protected his eyes. One of the splinters stung his cheek near the end of his neatly trimmed black mustache.

Luke looked over into the sightlessly staring eyes of the dead man who lay next to him and said, "Those amigos of yours are getting closer with their shots, José. Too bad for you that you're not alive to watch them kill me. Reckon you probably would've enjoyed that."

José Cardoña didn't say anything. He couldn't with a bullet hole from one of Luke's Remingtons in the middle of his forehead, surrounded by powder burns, and most of the back of his head gone where the slug had exploded out.

More shots rang out from the cabin about a hundred yards away, next to the little creek at the bottom of the slope. The sturdy log structure had been built for defense, with thick walls and numerous loopholes where rifle barrels could be stuck out and fired.

Luke had no idea who had built the cabin. Probably some old fur trapper or prospector. These mountains in the New Mexico Territory had seen their fair share of both.

Now it was being used as a hideout for the Solomon Burke gang. Luke had been on the trail of Burke and his bunch for several weeks. There was a $1,500 bounty on Burke's head and lesser amounts posted on the half dozen owl hoots who rode with him. If Luke was able to bring in all of them, it would be a mighty nice payoff for him.

Unfortunately, it didn't look like things were going to work out that way. Luke had tracked the gang to this cabin and had been crouched in the timber up on the hill overlooking the creek, trying to figure out his next move, when Cardoña tackled him from behind.

Of course, he didn't know at the time that his attacker was José Cardoña. All he knew was that somebody crashed into him and knocked him out into the open. Luke and the man who had jumped him rolled down the hill together, locked in a desperate struggle, even as the man screeched a warning to the others at the top of his lungs.

The big log, which had also rolled about twenty feet down the hill when it toppled sometime in the past, brought the two men to an abrupt halt as they slammed into it. Cardoña wound up on top. Luke barely had time to recognize the *bandido* from drawings he had seen on wanted posters when he realized that Cardoña was about to bring a knife almost as big as a damn machete down on his head. That would have split his skull wide open.

Without having to think about what he was doing, Luke palmed out one of his Remingtons, eared back the hammer as he jammed the muzzle against Cardoña's forehead, and pulled the trigger.

The point-blank shot blew Cardoña away from him. The dead outlaw flopped onto the ground behind the log. Luke had rolled over and started to get up, but just then a bullet whipped past his ear. Instinct made him belly down behind the log, and it was a good thing he did, because a second later more rifles opened up from the cabin and a volley of high-powered slugs smashed into the fallen tree. If it hadn't been there to give him cover, Luke would have been shot to pieces.

As it was, he was pinned down. The trees above him on the slope were too far away. If he stood up and made a dash for them, Burke and the other outlaws in the cabin would riddle him with rifle fire. If he tried to crawl up there, he would be an even easier target, because the grass was too short to conceal him.

No, he was stuck, lying here with a dead man for company and only a matter of time until some of those varmints slipped out of the cabin and circled around to catch him in a crossfire. Luke's craggy face wore a grim, fatalistic expression, but a ghost of a smile also lurked around his mouth.

He had been in plenty of tight spots during the years he'd spent as a bounty hunter and had always pulled through somehow, but he had known that his luck was bound to run out someday.

After all, he had already cheated certain death once. A man didn't get too many breaks like that.

From time to time, he rose up long enough to throw a couple of shots at the cabin. It was long range for a handgun, so he didn't really expect to do any damage. His nature wouldn't let him die without a fight, though. If he'd had his Winchester, he could have put up an even better one, but it was still in the saddle boot strapped to his horse, a good hundred feet upslope. Might as well have been a hundred miles.

"Blast it, José, I must be getting old, to let a clumsy galoot like you sneak up on me," Luke said.

Cardoña had been a big burly man built along the lines of a black bear. Like all the other men in Solomon Burke's gang, he had a reputation for ruthlessness and cruelty. He had killed seven men that Luke knew of during various bank and train robberies, and he was probably responsible for more deaths besides.

But he wouldn't be killing anybody else, and Luke took some small comfort from that. He tracked down outlaws mostly for the bounties posted on them, and he wasn't going to lie about that to himself or anybody else. It pleased him, though, knowing that because of him some men such as Cardoña were no longer around to spread suffering and death across the frontier.

More bullets pounded into the log. One of them tore all the way through it and struck a rock lying on the slope, causing it to whine off in a ricochet.

That brought a thoughtful frown to Luke's face. He didn't know how long the log had been lying here. Long enough to be half rotten in places. He saw grubs and other insects crawling around on it.

He holstered the Remington he was still holding and drew a heavy-bladed knife from its sheath on his left hip. He attacked the log with the blade, hacking and digging at the soft wood.

It didn't take him long to break through, and he saw what he'd been hoping to see. The log was partially hollow. Luke began enlarging the opening he had made. The hollow part ran all the way to one end of the log. He could see sunlight shining through it.

It took fifteen minutes of hard work to carve out a big enough hole for him to fit his head and shoulders through it. By the time he was finished, sweat was dripping down his face.

Luke sheathed his knife and looked over at Cardoña.

"*Adiós, José.* If I see you again, I reckon it'll probably be in hell."

He wormed his way through the opening into the hollow log. The men down below in the cabin hadn't been able to see what he was doing, and he could only hope that none of them had snuck around to where they could observe him. If they had, he was as good as dead.

That was only one of the risks he was running. Any chance was better than none, though. He began shifting his weight back and forth as much as he could in those close confines. He felt insects crawling on him. His nerves twanged, taut as bowstrings. The log began to rock back and forth slightly.

Luke bunched his muscles and threw himself hard against the wood surrounding him. Over the pounding of his heart, he heard a faint grating sound as the log shifted even more.

Then, suddenly, it was rolling.

Luke let out a startled yell, even though rolling the log down the hill was exactly what he'd been trying to do. Up and down switched places with disconcerting rapidity. He hoped he wouldn't get sick before he got where he was going.

There was nothing between the log and the cabin to stop it. The crazy, bouncing, spinning, dizzying ride lasted only a few seconds.

The log crashed into the side of the cabin with a loud cracking sound. Luke bulled his way out of the broken trunk, pulling both Remingtons from their cross-draw holsters as he did so.

He had counted on the log busting open. Otherwise he would have had to crawl out through the opening he'd hacked into it with his knife, and by the time he had done that, Solo-mon Burke and the other outlaws would probably have been waiting for him with ready guns and evil grins.

Luck was with him, though, and the log had split open enough for him to get out of it in a hurry. He was on his feet with irons in both hands when one of the outlaws appeared in the doorway, unwisely rushing out to see what had happened.

Luke shot him in the chest with the left-hand Remington. The slug drove the owl hoot back and made him fall so that his body tangled with the feet of the man behind him. Luke blasted that hombre with the right-hand gun.

Then he pressed himself against the cabin wall and waited. Where he was, the men inside couldn't bring their guns to bear on him from those loopholes, and the log walls were too thick to shoot through. If anybody tried to rush out through the door, he was in position to gun them down.

He didn't think the cabin had any other doors or windows. If the door was the only way out, he had them bottled up.

Of course, he couldn't go anywhere, either. It was a stalemate . . . but that was better than him being stuck behind that log and his enemies having all the advantage.

As the echoes of the shots rolled away through the mountain valleys, a charged silence settled over the scene. Luke might have been imagining it, but he thought he heard harsh breathing coming from inside the cabin.

After a few tense minutes, a man called, "Who the hell are you, mister?"

"Name's Luke Smith," Luke said. They already knew where he was, so he wasn't giving anything away by replying.

"I've heard of you. You're a damn bounty hunter!"

"Am I talking to Solomon Burke?"

"That's right."

"Who are the two boys I killed in there?"

Burke didn't answer for a moment.

"How do you know they're dead?" he finally asked.

"Wasn't time for anything fancy," Luke said. "They're dead, all right."

Again Burke hesitated before saying, "Phil Gaylord and Oscar Montrose."

"José Cardoña's dead up on the hillside. I blew his

brains out. That's nearly half your bunch gone over the divide, Burke. Why don't you throw your guns out and surrender before I have to kill the rest of you?"

That brought a hoot of derisive laughter from inside.

"Mighty big talk, Smith. You step away from that wall and you'll be full of lead in a hurry. How in blazes are you gonna kill anybody else?"

"I've got my ways," Luke said. He looked along the wall next to him. One of the loopholes, empty now, was within reach.

"You can go to hell," Burke said. "We've got food, water, and plenty of ammunition. What do you have?"

"Got a cigar."

"Well, go ahead and smoke it, then," Burke told him. "It'll be the last one you ever do."

Luke kept his left-hand gun trained on the doorway. He pouched the right-hand iron and reached under his coat, bringing out a thin, black cigar. He bit off the end, spit it out, and clamped the cylinder of tobacco between his teeth. Then he fished a lucifer from his pocket and snapped it to life with his thumbnail. He held the flame to the end of the cigar and puffed until it was burning good.

"Smell that?" he asked.

"Whoo-eee!" Burke mocked. "Smells like you set a wet dog on fire."

"It tastes good, though," Luke said. "I've got something else."

"What might that be?" Burke asked.

Luke took another cylinder from under his coat. This one was longer and thicker than the cigar, wrapped tightly in dark red paper. A short length of fuse dangled from one end. Luke puffed on the cigar until the end was glowing bright red, then held the fuse to it.

"This," he said around the cigar as the fuse began to sputter and spit sparks.

He leaned over and shoved the cylinder through the empty loophole. It clattered on the puncheon floor inside the cabin.

One of the other men howled a curse and yelled, "Look out! That's dynamite!"

Luke drew his second gun and swung away from the wall as he extended the revolvers and squared himself up. As the outlaws tumbled through the door, trying to get away before the dynamite exploded, he started firing.

They shot back, of course, even as Luke's lead tore through them and knocked them off their feet. He felt the impact as a bullet struck him, then another. But he stayed upright and the Remingtons in his hands continued to roar.

Solomon Burke, a fox-faced red-haired man, went down with his guts shot to pieces. Dour, sallow Lane Hutton stumbled and fell as blood from his bullet-torn throat cascaded down the front of his shirt. Young Billy Wells died with half of his jaw shot away. Paco Hernandez stayed on his feet the longest and got a final shot off even as he collapsed with blood welling from two holes in his chest. That last bullet rocked Luke as well.

He swayed and spit out the cigar but still didn't fall. His vision was foggy, but he couldn't tell if that was because he'd been shot three times or because clouds of powder smoke were swirling around him. The Remingtons seemed to weigh a thousand pounds apiece, but he didn't let them droop until he was certain all of the outlaws were dead.

Then he couldn't hold the guns up anymore. They slipped from his blood-slick fingers and thudded to the ground at his feet.

He might not live to collect the bounty on these men, he thought as he stumbled through the cabin door, but at least they wouldn't hurt anybody else. The single room inside was dim and shadowy.

He saw a table, and beside it lay the cylinder he had

shoved through the loophole. The fuse had burned out harmlessly, because the blasting cap on the end was just clay and the "dynamite" was nothing more than a piece of wood with red paper wrapped around it. Luke had used it a number of times before, because outlaws tended to panic when they thought they were about to be blown to Kingdom Come.

He ignored the fake dynamite as he stumbled across the room. His attention was focused on the table, because sitting on it was the thing he had hoped to find in here.

It took Luke a couple of tries before he was able to snag the neck of the whiskey bottle. He lifted it to his mouth. His hand was shaking enough that some of the liquor spilled over his chin and throat, but he got enough of the fiery stuff down his throat to brace himself.

He leaned on the rough-hewn table and tried to take stock of his injuries. He was hit low on the left side. He couldn't tell how bad, but there was a lot of blood. A bullet had torn a furrow along his left forearm, too, and the blood from that wound ran down and dripped from his fingers. Then there was the bullet hole high on his right chest that was starting to make his arm and shoulder on that side go numb.

He needed to stop the bleeding before he did anything else. He didn't have much time, either, because his hands were going to quit working soon. He pulled the bandanna from around his neck and used his teeth to start a rip in it. He tore it in half and managed to pour some whiskey on the pieces. Then he pulled up his shirt and felt around until he found the hole in his side. He wadded up one piece of the whiskey-soaked bandanna and shoved it into the hole.

But that was just where the bullet had gone in. He could tell that it had gone all the way through. Wincing in pain, he located the exit wound and pushed the other piece of bandanna into it.

That left the hole in his chest. All the gun thunder had deafened him for a few moments, but his hearing was starting to come back now. He listened intently as he breathed, but he didn't hear any whistling or sucking sounds. So the slug hadn't pierced his lung, he decided. That was good.

The bullet hadn't come out, either. It was still in there somewhere. Not good, he thought. Fumbling now, he pulled his knife from its sheath and used the blade to cut a piece from his shirttail. He was damned lucky he didn't slice off a finger or two in the process, he thought. He took the bottle, upended it so that whiskey poured right over the wound, and then bit back a scream as he crammed the piece of cloth into the hole.

That was all he could do for now. His muscles refused to work the way he wanted them to. He had to lie down and get some rest. There were a couple of bunks in the cabin, built against the side walls. He took an unsteady step toward one of them.

Before he could reach the bunk, the world suddenly spun crazily around him. The floor seemed to tilt under his feet. His balance deserted him, and he crashed down on the puncheons, sending fresh jolts of pain stabbing through him.

He felt consciousness slipping away from him and knew that if he passed out, he probably wouldn't wake up again. He tried to hold on, but a black tide swept over him.

That black surge didn't just wash him away from his primitive surroundings. To his already fevered mind, it seemed to lift him and carry him back, back, a bit of human flotsam swept along by a raging torrent, to an earlier time and a different place. The darkness that surrounded him was shot through with red flashes, like artillery shells bursting in the night . . .

Chapter One

The bombardment sounded like the worst thunderstorm in the history of the world, but unlike a thunderstorm, it went on and on and on . . .

For long days now, that devil Ulysses S. Grant and his Yankee army had squatted outside Richmond, pounding away at the capital city of the Confederacy with their big guns. Half the buildings in town had been reduced to rubble, and untold numbers of Richmond's citizens were dead, killed in the endless barrages.

And still the guns continued to roar.

Rangy, rawboned Luke Jensen felt the floor shake under his feet as shells fell not far from the building where he stood. Once this had been one of Richmond's genteel mansions, not far from the capital itself, but recently it had been taken over by the government. One particular part of the government, in fact: the Confederate treasury.

Luke was one of eight men who had been summoned here tonight for reasons unknown to them. They were waiting in what had been the parlor before the comfortable, overstuffed furniture was shoved aside and replaced by desks and tables.

In the light of a couple of smoky lamps, Luke glanced around at the other men. Some of them he knew, and some he didn't. The faces of all of them bore the same weary, haggard look, the expression of men who had been at war for too long and suffered too many defeats despite their best efforts.

Luke knew that look all too well. He saw it in the mirror every time he got a chance to shave, which wasn't very often these days.

For nearly four long years, he had worn Confederate gray, ever since the day he had walked away from the hardscrabble farm tucked into the Ozark Mountains of southwestern Missouri and enlisted in the nearest town. Behind him he'd left his father, Emmett, and his little brother, Kirby, along with his mother and sister.

It had been hard for Luke to leave his family, but it was the right thing to do. Fighting for the Confederacy didn't mean that a man held with slavery, although he figured that was what all those ignorant Yankees believed. Luke didn't believe at all in the notion of one man owning another.

But at the same time he didn't think it was right for a bunch of Northern politicians in By-God Washington City to be telling Southern folks what they could and couldn't do, especially when it came to secession. All the states had joined together voluntarily, back there when they'd won their freedom from England, and if some of them wanted to say "thanks, but so long" and go their own way now, it seemed to Luke that they had every right to do so.

Even so, if they'd just kept on wrangling about it in the halls of Congress, Luke, like a lot of other Southerners, would have pretty much ignored it and gone on about his business. But no, Abraham Lincoln had to go and send the army marching into Virginia, and the battle along the creek called Bull Run that resulted was the last straw as far as Luke was concerned. He'd been raised to avoid trouble if he could, but when a Jensen saw something wrong going on, he couldn't just sit back and do nothing.

So for four years, he'd been a soldier and fought against

the Northern aggressors, slogging along as an infantryman for a while before his natural talents for tracking, shooting, and fighting got noticed and he was made a scout and a sharpshooter.

He knew that three of the men waiting in the parlor with him were the same sort because he was acquainted with them. Remy Duquesne, Dale Cardwell, and Edgar Millgard were good men, and if he was being sent on some sort of mission with them, Luke was fine with that.

The other four had introduced themselves as Keith Stratton, Wiley Potter, Josh Richards, and Ted Casey. That was all they'd said, so Luke hadn't really formed an opinion about them. He didn't blame them for being closemouthed, though. He was the same way himself.

Remy fired up a cigar and said in his soft Cajun accent, "Anybody got an idea why they brought us here tonight?"

"Not a clue," Wiley Potter said.

"The treasury department has its office here now," Dale Cardwell pointed out. He smiled. "Maybe they're finally going to pay us all those back wages we haven't seen in months."

That comment drew grim chuckles from several of the men. Remy said, "I wouldn't count on that, my frien'."

Luke didn't think it was very likely, either. The Confederacy was in bad shape. Financially, militarily, moralewise . . . everything was cratering, and there didn't seem to be anything anybody could do to stop it. They would fight to the end, of course—there was no question about that— but that end seemed to be getting more and more inevitable.

The front door opened, and footsteps sounded in the foyer. Several gray-clad troopers appeared in the arched entrance to the former parlor. They carried rifles with bayonets fixed to the barrels.

A pair of officers followed the soldiers into the room.

Luke and the other men snapped to attention. Luke recognized one of the officers as a high-ranking general. The other man was the colonel who commanded the regiment in which Luke, Remy, Dale, and Edgar served.

The two men in civilian clothes who came into the room behind the general and the colonel were the real surprise, though. Luke caught his breath as he recognized the president of the Confederacy, Jefferson Davis, and the secretary of the treasury, George Trenholm.

"At ease," the general said. Luke and the others relaxed, but not much. It was hard to be at ease with the president in the room.

Jefferson Davis gave them a sad, tired smile and said, "Thank you for coming here tonight, gentlemen," as if they'd had a choice in the matter. "I know you'd probably rather be with your comrades in arms, facing the enemy."

Luke saw Stratton and Potter grimace slightly and exchange a quick glance, as if agreeing that was the last thing they wanted to be doing tonight.

Davis went on. "I've summoned you, though, because I have a special job for you."